About the Author

Award-winning author Heather Peck has enjoyed a varied life. She has been both farmer and agricultural policy adviser, volunteer covid vaccinator and NHS Trust Chair. She bred sheep and alpacas, reared calves, broke ploughs, represented the UK in international negotiations, specialised in emergency response from Chernobyl to bird flu, managed controls over pesticides and GM crops, saw legislation through Parliament and got paid to eat Kit Kats while on secondment to Nestle Rowntree.

She lives in Norfolk with her partner Gary, two dogs, two cats, two hens and a female rabbit named Hero.

Also by Heather Peck

THE DCI GREG GELDARD NORFOLK MYSTERIES

Secret Places
Glass Arrows *
Fires of Hate **
The Temenos Remains **
Dig Two Graves **
Death on the Rhine (novella) **

BOOKS FOR CHILDREN

Tails of Two Spaniels **
The Pixie and the Bear

* Shortlisted for the East Anglian Book Awards Prize for
Fiction 2021
** Winners of Firebird Book Awards

MILESTONES

Heather Peck

Ormesby Publishing

Published in 2024 by Ormesby Publishing

Ormesby Publishing

Ormesby St Margaret

Norfolk

www.ormesbypublishing.co.uk

British Library Cataloguing in Publication Data

A CIP catalogue record for this book is available from the British Library.

Page design and typesetting by Ormesby Publishing

With thanks to Gary

for everything

Acknowledgments

Many thanks again to my beta readers Geoff Dodgson and Gary Westlake for their constructive criticism and extremely helpful comments. This book is all the better for your help.

Thanks also to Sharon Gray at CluedUpEditing for her meticulous and sensitive proof editing, and to Helen Morrish for the cover design.

A life is shaped by a thread of decisions.

If you don't like it do you change the decisions, or snap the thread?

Aelfwyth has lived through some events that shook the world, and others that shook only hers.

Now she's reviewing how her decisions changed her life ...

Contents

Glossary

ANPR: Automatic Number Plate Recognition

APB: All Points Bulletin

Budgie bell: In the late '60s/early '70s, there was a vogue for teenage girls to wear budgie bells among their beads.

CPS: Crown Prosecution Service

DG: Director General

LOS: Light Opera Society

PA: Personal Assistant

QMC: Queen Mary College was a college of the University of London in the 1970s

VAD: stood for Voluntary Aid Detachment and was the acronym applied to volunteers who nursed soldiers in World War 2. It was still in use in the Red Cross in the '70s.

1

STARTING POINT: The Crowning of a Queen

I was born on 2 June 1953. My mother always followed up a statement of my date of birth with the comment: 'And made me miss the coronation as well.'

What it was 'as well' as, varied depending on the year, the time, her mood and many other things. Suffice to say, I was left with an abiding sense of shame that, somehow, I was to be blamed for the inconvenience of the day I chose to arrive.

Coronation was, in due time, followed by christening and the first emitting of the exclamation to which I became inured: 'What?' followed by 'How on earth do you spell that?'

Thanks in part to my mother's desire for a name that sounded Saxon, and my father's inability either to listen properly or spell accurately, the name on my birth certificate is 'Aelfwyth'. As a result, I've spent my life answering to a range of imaginative abbreviations, Ellie, Al, Elf and Wythy among them. Elf tended to win.

The road between then and now has twisted, turned and sometimes come close to a dead stop. I've walked it in full sun with a song in my heart, and I've sat on the verge with my head in my hands praying for it all to end.

Both joys and despairs are measured in milestones: markers of events that changed my path. And perhaps because I arrived on such a special day, I find a number of my significant dates are inextricably linked with other days when the world, or at least a lot of it, could say, *I know where I was when...* Which is why the story that follows is paced by milestones both personal and global.

And why I recall my first contact with the 'five towns flasher' not in a particular year, but next to the death of Kennedy.

2

MILESTONE 1: The Death of Kennedy

Friday 22 November 1963. I was an independent ten years old. Judging from the children around me today, most modern parents would be shocked at how much liberty I enjoyed. Brown hair in plaits bouncing on my shoulders, and shod in my Start-Rite lace-ups, with tartan trews (the ones with straps under your feet) topped by a hand-knitted woollen jumper and a duffle coat for warmth, I would sally forth after breakfast knowing that, on a non-school day, I was free to do whatever I liked, wherever I liked, provided I showed up for meals on time. School days were different of course, in that the trews would be replaced by a skirt. The rest of the ensemble would be identical.

That Friday I'd been to school and was walking home with my best friend Katy. Katy's mum worked in a potbank, or pottery factory to you. I'd visited with Katy and watched her mum painting flowers and foliage freehand onto china cups. She was a talented artist paid piece rates, which was another way of saying not very much. Katy often came home with me when her mum was working late. That day the sun was setting as we came out of school, and we could see the pink glow over the playground. Without discussion we turned away from home and went up the rough track that led away from the town's streets and to the area of waste ground and untended fields we called the Banks. The first part of the path bordered an old quarry now half-full of rubbish from the potbanks: broken china, the remains of clay moulds, and anything else that the factories regarded as waste. The shattered cups and plates formed a sharp-edged scree which we used to ski down on the heels of our school shoes, which suffered accordingly.

That evening we walked past the quarry on to the narrow path that led down the hill toward the railway line, canal and ironworks. The flare at the top of the ironworks was burning much brighter than the sunset, and looking at it spoiled my night-sight, so that when I looked up it was several seconds before I saw the man standing in the middle of our path. And several seconds more before I saw what he was doing.

His face was strangely vacant, yet at the same time, excited. His eyes shone lurid in the iron flames when he turned his head to glance over his shoulder. There was nothing and no one behind him. He turned back with that vacant smile, which grew wider as a movement of his hands attracted my attention lower. He was fumbling at his trousers, and I didn't at first see what he was doing. Katy was more worldly-wise and pulled at my arm.

'Come back, Elf. We need to go back. Come on.'

I was slow to react. Slow to appreciate what I was looking at. And when I did, I was more puzzled than afraid. *Why was he waving a sausage around? Why?* Belatedly I realised what I was looking at and why the vacant smile was revolting me.

'Elf,' repeated Katy urgently, and we both turned and ran up the rough soil path that we could scarcely see as the sun set behind us. It was now too dark for running. Katy stumbled and I almost fell over her. Then she really fell, and I had to jump to avoid treading on her. Now it was my turn to tug her arm, but before she could get up, the man was upon us. He stopped right by us, the sausage looking bigger and somehow angry. He was gasping and laughing at the same time, as he stood over Katy, the sausage still waggling and dancing. For a split second I almost ran away, then I did what I still think was the bravest thing I've ever done. I stayed with my friend, and I swung my school satchel hard, clutching the strap so tightly the buckle cut into my hand.

The bag full of books hit him in the head. He snarled, staggered, and then was gone. I pulled Katy to her feet, and we both ran without looking back.

We didn't stop running until we regained the high road by the school. Then we stopped to get our breath back and to listen. There was no sound of running feet. No sound of panting or shouting. We peered up the track in the dusk but could see nothing. Without any discussion, we both turned and went to our respective homes.

When I got home I was late for my supper. I got a hurried telling off from my parents, who were going out, a plate of beans on toast, and an evening in front of the telly with my babysitter. She was a teenager named Sophy, and I rather despised her as not very bright. She was, however, five years older than me and so assumed to be more responsible.

I doubted it, but my opinion wasn't sought. The main advantage of her as babysitter, from my perspective, was that she liked the same sort of TV as me, and, in the interests of a quiet life, would let me stay up to watch provided I got into my pyjamas and was willing to scuttle off upstairs when we heard my parents return.

I considered telling her about our encounter with the man with the sausage, but because I'd hit him, I decided to say nothing. Given I wasn't allowed even to hit my little sister, I was pretty sure assaulting a grown-up with a school satchel was on the forbidden list. Then Sophy raised the subject herself.

'You shouldn't stay out after dark,' she announced self-importantly, just as I was finishing my beans and looking forward to my afters – which I hoped and had reason to believe would be a slice of ginger cake.

'Why not?' I asked, heading for the cake tin.

'Because the flasher is still about. They haven't caught him yet. Didn't you know?'

'What's a flasher?' I asked innocently. Sophy paused, surprised. She often forgot I was younger than her.

'You know,' she said. 'A nutter. A weirdo. A man who gets a kick out of waving his willy about.'

'Willy?' I said, still slow to catch on.

'Oh, for goodness' sake,' said Sophy. 'You know. Willy, dick, todger, privates!'

'Oh.' It was a long sigh of realisation from me. Realisation that it was the flasher Katy and I had met that evening. The flasher that I'd probably knocked into the quarry with my satchel.

I opened my mouth to tell her all about it, but was interrupted by a news flash on the telly. It was just before 7pm and right at the end of the news programme the words, 'News has just come in that President Kennedy has been shot,' echoed round our little sitting room.

Our conversation was over. Tiny bits of more news came in during the evening, about Dallas and the president's poor wife sitting next to him in the car. Sophy was so excited she forgot to get me into my pyjamas. When my parents got home from their choir practice, their attempts to tell us both off for our failure to observe my proper bedtime were shouted down as we communicated our thrilling news. They didn't believe us at first. When they heard it for themselves, my going-to-bed routine was disrupted some more. When I did eventually get to bed, I was very tired, and fell asleep almost immediately.

I didn't see Katy that Saturday as we to visit relatives; and I never saw her on a Sunday, which was devoted to chapel and Sunday school. So, it was Monday and the mid-morning break before we had chance to discuss our experiences of Friday evening.

'Have you heard the news?' was Katy's opening question.

'You mean the President?' I asked. 'Yes, of course I have.'

'No!' She was scathing in her dismissal. 'No, I mean about the flasher.'

'You mean the man we saw Friday?' Despite myself I shuddered a little. 'No. What've you heard? Have you said anything?'

'No. And we mustn't. They found him on Saturday. In the quarry. He was at the bottom of the quarry, and he was dead.'

I stopped in my tracks and stared at Katy with my mouth open.

'What d'you mean? We didn't see the flasher after all? Or were there two of them?'

'No.' Katy shook her head impatiently. 'When you came back for me, and that was very brave of you, Elf. I meant to say. But when you came back, you hit him with your satchel.'

'Yes.' I still didn't see what she was getting at.

'Well, he disappeared, and I think he must've fallen into the quarry. You know, where all the broken china is. I think he must have got cut and bled to death down there.'

'Is that what they said?'

'They just said he'd bled to death. I heard my brothers talking about it. "Best thing," they said. "God's judgment." '

'But you think I killed him?' I was still struggling to take it in.

'No, Elf. You didn't. You saved me, and then somehow, he got cut. It might've been someone else or it might've been an accident. But it wasn't you. I do think we should keep quiet though. Otherwise, there'll be a lot of questions and they'll stop us going around together.'

'Okay. I promise,' I said, feeling something more than just a yes was called for.

'Cross your heart and hope to die?' asked Katy, pulling a wet finger across her throat in the traditional way. I licked my finger too.

'Cross my heart,' I agreed.

3

MILESTONE 2: History's Child

I was eleven years and nearly eight months old when Churchill was buried – still young enough that I counted months as well as years. But old enough that on my previous birthday I'd had a big argument with my mother about being 'a teenager'. I thought being well into double figures made me a teenager. I was desperate to join the golden group that was having such a good time dancing to the Hollies, the Beach Boys and the Rolling Stones. My mother, ever the spoilsport, said I wasn't a teenager until I was thirteen – emphasis on the last syllable. With a lot of muttering and a mulish expression, I had to concede the point.

At nearly twelve, however, if you stretch a small point, I was old enough to take in that this event was a big deal. Cue lengthy lectures from my parents' generation and the generation above, about how he'd 'saved us during the war'. I wasn't clear exactly how, but I soaked up enough of the largely conservative attitudes around me to mount a stout

—

defence when one of my fellow pupils at the girls' grammar school complained about the cancellation of her favourite TV programme.

Among all the pomp and circumstance, one phrase stuck in my mind above all the others. My father had read it out to me. The American president had said:

As long as men tell of that time of terrible danger and of the men who won the victory, the name of Churchill will live...

He is History's child, and what he said and what he did will never die.

'History's child.' Those two words rang in my ears for days. I decided I too wanted to be a child of history, not just someone ordinary. Someone forgotten.

By this time, I was in my first year at the grammar school, or high school as the one near our home was called. My daily routine now involved a half hour walk down the high street, all the way from our front door to the school entrance gates at the far end of town. Then half an hour back again at the end of the day. There was no money for a bus fare. I could, I suppose, have spent my pocket money on buses, but I always had a much better use for my cash. School turned out at 4pm, and notwithstanding the substantial school dinner we were served in the middle of the day – usually meat, two veg and a stodgy pudding – I would be starving by the time I started to walk home. There were several options for a snack, even with my very limited financial resources. A bar of Cadbury Dairy Milk at the sweet shop only cost a few pennies. You could get four gobstoppers for a penny, or a sherbet fountain for threepence. If I managed to get past the sweet shop, then there was the chippie, where I could get a hot, battered potato fritter for tuppence. Finally, for the days when I was really flush, probably because I'd washed my father's car – 6d if I helped my dad; a whole shilling if I did it on my own – finally, as I say, there was the pie and pasty shop, where a sausage roll or a pasty, hot from the oven, could be bought, and consumed in the street.

Katy and I always shared whatever we could afford. If it was gobstoppers then we got two each. If it was a pasty, then we pulled it in two, scalding our fingers on the glutinous veg and meat filling. That day, after Churchill's funeral, we'd treated ourselves to a sausage roll and wandered through the back lanes toward home, munching, with more delight than you can imagine, on its greasy delectableness. We'd reached the sucking-our-fingers stage, when we were joined by Katy's favourite brother, Jake. He was three years older, tall, dark and handsome. In those days, the heroes of romantic fiction were invariably tall, dark, handsome and had strong white teeth. They were also usually named Derek. The description would have fitted Jake, even to the teeth.

'Well hi,' said Jake. 'How's the flasher murderer?'

I glared at Katy. That was supposed to be our secret. This was the first inkling I'd had that she hadn't kept her word. 'You told,' I said accusingly. She had the grace to look embarrassed but said nothing.

Jake went on. 'Not a girl to mess with, are you, Elf? Seen any more todgers recently?' Clearly, he thought it was a huge joke. Now I know that teenage boys aren't noted for their sensitivity. Then, I just thought he was a prat. I stuck my nose in the air and kept walking.

'Want to see mine?' he asked. Favourite brother he may have been, but even Katy was shocked by this.

'Jake!' she exclaimed, just as I turned round. I was filled with a level of rage I'd rarely felt before and was about to punch him on his handsome nose, when I tripped over something half hidden in the hedge beside us. I don't think that would have stopped me desecrating his good looks, except that whatever it was I'd tripped on, whimpered. I stopped dead, bent down, then kneeled on the path, horrified.

'What is it?' asked Katy.

'It's a dog,' I said. 'A little dog, and it's all burned, poor thing.'

'Is it dead?' asked Katy. 'Leave it.'

'No it's not dead, and no, I'm not leaving it.' As I looked more closely, I realised it was a small spaniel-type dog. 'It looks like some monster has tied a firework to its tail, then let it off,' I exclaimed. 'It's got burns on its tail and back. And it's terrified. How can people be so cruel.'

'Leave it,' said Katy again. 'It might bite you.'

'No, she won't,' I contradicted her. 'I'm not leaving her. Don't be so horrid.' I looked round at Jake. It suddenly seemed to me that he was being suspiciously quiet, and he was looking a bit shamefaced. I stood up, and as he stepped back, I grabbed him by the front of his jumper. 'You know something about this,' I said. It wasn't a question.

'No! I...'

I didn't believe him. I knew I was making assumptions, but I was certain I was right.

'Know this, Jake Swingewood. I'm a witch. Remember the flasher? It's not a good idea to cross me. So spread the word. Anyone *ever* does anything like this again to any animal on my patch, they'll be sorry. My word on it. Now,' I added briskly, 'you can carry her home for me, and if she bites you, it's no more than you deserve.'

The little spaniel didn't bite anyone. Jake carried her to my home without a murmur, then handed her over to my mother at the door. He left without a word. My mother was horrified too, and so was my father, but in a different way.

'She needs a vet,' my mother said.

And my father replied, 'We can't afford a vet. Give her to me.'

'No,' I said, guessing that his next actions would probably involve a sack and a lot of water. My father wasn't actively cruel, but he could be callous. He wasn't very empathetic to humans, let alone animals. Luckily my mother sided with me.

'Let me have a look,' she said. 'Perhaps we can help without needing to bother a vet.'

Very gently Mum and I washed the little spaniel in tepid water and assessed the damage. 'She must be very sore, and she's terrified,' my mum said, 'but the burns aren't too deep.' She dug around in the drawer near the gas cooker and came up with the tube of anti-burn ointment she kept there, strategically placed for a house full of clumsy people. She used the whole of the tube, and then we carried her upstairs, and laid her on an old sheet on my bed. The dog had refused all the food we'd offered and only drunk a little water.

'She might still die,' my mother said. 'She's very shocked. I don't want you getting all upset if she doesn't make it. We've done our best. And you did a very good thing bringing her here.'

I took no notice and curled up next to the dog. Looking at her in the stronger light of the kitchen, I'd concluded she was probably a cocker cross something else, perhaps a terrier. She was part gold and part white, with one brown eye and one blue one. I loved her with all my heart.

'I'm sorry you hurt,' I whispered in her ear, 'but you're going to get better, and no one will ever hurt you again, or they'll have me to answer to.' The dog looked at me out of a blue eye, then sighed and closed it. 'I'm going to call you Magic,' I said. 'You can be my familiar.' Even through the worry, I grinned a little. It was hilarious that Jake had believed me, about being a witch.

That's why I remember the day they buried History's child. It was the day I became a witch and acquired Magic.

4

MILESTONE 3: The Six Day War, June 1967

The announcement of war terrified me. We were the generation that grew up on stories of rationing, the Blitz, the gallant few and the trenches. We also knew about 'the bomb'. Thanks to my parents' philosophy of 'We don't care what she's reading, so long as she's reading', I'd already read both *Hiroshima* and Nevil Shute's *On the Beach*. Possibly they weren't the best reading matter for a thirteen-year-old girl, as I had accepted unquestioningly the accuracy of their depictions of nuclear war. As far as I was concerned, *Hiroshima* described in agonising detail what was about to happen to my town in the Potteries if we got a direct hit. And if by any luck the bombs fell further afield, then the radiation would still get us, as described by Mr Shute. As far as I was concerned, my life was effectively over before it had begun.

I don't think my parents ever realised just how terrified I was. They put my obsession with the news down to intelligent interest rather than panic. I even looked back through the pile of newspapers by the back door, to see how this could have happened. How could the world walk blindly into war again, without anyone noticing? I scoured the newsprint for clues, but all I could find was something about an Egyptian named Nasser telling the United Nations to get out of Egypt, which in the face of it seemed fairly reasonable; and then a threat to close the Suez Canal again. That sounded more serious, but was it worth killing the whole world for?

After announcing the war had started, the BBC announced that Israel had bombed Egyptian airfields and invaded somewhere called Sinai, which I vaguely remembered from the Bible. This was David and Goliath stuff. Little Israel, all on its own, was battling the massed ranks of the Arabs. Nuance and detail were lost to thirteen-year-old me, tucked away in the English Midlands and in the throes of my first love affair. Because if I'm honest, what a certain Peter Lynch was doing and thinking was of as much interest as the threatened Armageddon. Perhaps all the more so, as I was anticipating a short life!

Peter had fair hair, classically regular features and brown eyes. At least, I think they were brown. I'd struggled to get close enough to be sure. He was taller than me, which was another tick in the box, as I'd recently had a growth spurt and at 5ft 9 was taller than many of the boys my own age. Peter was three years older and therefore, by definition, sophisticated and desirable. He played cricket for his school and was also on the running team. When I met him, he was learning the guitar and sang in a folk band with other boys mostly of a similar age. They were regulars in the concerts put on by the local church and had even been known to play in church services, when the song of choice was usually 'Kumbaya'. Anyone who grew up at the same time will probably remember its dual advantages of broadly religious content and simple guitar chords.

The war, or what I assumed was the beginning of world war three, began on a Monday. By the Friday, the Israelis still seemed to be doing OK, no one else had yet joined in, and I began to breathe easier. I was surprised, but pleased, to find that the planned Summer Concert at our church was going ahead and we were all still going. For a while I forgot my wartime preoccupations in favour of a comparative assessment of my wardrobe. There was my favourite dress: a black and white '50s-style option with a V-neck, wide skirt and broad belt, inherited from a young aunt. I loved it but set it aside with a big sigh. Rather outré for Peter, I thought. He was unlikely to go for a retro look. All the rest of the choices, a massive three, were minis. There was a cream, lacy mini over a coffee underskirt – very sophisticated I thought, but quite long for a mini, only just above my knee. There was a blue crimplene affair, which had been much improved by the removal of the bow that had 'adorned' its midriff but wasn't exactly exciting. Then there was the one my mother had made me. Dark green background with small flowers, it was a shift dress with puff sleeves to a narrow cuff, and very short because when she'd been pinning the hem I had consciously dropped my shoulders as far as they would go. With shoulders in a more normal position, the dress was a good deal shorter than my mother had intended. My father hadn't seen me in it yet, and I foresaw problems when he did. The green dress it was, with block-heeled shoes and a cream clutch bag, which I would probably forget somewhere, but who cared?

Using the imperative that I watch the news before I went upstairs to change, I managed to delay my evening preparations to the last minute. The news was more of the same. The Israelis were hanging on and, so far, no sinister mushroom clouds had been seen. I changed into the green dress, and to bolster my confidence, decided that green would be a colour of good omen for a witch. My familiar, Magic, viewed my changed clothes with a gloomy air. She knew what that meant. An evening on her own with just a bone for company. I added some strings of beads, contemplated a budgie bell on a leather thong, but decided that would be a step too far for my father. A few minutes more and pale lips, green eye shadow and black mascara made my face look, interesting. I was careful to wait for the second shout from my father that, 'Everyone's waiting. Hurry up, Elf,' before I ran downstairs, out the kitchen and jumped into the car.

'Are you wearing makeup?' my father demanded, looking over his shoulder; then, 'Good God, where did you get that dress from?'

'Mum made it,' I said smugly, which drew a sharp look from driving seat to passenger seat and a muttered, 'What were you thinking? It barely covers her knickers!'

'I've a good mind to send you back to change,' my father declared more loudly.

'Too late, we need to get going,' said my mother. 'She'll be fine. It *is* a church do, remember.'

'Precisely,' my father replied. 'What the minister will think, goodness knows.'

'There'll be lots there with much shorter skirts than me,' I started, but my mother shook her head sternly and I took the hint. The drive was completed in silence.

The church concert proceeded in much the usual pattern. There was an introduction from the minister, explaining what we were fundraising for, and a short prayer. I don't know what that was about, as I wasn't listening. I was craning my neck to see if Peter was there. Good. He was on the front row, sandwiched between Rob (guitar) and Phil (flute). Obviously, the threesome would be performing. All three sported long hair – as in, over their collars – and velvet bell bottoms. I decided my dress decision was probably correct for today, and wondered if I could land some velvet bell bottoms for Christmas.

The concert continued in the time-honoured way. My honorary uncle Tom did a monologue. I forget which. But I know it would be either *The Green Eye of the Little Yellow God* or 'Sam, Sam, Pick Oop Tha' Musket'. He always did one or the other. Then the gentlemen's quartet would do some barbershop, and the ladies' trio would sing 'Three Little Maids from School Are We'. A rearrangement of personnel would produce a mixed quartet and three or four songs, one of which would always be a rendition of 'All in the April Evening'. The baritone, Uncle Eric, would then deliver a soulful 'Drink to Me Only', followed by Aunty Mollie, who would give – she always 'gave' her performances – a throbbing version of 'I Wandered Lonely as a Cloud'.

I fidgeted through all these offerings, hardly able to contain my impatience to hear Peter and the other two bring us into the '60s. There was a definite susurration when the minister announced, 'I'm delighted now to introduce Peter, Robert and Philip, who have formed a new band known as the Potters.'

There was some disappointment evident among an audience who were used to getting tea and cake after they'd wandered lonely. And some nervousness about what they were about to hear.

Pete, Rob and Phil took to the stage with minimum fuss. Rob, blue-eyed with a distinct look of a blond Paul McCartney, sat in the middle with his guitar. Pete and Phil stood to either side, Pete grinning confidently and Phil shaking floppy brown hair out of his eyes as he picked up his flute. Without further preliminaries they launched into their opening song: 'Leaving on a Jet Plane'. This was followed by 'Blowin' in the Wind', 'Both Sides, Now' and the final singalong of 'Kumbaya'. When the crowd was eventually released to its tea and cake, all the comments I overheard were complimentary.

Eschewing refreshment, I pushed my way down to the front where Rob and Phil were putting their instruments back into their cases. Pete was already surrounded three deep by other girls, and I couldn't get near him.

'You were great,' I said to Rob. 'I really enjoyed that.'

'We're going on to the White Swan,' he said. 'Would you like to come?' Would I! But I also knew there was no way my father would let me go to a pub.

'Sorry,' I said, gutted, 'but I'm here with the family,' and gestured over my shoulder. 'Maybe another time?'

'Sure,' he said, already losing interest, when Phil interrupted.

'Was that you adding a descant to "Kumbaya"?'

'Yes,' I said. 'I hope you don't mind.'

'No,' he said. 'It was good. Do you know anything else?'

'I know the descant to "Scarborough Fair".'

'You mean in the Canticle?'

'Yes. That's right.'

'Pete, come over here a minute. She can do the Canticle to "Scarborough Fair",' he said. 'Come and listen.'

'Where?' asked Rob practically.

'There's no one in the baby room,' I said, using the shorthand for the Sunday-school room.

'How appropriate,' sneered Pete, and I found my enthusiasm for his good looks waning.

'Come on,' said Phil, and pushed us all before him into the next room. Door firmly closed, he and Rob started on the introduction and Pete started singing. He had a pleasant tenor voice and sang in tune, otherwise it was pretty ordinary. Rob, on the other hand, was a skilled guitar player and put some nice harmonies in as well. Phil on flute, obviously couldn't join in the singing, but he nodded to me when the Canticle was due to start. I think I'd have been nervous, except that the scales had begun to fall from my eyes as far as Pete was concerned, so I had nothing to lose and just enjoyed singing.

At the end there was a pause, then Rob said, 'Wow! What else do you know?'

'I could harmonise to "Leaving on a Jet PLane",' I said. 'I know that one.'

'I don't know a descant to that,' replied Phil.

'Nor do I. Yet,' I answered. 'I'll make one up.' So I did, and that went really well too, except Pete had a face like a smacked arse.

'She's too young,' he said bluntly.

'Rubbish,' said Phil. 'She's not much younger than me. And we don't exactly have a wide pub circuit yet! By the time we get a wider audience, she'll be older too.'

Rob agreed, and that was that. The Potters became a quartet, briefly. I say briefly, because a few months down the line, Pete decided he didn't want to sing with a child – for which read, he didn't like being shown up by a better musician – and he moved on.

The war? You want to know what happened to the nuclear war I was confidently expecting? Funnily enough it ended the day after I joined the Potters. But by that time, my mind was wholly on other things.

5

The Aftermath of War

My first gig with the Potters was at a Methodist youth club and was pretty sedate. We sang a medley of traditional folk, modern folk and protest songs, with a few gospel songs thrown in as a sop to our hosts. The refreshments tended to church-bazaar standard – filled rolls, and cakes predominated, with the exciting innovation of sausages on sticks stuck into foil-covered grapefruit. The beverages were soft drinks or coffee. At least, the ones on offer were. Backstage, Pete had a secret stash of what I think was vodka in a lemonade bottle. He offered it round during the interval, which I was innocent enough to think was pretty cool, but after one sip I decided I just didn't like the taste, and I turned down all the subsequent offers. Phil and Rob weren't so keen either. Phil would have preferred a beer and planned a trip to the pub after the event. Rob was concerned that neat vodka and precise fingering weren't a good mix, and he prided himself on his guitar playing. So, Pete ended up doing a lot of the drinking on his own. By the second half of the programme, the effects were becoming evident.

We'd just embarked on our version of 'Melancholy Man', by the Moody Blues. Pete was singing most of the words, with me doing the 'aaah'ing, and even *this* audience noticed all the 'shtars' falling down into the 'shea'. At a nod from Phil, who was mirroring the 'aahs' with the flute, I joined in on the words and attempted to add some clarity. I had only moderate success, as Pete clearly resented my efforts and upped the volume until he was nearly bellowing the remainder of the song. When I left him on his own again vocally, to sing the chorus over the verse, he stopped dead, confused, then left the platform at a run and sounds of vomiting could be heard backstage. The song ground to a ragged halt as Rob stopped playing, leaving me to continue for a bar or two on my own. I stood in the centre of the stage, deeply embarrassed, and wondered what the devil to do.

Phil stepped forward and told our audience, 'I'm sorry that Pete has been taken ill, but don't worry, we'll be back on track as a trio in just a moment.'

He beckoned for Rob and me to come closer and muttered, 'Start "Sweet Thames" as a duet, and I'll join in as soon as I've checked on Pete.' Rob looked at me, we both nodded, and as Rob picked out the first few notes I started to sing. Phil waved to our fascinated audience and slipped backstage. He returned in minutes, gave us a thumbs up and, picking up his flute, started to play. At the end of the song we got a great round of applause, which I think owed a lot to sympathy, and under its cover Phil muttered, 'One of the WI is looking after Pete. He's drunk, silly sod. We'll carry on without him.'

When we'd rounded off our concert, with two encores, we went backstage. Pete was nowhere in sight but a mature lady wearing an apron and topped with an incongruous petalled hat was just finishing mopping the floor.

'His mother picked him up,' she said. 'Silly boy! But he's not the first and won't be the last.' She held out the empty lemonade bottle. 'I tipped the last of it down the sink,' she added.

'We're very sorry—' started Phil.

'Especially about the mess,' I chipped in.

But the lady snorted. 'Don't worry,' she said. 'I've seen worse. I was a VAD in the war. But don't let him do it again. It's not a good habit to get into.'

We assured her we wouldn't, although I had no idea what we could do about it, in reality. And as it turned out, we didn't get the chance. Pete never came back to the group. Rob put it down to embarrassment and not wanting to face us. Phil, kinder, said Pete had been thinking for a while about committing to his sport and didn't have the time for singing as well. I didn't know what to think. If anything, I agreed with Rob, but wanted to agree with Phil.

I knew in my heart that he resented me being the better singer and didn't like being outshone, even before the mortification of getting drunk and throwing up almost in public. But I still fancied him. The blond hair and blue eyes together with the practised charm still haunted my dreams. I had fantasised about coming to his rescue in some unspecified way and earning his undying love and gratitude. The fantasies had not survived the reality of alcohol and vomit. His rescuer had been an elderly ex-VAD with practical experience and a mop. Nonetheless, I sympathised with the mess he'd got into and made excuses for him. I preferred to believe that he had chosen to pursue his sporting ambitions, rather than hidden his blushes. Rob, Phil and I continued as a trio, with me as lead vocalist.

Apart from the singing, I had another preoccupation. My claim to be a witch, made in the heat of the moment, sat in the bottom of my mind like the worm in a bottle of mezcal. And like the worm, it added a tincture to everything I did. At first, the only people who knew about my witch claim were Katy and her brother Jake. And the only one who believed it was Jake. Not even me. Or actually, especially not me, as I knew I'd made the claim solely to scare the pants off him and bend him to my will that stressful evening I found Magic.

Then I stumbled on an odd book in the library, about water witches, and I thought, *Why not?* Perhaps I could be a witch, or at least, could practise witchcraft. Scaring people and bending them to your will were right up there with unbridled sex and dodgy goings-on with sacrifices and knives in the annals of witchcraft. I wasn't keen on the sacrifices and knives bit, and the unbridled sex seemed rather a long way off for me and thank goodness for that. But scaring the bad and stopping them doing bad things? I liked the sound of that. With the benefit of hindsight, I now realise that the idea of being 'special' was even more attractive, and having a secret, still more so. The combination was a winner.

The attraction of water witchery in particular, was that it was based in nature and seemed mainly to be benign rather than malign. I started to develop little rituals that I could complete in full view of everyone, without anyone noticing. In our house, every meal was accompanied by a glass of water. God forbid we should get to drink anything frivolous with food, like Tizer or even orange squash. As for alcohol – that came much later. For now, it was water, and before my first sip from the glass, and indeed before I filled a glass from a tap or jug, I said a little prayer of thanks to the goddess.

I am made of water. I am nothing without water. Water sustains me, refreshes me and supports me. I move with rainfall, river flow and sea tides. We are all one.

Then, with further reference to my library book, I created my shrine. This lived on my windowsill, and, after a few sharp words, people learned to leave it alone, writing it off as the sort of collection of important 'things' that many children collect. In the interests of harmony and peace, I forbore to point out that I wasn't a child any more.

At one end of my collection was half a scallop shell, purloined after my aunt's ambitious attempt at coquilles St Jacques. If anyone noticed there was usually a few drops of rainwater in it, they didn't say anything. That was for health and healing. Next was a hag stone, for protection. This was a particularly powerful hag stone, as it had been found and brought to me by my familiar, Magic. Occasionally she would take it back, regarding it as one of *her* stones, and I'd have to retrieve it from her bed and put it back in the shrine. If it had her slobber on it, that was an extra blessing. What was slobber after all, but water? Next to the hag stone was an arrangement of three cockles for love, and a limpet for confidence and strength. Finally, at the far end of the shrine, was a piece of green sea glass and a reed candle.

My preparations complete, I was all set to protect the weak and attract love. Pity I never got the chance to do the former, and I'd temporarily lost interest in the latter.

6

MILESTONE 4: Walking on the Moon

Over the couple of years Phil, Rob and I performed as the Potters, we grew very close. I wouldn't say we were very creative – mostly we sang songs that other people had made famous. Or we sang British folk songs and tried to give them a modern twist. We tried writing, but we weren't very good at it. The few songs of our own that we performed regularly were more than a little trite, for which I take full responsibility, as I wrote the words. Either Rob or Phil would provide a tune, or most often Rob *and* Phil, but they weren't going to set the world alight either. The best of them was a rather weird song about witchcraft for which Rob and Pete provided an eery, almost haunting melody. But it wasn't exactly mainstream, and audiences tended to look a bit bemused when we played it. It didn't matter. We were having fun, we rarely disagreed and none of us saw this as a long-term career choice. Rob wanted to teach music. Phil planned to be a solicitor, of all things, and I wanted to be either a vet or a farmer, depending on my mood at the time. But careers were some way off. I'd only just taken my 'O' Levels, as they were called then, and the boys were still studying for 'A' Levels.

By that time, we'd been together for two years and Rob had introduced a girlfriend into the mix. Jamie was short and curvy with long wavy brown hair and a sweet expression which, unusually, was an accurate reflection of her personality. We all liked her. But she couldn't carry a tune in a sack, which meant she was no threat to me or my place in the group. She came to every gig, loyally supporting Rob, who she thought was wonderful. Rob, for his part, thought she was the sweetest girl he'd ever met, and he idolised her. They were very happy together.

This left Phil and me as a twosome by default. The four of us often went out together, before and after gigs. I was still only sixteen, but we'd been visiting the odd pub together for some time. Our drinking was pretty moderate, not least because we didn't have much money. Mainly it was good to have somewhere to go for a chat and a giggle that wasn't a parent's sitting room. Phil and Rob would have a couple of pints of beer. Jamie and I would have shandies if we were strapped for cash, or martini and lemonade if we were well off. Then Rob and Jamie would go home with their arms round each other, and Phil would give me a lift home on his scooter.

Phil was a good friend to me. As well as the endless lifts to gigs and home again, he helped with my maths homework (never my strong point), listened patiently when I wondered how Pete was getting on, held his tongue when I bored on about how well Pete seemed to be doing with his cricket and running, and played tunes over and over when I was devising a new descant for an old song. Yes, you're right. I was completely blind to what everyone else could see.

If we were going with the traditional Moon in June romance, my revelation would have been a month earlier than it actually was. But unfortunately for the traditionalists among you, Neil Armstrong didn't take his giant leap until 21st July 1969. Phil had come round to ours to watch the moon landing on the TV. We all, my parents, Phil and I, watched Apollo 11 land on the moon around a quarter past nine on the Sunday evening. We knew a walk on the moon was planned, and the BBC had already announced that, for the first time ever, they would stay on air all night to broadcast this historic event. Around midnight, my father started snoring on the sofa and just before one in the morning my mother carted him off to bed, saying that they'd watch anything else in the repeats the following morning. She pointedly put a sleeping bag and pillow on the arm of the sofa.

'You're welcome to stay, Phil,' she said. 'Don't even think of driving home at this time of night. When you get tired of watching TV, just kip down on the sofa.'

Once she was safely out of the room, I looked at Phil and collapsed into giggles. 'Well that's told you,' I said. 'Clearly you're not to share my bed!'

He smiled, but he didn't laugh. 'Not yet anyway,' he said. I stopped laughing and looked at him hard. Perhaps it was the first time I'd looked at him properly for a long time.

I started to speak, stopped, then started again. I could feel the heat rising, all the way from my chest to my forehead. My tongue felt too big for my mouth, and I reached for my glass, just to create a diversion. It was empty. Phil leaned over with the bottle of Coke and topped it up.

'You don't need to say anything,' he said. 'I don't think you feel the same way. But I can wait.'

My face now scarlet, I gulped at the Coke. Some went the wrong way, and I choked. Ignored on the screen behind us, men in the command centre in Houston yattered on. Phil patted me on the back. I coughed, looked up through streaming eyes and realised that he was smiling, and that he had a look in his eyes I'd only seen before on Rob, when he looked at Jamie. He handed me his hankie to wipe my eyes. Too late, I realised I'd managed to smear it with mascara as well as tears.

'Come on,' he said. 'Let's watch this epoch-making event. It's not going to happen twice, and we have all the time in the world.' He sat back in the sofa, and as I leaned back, he put an arm around me, and gave me a little hug. It felt, good.

We both turned our attention back to the TV, although I have to admit that the warm arm round my shoulders had quite a lot of my attention too. My mind was whirling. How could I have missed how he felt? Suddenly I thought, *This is still the same Phil. The Phil I can say anything to.* And I spoke up.

'How could I have missed noticing how you felt?' I asked him. 'I'm sorry, Phil.'

'Don't be,' he said, on a half laugh. 'It gave me time to get close to you. To be a friend, and from what I've seen so far, couples who are friends first and lovers second last a good deal longer than the other sort. Look at Rob and Jamie.'

Instead, I looked at him. Not the flashy good looks that Pete had. But not the bad temper, the childish tantrums and the irresponsibility either. Phil was good and kind and, in his own way, I realised, quite handsome. His features were even, his mouth always smiling and his brown hair waved slightly into his collar. *Why don't I fancy him? No chemistry*, I thought sadly, and settled back to watch the TV.

Sometime between two and three in the morning, I dozed off. Phil woke me with a little shake around half three.

'It's about to happen, I think,' he said. 'You don't want to miss this.'

I rubbed my eyes and focussed rather blearily on the small screen. A space-suited figure climbed from the hatch on the side of the Apollo 11 capsule, paused and then stepped onto the surface of the moon. The picture wasn't terribly clear, but leaning forward we both saw his foot hit the moondust and heard those words you all know off by heart.

> *One small step for a man, one giant leap for mankind.*

I took a breath to say something, and it's lucky I did, because at that moment Phil took my face in his hands, leaned forward and stopped my breathing with a long kiss.

Did I say there was no chemistry? I was wrong. Sodium and water had nothing on how I felt at that moment.

7

MILESTONE 5: New Money

The next couple of years were among the happiest in my life. At school, I got respectable 'O' Levels and started my 'A' level studies. Rob and Phil had both moved on from school. Rob wasn't particularly academic, but excelled at his chosen subject, music. He played piano and percussion as well as guitar and remained set on a career teaching music. Jamie planned to be a primary school teacher. I still hankered after being a vet but knew in my heart of hearts that I was unlikely to get one of the hotly contested places to study veterinary science with my rather shaky physics and chemistry. Phil's plans to become a solicitor were also unchanged and he began a year working in a local legal firm as an office junior, to gain some experience.

Our social lives revolved around performing as the Potters. We sometimes went out as a foursome, but mostly Phil and I spent the weekends when we didn't have a gig either working on some new music at mine or at his parents' house, depending on who was in. Or going to the cinema and cuddling in the back row. We religiously split costs between us. 'Going Dutch' as it was known then. Not because Phil was mean but because I was stubborn.

'You don't earn any more than I do,' I pointed out. 'It's not fair expecting you to pay for everything just because you have a Y chromosome. Just wait till you're a rich solicitor. You can pay for everything then.'

'I intend to,' he said. It was the first time we'd spoken about the future. The first time either of us had mentioned spending it together. We were sitting on the old sofa at his parents' house. They'd gone out somewhere, and we knew we had the place to ourselves for an hour or two. This would normally have involved some petting of the type then referred to as 'top half only'. Neither of us were ready for anything more venturesome, notwithstanding the temptations, but on this occasion, we spent the time in serious conversation.

Phil took his arm from round me, apparently for the purpose of taking both my hands in his.

'I think you know I love you, Elf,' he said. 'I don't want ever to be away from you. But next year we'll be going to university, and I don't think I can bear to spend three years wondering who you're seeing and hoping just to spend time with you during the holidays. How would you feel about us going to the same university, or at least, the same city?'

I looked down at our hands. I took a deep breath, then let it go away without saying anything. For a moment I didn't know what to say. If I committed to Phil now, it would mean some of the university big adventure would pass me by. A big part of my life, of my life choices, would be done and dusted. Then

I thought about life without Phil, without his steady loving presence, without the laughter and the friendship. The words I'd just spoken without thinking came back into my head – the joking reference to our lives together when he was a solicitor.

The silence was starting to drag. I looked up from our hands, straight into his worried eyes.

'I think I love you too, Phil,' I said, knowing, as I spoke those words for the first time, that there would be no going back. 'Let's make a plan.' He heaved a huge sigh of relief, then whooped with joy.

'Let's do that,' he said. 'First thing is, what are you going to apply to do? I'm easy, I'm going to study law.'

'I'd love it to be vet science,' I said, 'but we both know that with my predicted grades for physics and chemistry, I'm not going to get a place. So, I'm going to study something I'll enjoy, then work out what to do with it later. So that means zoology.'

'Any thought about where?' asked Phil.

'I haven't got that far,' I said.

'Then, would you consider London? It would maximise our chances of finding courses for both of us'.

I thought about that. I hadn't considered London. I thought it a bit big and scary. If anything, I'd assumed I'd go somewhere like York or Bristol. When I voiced that thought, Phil had a solution.

'Let's go to London for a visit,' he said. 'Take a look around and see what we think.'

So that's what we did. After a lot of negotiation, and greatly to my surprise, my parents agreed to us having a weekend in London. They booked us two rooms in a B&B near Victoria Station, which, they assured us from the worldly-wise high ground of middle age, would be near to lots of places we'd want to visit.

We went down by train one Friday evening and went straight to the B&B, taking the Underground from Euston to Victoria. That was an adventure in itself. We dumped our rucksacks in our chaste single bedrooms and went straight out to find some supper. Given that cash was tight, we briefly considered a Wimpy, but eventually settled on a small Italian restaurant where we had the cheapest pasta option on the menu, followed by ice cream sundaes. Then we went for a wander through the streets and down to the river. That was our mistake.

Our walk along Victoria Street took us past Westminster Abbey, across Parliament Square and down to Westminster Bridge. I think what Phil had in mind was a romantic moment viewing the riverscape and the lights reflecting in the water beneath. The evening was quiet. A light rain earlier had left puddles on the pavement, but the sky was now clear enough for the moon to show as a semicircle through ragged clouds. The clock on the tower was showing a quarter to eleven, and Phil was just saying, 'Let's listen to Big Ben strike the hour,' when his voice trailed off. We were walking past the statue of Boudicca and her daughters when he stopped dead.

'Elf,' he said. 'I think there's someone in trouble on the bridge.' I looked in the direction he was pointing and saw someone on the wrong side of the parapet, clinging to the metalwork but facing outwards, downriver. I looked round to see if there were any police nearby but could see no one.

'What should we do?' I asked. 'Should I run to the Houses of Parliament? There must be some security guys there.'

'That might be too late,' said Phil, and started walking again, toward the person on the bridge. A car went past us, but there was no one else on foot.

As we got closer, the person looked up and their foot seemed to slip. They gasped, clutched the parapet harder, then looked up and shouted, 'Don't come closer!'

We stopped. I looked over at the river beneath, and I remember thinking how dark and threatening it looked.

'Can we help?' asked Phil. Then he added, 'We won't come any closer. Not unless you say so.' The figure looked out across the river again, then looked down at the water, like me.

'My name's Phil,' said Phil. 'What's yours?' He slid a foot along the pavement as he spoke and edged a little closer. There was a silence. 'This is Elf,' he added. 'We've only just arrived. We're here for the weekend.' He edged a little closer again, but then the figure turned back and looked at him. It was a girl, with long dark hair under a sodden hood. She looked thin and cold.

'Tell me your name,' said Phil again, as persuasively as he could. 'Let us help.'

'You can't help,' said the girl. Then added, unwillingly, 'I'm Sue.'

'Whatever the problem is, Sue,' said Phil, 'the answer isn't down there, believe me. Let us help, please.'

She looked away again, at the river. As she turned, her wet jacket fell open and revealed what I guessed might be part of the problem. Her stomach stuck out from her thin frame. It seemed she was pregnant. While she was facing away from him, Phil risked another two silent steps.

'Sue,' he said again, 'please let us help. Come and have a coffee with us. Get warm and dry and we'll help you find an answer. Everything will look better when you're warm and dry.'

I risked a small step behind Phil and added my two penn'orth.

'We'll both help,' I said.

'You can't,' said Sue. 'No one can. It's too late. No one wants us. No one cares what happens to us. It's best we just go.'

'We care,' I said, and Phil risked another step forward.

'I know what you're doing,' said the girl as she looked over her shoulder at Phil. 'It's not going to work.' And she let go of the parapet.

For a moment she seemed to hang there in the damp air, the moonlight reflecting from her eyes. A bus went past, drowning my scream in engine noise as Phil leaped forward to grab at her arms, her clothes. She slid through his hands and plummeted to the river below without a sound. The dark waters closed over her head and, although I hung over the edge watching closely, I didn't see her again.

Suddenly we were surrounded by people, crying out, shouting and, like me, hanging over the parapet. Phil was standing staring at the jacket in his hands, unable to move or speak. The bus driver came up to us and pushed his way through the small crowd of his passengers.

'Too late?' It was only half a question. I looked along the road to where the bus was parked unattended. 'The passengers shouted to me,' he explained. 'I'm sorry we were too late. I've radioed it in. The river police should be on their way.'

Even as he spoke, the bus passengers still hanging over the parapet shouted and pointed. A river police boat was approaching and circled cautiously near the bridge. Moments later, a police car pulled up alongside us, and after a brief word with the bus driver, came over to Phil and me. The driver shooed his passengers back on the bus and left with a roar of diesel engine. Phil held out the jacket to the first policeman from the car.

'This is hers,' he said. 'I tried to stop her, but she jumped anyway, and I couldn't hold on to her.' He was on the verge of tears, and I stepped forward to take his hand.

The policeman ran his hands through the jacket pockets and came up with a student card and a small purse. The card said 'Susan Harvey'.

'Did you know her?' asked the policeman.

'No,' I said, as Phil still seemed to be in shock. 'We came across her as we walked onto the bridge. We're here for the weekend, that's all. We tried to stop her from jumping and Phil tried to hold on to her, but her jacket came off in his hands.'

The policeman looked over the bridge at his colleagues in the boat below. One of them waved, then turned his thumb down.

'They haven't found her,' said our policeman unemotionally. 'They often don't. The currents are fierce in this river. I'll need you to come down to the station with me to make a statement. It's not far and it won't take long. You look like you could do with a cup of tea,' he added, looking at Phil.

Phil nodded. Then said, 'She was pregnant, I think. At least she looked it.'

I nodded. 'I thought so too,' I said.

'Ah,' said the policeman, then, 'Pity. That's two lives lost.'

We were taken by police car to Charing Cross police station. Our friendly constable was as good as his word. Cups of tea and a short statement later, and we were free to resume our weekend. They stopped short of providing us with a lift back to our B&B but pointed us at a bus stop in Whitehall for services to Victoria Street. We caught a No. 29, got off near Victoria Station and found our way back to our B&B rather later than we'd intended. The front door was locked but the landlady responded to our knocking, rather irritably.

'I wouldn't normally let you in, coming back so late,' she grumbled. 'I'm only making a special case for you, because you're so young. I've a daughter myself, and I wouldn't want her wandering the streets at night.'

'I'm sorry,' I said. 'It wasn't really our fault. We've had a very strange evening. We tried to stop someone jumping into the river, but we couldn't, then we had to talk to the police...' My voice trailed off as the enormity of what had happened hit me for the first time. 'I'm sorry,' I repeated, my voice shaking. 'We didn't know what to do.'

Tears suddenly began to pour down my face, and Phil put his arm around me; our roles reversed in a moment, he now the comforter, me the shaky one.

'We did our best,' he said to me, and the landlady stepped forward, her attitude transformed in an instant.

'You poor things,' she said, and put her arm round me too, from the other side. 'Come through to the kitchen and I'll get you a nice hot sweet tea. What a terrible experience.' She was still clucking like a fluffy fat hen when she sat me down by the kitchen table.

This room was much more homely than the minimalist settings of our bedrooms and the entrance hall. There was a cat on the table and a bowl of flowers in the window. Everywhere was very clean and scrubbed-looking, with wooden chairs round the table and a couple of chintzy armchairs facing a window into the small back garden. The cat, a tabby, stretched lazily as we came in, then jumped down to the floor and left through a cat flap in the back door.

'You two, sit down there,' she said, 'and I'll soon get the kettle boiled.' We sat in the armchairs, and she bustled round pouring boiling water into a brown teapot and putting sugar and milk on the low table between the chairs. 'Just get that down you,' she said, 'and then off to bed, the pair of you. You both look like something my cat brought in.'

I saw Phil heave a sigh of relief. I think he'd been worrying about a long session recounting all the events of the evening to the Victoria Street gossip. As it was, we drank our tea, heavily sugared by our hostess 'for shock', then she shooed us off to bed. She asked only one question.

'Was it a man or a woman?' she asked.

When we said, 'A young woman,' she sighed and shook her head.

'So sad,' she said. 'So very sad.'

She watched as we went up the stairs, then we heard the kitchen door click as we turned the bend in the landing to our two small rooms. Phil hugged me again, then I pulled him toward my door.

'I don't want to be alone,' I said. 'Stay with me, Phil.' He looked into my face, then nodded.

'But just to sleep,' he said. 'I'm not taking advantage of how you're feeling, let's be clear on that.'

'Just to sleep,' I agreed, and went into my tiny room. By the time I'd cleaned my teeth and got ready for bed, he'd rejoined me. He looked a bit embarrassed.

'I haven't any pyjamas,' he said. We were both whispering to avoid waking anyone. 'I was expecting to sleep alone.'

'You're too good to be true,' I said.

'No, just terrified of your father,' he said with a grin. I smiled too.

'Just come here.'

He slipped out of his shirt and jeans, and got into bed with me, his pants still on. The single bed didn't seem to matter too much. He turned me so my back was cuddled into him and put his arms around me.

'Go to sleep,' he muttered into my hair. 'I love you.'

Contrary to my expectation, I fell asleep almost immediately, but woke suddenly only an hour or two later. My heart was beating so fast I thought I might faint, even though I was lying down. The nightmare that had woken me with a shout was still hovering round my head. I could see the girl's head disappearing under the dark water of the Thames, just as I had earlier. Only this time I could also see hands around her neck and the long slim arms of the water goddess disappearing into the gloom beneath as she pulled the girl down, to die in the slime. I screamed again, and Phil said, 'Hush! Hush Elf, I've got you, you're safe. You're safe.'

'She's after the baby,' I babbled. 'That's why she dragged her down. She wants the baby.'

'Who wants the baby?' asked Phil. 'Who's dragging anyone down. Wake up, Elf. You're safe here and no one dragged anyone down. She drowned because the river runs fast there, and the currents are dangerous. That's all.'

I came to myself slowly. 'I had a dream,' I said.

'You had a nightmare,' he said. 'But it's all right now. You're safe with me.' We fell silent as we heard voices in the corridor.

One said, 'Did anyone hear a scream?' We didn't hear the muffled response clearly, but we kept quiet, and the voices went away.

'Try and go back to sleep,' said Phil into my hair. 'I'm still here. No harm can come to you while I'm around.' I settled down again, hoping for sleep but not really expecting it.

Unsurprisingly we got up late the following morning. When we went downstairs, we were cornered by the landlady.

'I thought you needed a lie-in,' she said, 'but I've kept some breakfast hot for you. Go through to the dining room.'

It was the first time we'd seen the dining room. It was a small room at the front of the house, with four mismatched wooden tables and Windsor chairs. One table was still set for breakfast, and she soon reappeared with hot plates covered in a generous supply of eggs, bacon, sausages, mushrooms, tomatoes and fried bread.

'Get yourselves round that,' she said, 'and I'll be back with some toast. Then get yourselves off outside for a day's sightseeing. It's a lovely day. I recommend the Tower of London, followed by the zoo.' She bustled away, then suddenly turned back. 'Meant to say,' she added, 'I don't take this new funny money, so I hope you've got some of the proper stuff.'

We looked at her, confused. 'What do you mean?' I asked. Phil, correctly anticipating the answer, began to grin.

'I mean this new decimal stuff. I don't believe in it. Pounds, shillings and pennies have always been good enough for me, and they still are. They've got the Queen's head on them after all!'

'So have the new coins,' I started to say, but Phil shushed me.

'I'm sure we can pay you as you'd like,' he said, and got us outside before we started laughing.

The rest of our stay was a lot more like my expectations. We dutifully visited the Tower and the Zoo, but we also spent some time wandering round the outside of some London University colleges, trying to get a feel for what it might be like to study here. We ate in Chinatown, and in a greasy spoon hidden behind Kingsway. Without any further discussion, we spent our second night in each other's arms again. Then on Sunday evening, having paid our bill with one-pound notes, we headed for Euston and the train home.

As our train dawdled home through late-running Sunday evening rail works, Phil flicked through the newspaper he'd picked up at the station. It was a Saturday evening edition. Somewhere around page five, he suddenly froze, looked at me over the paper, then came to a decision and laid it out flat on the table in front of us.

'Look,' he said, and pointed with his long, flute-player's finger. It was a short item, noting that the body of a young girl had been pulled out of the river near Greenwich in the early hours of Saturday morning. It was believed she'd jumped into the river from Westminster Bridge. She had not so far been formally identified. I read it without saying anything, then leaned back in my seat and closed my eyes. I could still see her head disappearing under the water. And I couldn't get the image of her swollen belly out of my mind. *How long after she drowned would the baby have lasted?* I wondered. *What would it have known as the blood slowly stopped flowing through its veins?* I only realised I was crying when Phil put his arms around me again and kissed away the tears.

The first thing I did when I got home was cuddle Magic. I swept the shells and pebbles off my windowsill and dumped them in the wastebin; I was having no more to do with any water goddess. Then I filled in my application forms to study zoology at various colleges of the University of London.

8

A New World, 1971–72

We both started at university in London in the autumn of 1971. Our grand plan had worked a treat. We both enrolled at Queen Mary College, which was then part of the University of London. My dodgy physics and chemistry meant that my applications to swankier London colleges got nowhere. Phil had offers from a couple of places but held back from accepting any until he knew what was happening to me. I was luckier than I realised at the time, to get a place at QMC. They were early adopters of a course-unit system. That meant, provided I did a minimum of course units from my designated faculty – Biological Sciences – I was free to choose other units from elsewhere in the college. For an intellectual gadfly like me, this was perfect. I got to study history and philosophy of science as well as geology. Unfortunately, I also had to study statistics and computing, both of which bored me rigid. I pretty much gave up on learning Fortran, a popular computer language, when my first program was spat back at me with error printed all over it. Just because I'd put a full stop at the end of a line! I declared then that I wasn't going to go near a computer until they spoke English. And I didn't.

Statistics was nearly as bad for a firm believer in the axiom that 'enough statistics proves your case'. I learned enough to get by and deployed biological warfare on the day of the exam to improve my chances of passing. I'd learned that the pass mark was adjusted depending on the overall performance of the examinees, so I attended the exam at the end of my first year dressed in very short hot pants as a distraction for my, mainly male, co-examinees. I don't know if it worked, but I did scrape a narrow pass. (At nineteen I had very good legs!)

Phil turned down offers from a couple of other colleges to accept one at QMC. The Law Faculty was a bit further down the Mile End Road than Biological Sciences, so we weren't right on top of each other all day. But we did meet up for lunch a couple of times a week, and we both got involved in musical clubs: me in the choir and Light Opera Society, Phil in the orchestra. I had toyed with the idea of joining the Drama Club, but found it stuffed full of wannabe luvvies, drifting about quoting Oscar Wilde and waving cigarette holders. When I suggested, a couple of years later, that the next Light Opera Society production should be Patience, I was being more than a little mischievous. The LOS, by contrast to the mannered extremes of the Drama Club, was made up of down-to-earth scientists and lawyers who enjoyed acting, singing and having a good time.

The master stroke, and this was down to Phil doing his homework, was finding a hall of residence we could both live in.

I started my first year in London in a Methodist hostel in Kings Cross. It was grim! My fellow residents were mainly low-paid workers from the immediate area, and while friendly they had little time or energy for a student. The area itself, apart from the railway stations of Kings Cross and St Pancras, consisted mainly of cheap cafes and odd little shops. At night it became the haunt of prostitutes and druggies. I was naively oblivious to the latter, but even I noticed the plethora of women dressed in skimpy skirts, tight tops and high-heeled boots that were intended to look like patent leather but were plainly plastic. Sometimes I'd almost trip over one asleep on the pavement. Often it was obvious they had no underwear. I'm ashamed to say that I always walked on by, confused and scared. Occasionally I would be stopped by a passerby and asked, 'How much?' I would rush on, shaking my head. Once I even responded with an absurd, 'Not today, thank you!'

After a couple of weeks, an increasingly worried Phil took steps to remedy the situation. He had been placed, by his solicitous parents, in a church-run hall of residence in North London. He had words with the hall management, explaining how concerned he was about me, and succeeded in getting me a scarce vacancy.

That change revolutionised my feelings about uni. I'd been getting depressed about my living conditions even as I enjoyed my studies and other college activities. Having somewhere to stay that was safe and full of young people also studying, or working in London for the first time, was bliss. The church hall even had musical events of its own, with a tiny choir and a couple of groups. Phil was much in demand as accompanist.

We re-formed as a duo, singing at every organised concert at the hall, and many disorganised ones too.

We became recognised as an established couple and were invited to everything together. Occasionally a new resident would flash his or her eyes at one of us but would soon be warned off by one of our many friends. I didn't mind that. Having Phil as my steady was reassuring and comforting. And Phil, as far as I could see, continued to be absolutely devoted to me. It could have been boring, except that I had so much else going on in my new life, that I had no time to worry that we'd become like an old married couple while still only nineteen.

Except, of course, that we weren't a married couple, and there was a world of unresolved sexual tension in our relationship. The genders in the hall were carefully segregated, with rooms on different floors, and there was a strict rule that no one was to be in a room belonging to a member of the opposite sex after 11pm at night. If the aim was to prevent intercourse, then it was a transparently stupid rule. Even in 1971 there was no assumption that sex could only happen after 11pm. Nor that it couldn't happen between two people of the same gender. Moreover, we were all over the age of consent and it was no one's business what we got up to.

The warden, when challenged, maintained that it was to prevent excessive noise late in the evenings, and turned a strategically deaf ear when it was pointed out, by me as it happens, that two women chatting together would probably make more noise than a man and a woman.

Nonetheless, this mixed hall was not the hotbed of riotous free love that you might have assumed. In fact, looking back, most of us were both naive and repressed. So what Phil and I got up to in our moments together that didn't involve musical instruments, remained pretty innocent by any standards, until we took our first proper holiday together the following summer.

As the long summer break of 1972 approached, Phil was a little irritated to discover that my study choices meant I had to go on a field course.

'I thought we'd have the whole summer together,' he complained. 'Did you have to pick a study unit that involved a field course?'

'Yes, I did,' I replied, a little irritated in my turn. 'In fact, I picked two. There wasn't much choice left if I avoided all field courses, so you might as well get used to the idea that I'll have a few over the next couple of years.'

'You picked two?' That was the part of my sentence he focussed on. 'Do you have two field courses this summer?'

'No. One in the summer and one in the autumn,' I said. 'Freshwater Biology in Ross-on-Wye this summer, and Marine Biology in St Andrews in the autumn. As I said, I couldn't avoid it without missing out on some really interesting courses.'

'Oh. Okay.' He calmed down. 'In that case, let's plan a holiday for when you get back from Ross-on-Wye. Where shall we go?'

Shortage of money dictated a UK holiday. We considered camping, but, as our transport was still limited to two wheels, albeit upgraded from a scooter to a motorbike, we opted for a tour of Scotland staying in B&Bs. On the assumption that Scots landladies might be a little strait-laced, I bought a plain gold ring in Woolworths, then went off for my field course.

I had a whale of a time. The two lecturers conducting the course were young and dishy. I quite fancied one of them, but both were married and non-predatory. We did a lot of paddling around in rivers, pools and streams. We collected a lot of insect samples and measured water quality. Then we were challenged to carry out an individual project, the only proviso being that we had to agree its title and objective with one of the lecturers. Slightly tiddly on cider, I put forward as my project *An investigation of the incidence of hippopotami in the River Wye* complete with research strategy and project plan. When this was rejected with the derision it merited, I defended my choice by pointing out that they had repeatedly argued a negative result was as valuable as a positive, and asked 'Has anyone actually proved that there are no hippopotami in this river?'

I still didn't get my way, which was why I spent the following three days counting the contents of a fish trap in a fishpond at six-hourly intervals, day and night. I had to mark the fish, when caught, by snipping a little cut in one of their fins, then by application of a complicated formula dependent on how many times I re-caught the same fish, calculate how many fish were in the pond. Short of draining the pond, I didn't see how they were going to check whether I was right or wrong, but I'd pushed my luck to its limits by then and obediently embarked on the project.

The fish I was surveying were rudd. The pond also contained a few tench, which sometimes made it into the trap and had to be released back into the pond without marking. For those who don't know, the tench is a very slimy fish, and if there is a more unpleasant sensation than picking up an unexpected tench in the dark at one in the morning, in the rain, I'm struggling to think of it.

On the last night, I was heading back to our hostel, wet and tired, and, if I'm honest, still a little light-headed from the scrumpy consumed between the 18.30 and 00.30 counts, when I spotted a police car, complete with blue flashing lights, parked askew the narrow lane.

I stopped dead, rearranged my rucksack (which contained my precious notebook with the earth-shattering conclusions of my ground-breaking project) and then walked forward cautiously. The rain was still pouring down steadily, and my hood was up, obscuring my peripheral vision. The blue lights splintered in the water on my glasses, and I took them off for a moment to wipe them clear. Back on, I peered through the damp lenses again, and even to my slightly fuddled brain, the car looked empty. I went closer, looked in, and then shrieked as a large figure pounced out of the hedge, bounded over the intervening roadway and pinned me face down on the car bonnet, with an arm twisted painfully behind me.

'Got him,' my captor shouted and a colleague in blue materialised from the other hedge. He shone a very big, bright torch on me then said, 'Don't think so, Barry. It's a girl.'

Barry let go and stood back, swearing. I stood up, rubbing my arm, and also swearing, then demanded, 'What the devil did you do that for?'

'Mistaken identity,' said the second policeman.

My erstwhile captor said, 'Sorry, miss. Thought you were our flasher. We've had a lot of complaints of a sexual offender round here.'

It brought back unpleasant memories for me, of a certain marl pit and the swing of a satchel. I shook the thoughts off, still rubbing my arm, and as the light focussed again on my face, the first policeman said, 'Hang on a minute, don't I know you from somewhere?'

'I shouldn't think so,' I said, or rather snarled. It was beginning to look as though something was going to be pinned on me, even if flashing wasn't looking likely. But the constable persisted.

'I never forget a face. I'm sure I've seen you somewhere.'

His colleague switched his torch toward the man who'd grabbed me, and in the rain-sodden partial light, my memory clicked too.

'The Thames!' we both said.

'The jumper,' he added.

'What're you doing in Wales?' I asked.

'Transferred a few months ago on a temporary secondment,' he said. 'What about you? Is your boyfriend here as well?'

'A freshwater biology field course, and no he isn't. He's studying law,' I said. 'What happened about the girl who jumped?'

'Lovely as this touching reunion is,' interrupted his mate, 'we still have a flasher to catch, and time's passing.' He turned to the car and got in, turning his torch off.

'How much longer are you here?' asked my constable. 'I'm off tomorrow night. See you in the Prince's Arms down the road here? Around seven? I can tell you then.'

'Okay,' I said. It was all moving too fast for me. 'See you then.'

It was after two in the morning by the time I got back to the hostel. I woke my roommate as I got into bed.

'What kept you?' she asked, looking at her travel clock sleepily.

'Got picked up by a policeman. I'm seeing him tomorrow,' I replied.

'Pull the other one,' she said, and rolled over in her bunk, wrapped in her sleeping bag like a chrysalis.

***

I did my final pond recording at midday the following day, then retired to bed for a nap before our end-of-field-course knees-up in the pub that evening. Which was, not entirely coincidentally, the pub where I was to meet my copper.

We'd already been in the pub for over an hour when the policeman turned up. Even out of uniform he stuck out like a sore thumb among the long-haired and fairly scruffy students. His short hair would have been enough, but the clean-shaven face and neat short-sleeved shirt above pressed jeans were also noteworthy. He looked round, quite unfazed by the cacophony, and spotting me, came over with a wave. The crowd parted before him, with good-humoured catcalling when they realised I was the destination.

'Hi,' he said. 'It's good to see you. Can I get you a drink?'

He shepherded me to the quieter end of the bar, and then leaned his elbow on it, cutting me off from the rest of the crowd. 'What're you drinking?' he asked, then added, 'I suppose I should introduce myself. I'm Bob Manners.'

'Bob the Bobby,' I said before I could stop myself, then laughed at his face. 'I guess you've heard that before.'

'A few times,' he agreed, handing me the white wine spritzer I'd asked for. He took a swig of his Guinness, then looked round. Despite the crowd, or perhaps because of it, there were a couple of seats empty at a table in the corner.

'Shall we sit down?' he asked and led the way over. Now I could see him in a better light, I gave him a good looking over. The short hair was brown, and so were his eyes. He was taller than me and heavyset without being fat. I guessed he was packing quite a lot of muscle. When he sat down and leaned back, I noted that his stomach under his shirt was perfectly flat. He was fit, in more ways than one. I quite enjoyed being seen with him and noticed that my enjoyment was reflected in envious looks from the girls and slightly aggressive posturing from some of the boys.

'I've wanted to ask you about that girl,' I said. 'The jumper. I've always wondered if you found out any more about her. I looked in the papers, but I couldn't see anything.'

'There was an inquest,' he said. 'We had to provide your statements and our own, but it all went through quickly and nothing much was reported in the papers. Just a short note at the bottom of a page, saying that the verdict was suicide. It was a very sad case.'

'I'm surprised you remember it,' I said. 'I'd have thought you saw a lot of that sort of thing.'

'Probably not as much as you think,' he said, drinking some more of his Guinness. 'But in any case, the inquest only happened a few months ago. It takes quite a while before a case comes in front of the coroner, you know.'

'I didn't, but I suppose I should have guessed,' I said.

'Also,' he started again, then stopped.

'Also what?' I asked.

'It's not pretty,' he said. 'That's why it stuck in my mind. Are you sure you want to know?'

'I do now,' I said. 'Otherwise, my imaginings will probably be worse.'

'You remember she was pregnant?' he asked.

'Yes, of course. It was very obvious.'

'Well, at the inquest, it came out that the father of the baby was her elder brother.' At first, I couldn't say anything. I just stared at him with my mouth open.

'Her brother?'

'Her brother. At least, her mother said so, and there was an enormous row, there in the coroner's court, between the mother on one side and the father and brother on the other. The coroner had to suspend proceedings for a while to calm things down.

'But how was it proved?' I asked.

'It wasn't. The mother made the allegation; it was denied, hotly, by the brother and the father, but the mother said she could bring witnesses to the fact they'd been having an inappropriate relationship and produced the girl's diaries. The coroner reviewed the evidence and it contributed to his conclusion of death by suicide. And that was the end of it.'

'Wasn't the brother charged? I thought incest was an offence?'

'It is. But if she was willing, then it's an offence in both directions, if you see what I mean. And since she was dead, there was too little evidence to prosecute. It basically came down to the mother's accusations and some ambiguous diary entries. The CPS – the prosecution service – concluded that it wasn't in the public interest to prosecute.'

'Should you be telling me this?' I asked.

'It's in the court record,' he replied. 'But what have you been doing this last year?'

I explained about my course and Phil. He looked interested when I mentioned London.

'My secondment finishes in a couple of months,' he said. 'Might we meet up when I'm back in London?'

'Well,' I hesitated. 'I'd be happy to meet up for a drink,' I said, 'but you do realise that Phil is my steady boyfriend?'

'For now,' he said cheerfully. 'You never know what the future might hold. Could I have your phone number, Aelfwyth?'

'You remembered my name,' I said just a little pleased. He laughed.

'It's not easy to forget,' he said. 'But the phone number?'

'Okay,' I said, 'provided you call me Elf. No one calls me Aelfwyth except my gran.'

'Elf it is,' he said, flourishing a couple of cards. 'Here's my number. You keep one and write your number on the other for me.'

'You're persistent,' I said, writing.

'Yes,' he said. 'Believe it.'

9

Scotland 1972

After my return from the field course, I went to my parents for a few days, then Phil and I loaded up his motorbike with luggage for our holiday in Scotland. It wasn't a lot. The bike had one pannier either side, and one on top of the fuel tank. We decided that we'd have one pannier each for clothes, and that toiletries could go on top of the fuel tank, together with a picnic lunch for the journey, and other odds and ends, like my shoes.

'How many shoes do you think you need on a bike?' demanded Phil.

'I'll wear my ankle boots,' I said, 'and then I'll need a pair of sandals for good weather and a pair of smart shoes for when we go out.'

'Who says we're going anywhere you'll need smart shoes?' he demanded. But he was smiling, and I noticed that he'd packed a decent pair of shoes as well as trainers. Otherwise, my capsule wardrobe, of which I was rather proud, consisted of one dress, rolled round tee-shirts, a spare pair of jeans, a pair of shorts, and undies. I'd decided a tee-shirt and pants would also do as pyjamas. Socks filled the corners of the pannier.

We headed up the M6 shortly after eight in the morning, fully armoured in bike overalls on top of everything else. That summer had been hot by English standards, but at that time in the morning, at the beginning of September, it wasn't too warm. We made good time up the motorway, stopped in a service station to eat the sandwiches my mother had provided (corned beef and tomato plus cheese and onion crisps, and an apple each) then carried on north. We reached Gretna Green by evening, exchanged the usual jokes about cutting out the waiting and getting married there on the spur of the moment, then found our first bed and breakfast place. It was a small cottage and only had two rooms to let. The other was vacant for the moment, so we had the bathroom and indeed the little lounge downstairs, all to ourselves.

Our hostess regarded us with some suspicion but didn't challenge our statement that we were 'Mr and Mrs Waters'. We dumped our panniers in the bedroom, noted with some amusement the single beds, and took ourselves off to the pub just down the road for some supper.

The menu was '70s exotic, by which I mean things 'in a basket', usually sausages, scampi or chicken – always accompanied by chips and some rather tired salad. If you're reading this in the twenty-first century, you may wonder where the vogue for food in a basket came from. So did we, even at the time. In fact, a favourite joke was that the first course would be 'minestrone in a basket'. You may also think that the baskets must have been a nightmare to fit into the dishwashers of the day. The sad reflection is that they probably didn't get washed.

The lining paper napkins would be removed and a fresh one put in. That was probably about it. Even more surprising to a modern audience, is probably the lack of burgers. At that time, they were generally only found in a Wimpy, and certainly hadn't made it to rural Scotland.

We happily ate our prawn cocktails followed by sausages (me) and scampi (Phil) in the baskets, followed by Black Forest gateau, and wandered back to the cottage for an early night.

***

Up in our tiny bedroom with the single beds, we wriggled past each other in the clumsy process of undressing, washing, cleaning teeth and using the other facility with, in my case at least, significant embarrassment about what I was doing being audible. I even ran a tap to hide the sounds. It makes me laugh now, but I was so bashful.

By the time I'd finished all my going-to-bed preparation, Phil was already in the bed nearest the window, covered to his waist by the sheet and leaning on the headboard. I was in my tee-shirt and pants. Black, in case you're wondering. I hesitated en route to the other bed, but Phil held his sheet to one side with an inviting gesture, and I got in.

We fitted together like a neatly dovetailed joint in a piece of carpentry. My head was resting on his shoulder and my arm across his chest. I put my feet on his legs, and that got a reaction.

'God, they're cold,' he exclaimed. 'What've you been doing out there? Bathing in cold water?'

'My feet are always cold,' I said. 'Especially after a bike ride. You'd better get used to them. What's the point of having a hot man if I can't warm my feet on him?'

'Okay,' he said with a shiver. 'I'll be brave.' Then he wriggled round a little, kissed me long and hard, and all concerns about cold feet flew out the window.

When I woke in the morning, I was alone in the bed by the window. I looked round and Phil was fast asleep in the other, cocooned in rumpled blankets like a fuzzy-topped caterpillar. As soon as I swung my legs out of the bed he woke with a grunt, looked up, and gave me the biggest smile ever.

'You'll have to marry me now,' he said.

'I can't,' I replied, and he shot up in bed, looking panicked.

'Why not? I always thought, I mean, you know I've loved you for absolutely ever, I thought—'

I interrupted. 'You haven't asked me,' I said, practising my demure look. He leaped out of bed, careless of his state of undress, kneeled in the narrow space between the two beds and took my right hand in his.

'Elf, spinster of the parish of Stoke, would you please do me the honour of becoming my wife? You minx,' he added as an afterthought.

I looked down into his eyes, smiled, and then said, 'Yes.'

The romantic moment was ruined seconds later by the sound of heavy footsteps on the stairs and a bang on the bedroom door.

'Breakfast ready,' announced our hostess in stentorian tones, then the footsteps descended the stairs again. We dressed hurriedly and ran downstairs. Bowls of cornflakes, the milk already added, were on the table. We looked at each other, and both got the giggles. Phil sat down and manfully attempted to eat the soggy mess. I didn't even bother, but just pushed the plate away. I was still laughing when the lady of the house returned, carrying two platters laden with eggs, bacon, mushrooms, tinned tomatoes and something square I couldn't immediately identify.

'You don't like the good cereal then?' she demanded of us both.

'No thank you,' I said. Then, as inspiration struck, 'I'm lactose intolerant, you see.'

'Oh,' she said, and put the plates down in front of us with a hint of a bang. 'Could've said that last night,' she was muttering as she took the rejected mess of milk and cornflakes out with her. In view of her culinary approach, I was relieved to see that the breakfast fry-up had not been pre-decorated with ketchup. Actually, it smelled and looked wonderful. Except I still didn't know what the square item was.

'What do you think this is?' I said, prodding it suspiciously. Phil cut a bit off and put it in his mouth.

'It's sausage,' he exclaimed. 'Rather good sausage actually, just a funny shape.' Much relieved, I tucked in too.

Rather later in the day than we'd intended, we headed north and west toward our next stop in Oban. It was a miserable ride: cold, wet and windy. Holding the bike steady in the gusts that hit us on exposed roads was wearing Phil out, and rain on his visor made it difficult to see. I just crouched on my pillion, thankful that my overalls kept me more or less dry, but very conscious of rain dripping down the back of my neck and my cold hands holding on to Phil's hips.

Disaster struck just outside Oban. The traffic was heavier here, at least heavier than we'd seen during most of our lonely ride. A car overtaking too close in the flying spray forced Phil to brake sharply. I didn't realise it at the time, but, as I saw later, our rear wheel was at that precise moment crossing a manhole cover. With no grip for the wheel as Phil braked, the bike suddenly slid sideways. As far as I was concerned, one moment I was sitting on the back of the bike, looking forward to a hot bath and a hot meal. The next, I was sliding down the road on my bottom at some speed. In front of me was Phil, and in front of him was the bike, sparks flying as it slid.

I was too shocked to think of anything except the vague hope that sparks weren't flying off me as well. Phil, much quicker-witted, was on his feet and running toward me before I'd even ground to a halt. The fact there was traffic close behind us had not even crossed my mind.

He reached me, disregarded my bleats and, seizing me by one hand, yanked hard on my arm to swing me out of the way of the oncoming traffic. Which left him in the middle of the road facing a large white van.

I freely admit I closed my eyes and waited for the sound of a collision between metal and flesh. Time ran slow. Even the rain seemed suspended in the air. There was a deafening squeal of brakes, and I opened my eyes to see the van skewing sideways as it braked hard on the wet road. Then the driver, realising that he'd made things worse by turning the van broadside on, took his foot off the brakes and the van shot forward until it came to a dead halt on the verge opposite.

Phil hadn't been hanging about either. He'd leaped for the side of the road, fallen over me, and was now in a heap against a holly bush, from which he extricated himself with some care and much swearing. The bike had ended up in the ditch further down the road. I became aware that a couple more vehicles had come to a halt in the road behind me as Phil and I crossed over to the white van.

The van had not escaped unharmed. The radiator had seen better days and steam was rising from it, while a thin trickle of oil suggested some other damage. And judging by the deep ruts in the soft verge, it would need a good pull to extract it from its current resting place. The driver was still holding the steering wheel when we reached him but let go and released the door catch as we came level with the cab.

'God, you gave me a fright,' he said. 'You all right, mon?'

'I'm fine, thanks to you,' said Phil. 'What about you?'

'I'm okay,' replied the man. As he got out of the van, we saw he was wearing green overalls with a tractor logo. 'I think the van's buggered tho'.'

'I'm sorry,' said Phil. 'It was another car coming too close that pushed my bike over, and he's disappeared of course.'

'How is your bike?' asked the van man.

Behind him the driver from one of the other cars asked, in an officious tone, 'Is anyone hurt? Do we need to call for an ambulance? There's a phone box a little way back.'

'We're fine,' I said, only now becoming aware that I had a sore patch on one hip and that my right wrist ached. Neither of which qualified for the attentions of an ambulance crew.

'What about you?' I asked the van driver.

'No, I'm fine,' he said. 'Except for feeling a bit shaken up. Although how fine I'll be after the boss sees his van, I'm not so sure.'

Phil had gone to pick up the bike and assess the damage. As he wheeled it back up the road he called, 'I think it's okay. Just a bit scraped. We're lucky it fell handlebars up, otherwise the brakes and everything would have been scraped off. As it is, I think we can carry on. But you'll need my insurance details,' he said to the van driver. 'It was our fault you ended up in the ditch.'

The officious car driver interposed himself again. 'I've a notebook and pen,' he said. 'And if it would help, I can run you back to the call box to ring for assistance.'

'If you're offering,' said the van driver, 'it would be even better if you could drop me at the farm just down the road. That's where I was going. The boss will probably come out with a tractor to haul the van out of the ditch. We won't need to bother a recovery company. Once he's stopped shouting at me,' he added, but there were the beginnings of a smile on his face.

Phil finished writing his contact and insurance company details on the proffered notepad and started apologising again.

'It wasn't your fault,' said the van driver. 'And in the end, no one got hurt. I'm just glad I'm not having to scrape you off the road.'

All the formalities completed, Phil found to his relief that the bike would start, and we set off again, rather slowly and sedately. Behind us, the van driver got into the car and for a few miles they followed us through the steadily diminishing rain. After some minutes, the car flashed its lights and turned into a farm drive. We carried on toward Oban.

What with the hold-up, the weather and our unnaturally steady pace, it was late by the time we arrived at our next B&B.

The landlady couldn't have been more different than the last. She exclaimed in horror when we explained why we were late. She insisted on carrying our battered and muddy panniers up to our room for us, ran us a hot bath, and declared that she could 'rustle up' something for supper.

'You can't possibly go out again after an experience like that, you puir wee things.'

A few minutes later she was shouting up the stair, 'Do you need any plasters or bandages? Are you hurt at all? I have a first aid certificate.' When we declined with thanks, she seemed positively disappointed that she wasn't going to get an opportunity to practise her first aid. In fact, on inspection of our respective tired and chilled bodies, the damage was limited to a graze on my hip, some bruises on Phil and my slightly sprained wrist. A hot bath made us both feel a lot better, and we went downstairs feeling a lot more cheerful. A delicious smell greeted us in the hall, and as we hesitated, not sure where to go, our hostess emerged from the door at the end.

'Come you in and eat in the kitchen. I'm afraid it's not much of a meal, but it'll stick to your ribs, I can promise that much,' she said.

The 'not much' turned out to be piping hot pea and ham soup, which was what we'd smelled in the hall, followed by thick ham sandwiches and a plate of what looked like homemade fruitcake. A large, fat ginger cat sitting by the old range watched our every move, as our hostess plied us with more soup, more sandwiches and more cake, until we could scarcely move. I reflected that if a remedy for shock and incipient hypothermia was needed, homemade pea and ham soup should be up there in the front row.

Unfortunately, the following morning revealed a bigger problem with the bike than we had realised. The crash had not been without consequences after all. Something important seemed to have cracked – don't ask me what. I don't have a Y chromosome, so maintain that I can't be expected to get down and dirty with anything oily. Suffice it to say, that our tour came to an abrupt halt.

We had intended to stay in Oban for a week before moving on further north. The revised plans still gave us a week in Oban, but after that we would have to go home ignominiously by recovery vehicle with the bike resting on the back. Phil shrugged off both the damage to his bike and the rearranging of our plans.

'Let's go to Mull and Iona,' he proposed. 'We can make the most of our trip, even if it's going to be shorter than we planned.'

After the disaster of our bike ride to Oban and the disappointment of the change to our plans, the trip by ferry to Mull and on to Iona was a return to paradise. The sun shone, the waves sparkled and every possible happy cliché was fulfilled. On Mull, we wandered hand in hand round the harbour and enjoyed a tour of the Tobermory distillery, complete with tastings and lessons on blending malts. On Iona, in the afternoon, we walked for miles and just before closing time, stopped in a little craft shop near the abbey. I was poking around among the hand-thrown mugs and jugs, while Phil was occupied elsewhere in the shop. We left just as it closed, and had to run for the ferry, boarding it just as it was ready to leave.

Halfway back across the sea to Oban, we were leaning on the rail admiring the view again, when Phil turned me to look at him and pulled something from his pocket.

'One day, I want to give you a proper grown-up engagement ring, but for now, I'd be really happy if you'd wear this.' It was a silver ring decorated with blue enamel. Something was engraved inside it, but when I peered at it, I couldn't make it out.

'What does it say?' I asked.

'It's written in ogham,' said Phil. 'The ancient Celtic tree script. It says "For ever".'

I removed the Woolworths gold-coloured ring from my left hand and slid the silver and blue ring onto my finger. It fitted perfectly.

'That's a relief,' said Phil. I was crying when I looked up at him.

'Thank you,' I said. 'I'll always wear it.'

10

MILESTONE 6: The Three-Day Week

Back at uni after our rather more eventful than planned summer break, we continued much as before. Studies took up a lot of our time. Social activities, often together but sometimes apart, also took a lot of energy. Back in the Light Opera Society, I would have been happy to be in the chorus, but, rather to my surprise, found myself cast as Lucy Lockit in *The Beggar's Opera*. Phil was in the orchestra, and we made a lot of friends during rehearsals and drinks in the student bar that usually followed. One of our regular drinking companions wasn't a student. Rather surprisingly, it was Bob Manners, or Bob the Bobby, originally met on Westminster Bridge, and whose acquaintance I had renewed near the banks of the Wye. When his shifts permitted, he often joined us for a drink and soon found himself dragooned into joining the group of practically-minded enthusiasts who built stage sets and managed lighting. He somehow managed to make his admiration for me clear, without overstepping the mark and upsetting Phil. After a while, he started bringing a girl along with him to the more social events. It was rarely the same girl more than three occasions running, but it did make life easier.

The Beggar's Opera was eventually performed to considerable student acclaim and with only one setback, which luckily remained more or less invisible to the audience.

I should perhaps explain that this was a contemporary-dress version. I wore Laura Ashley. The chorus of tarts wore satin halterneck dresses in primary colours, and Macheath was resplendent in a tight, white, denim suit. It was the tightness that was his undoing. All went well until the last night, when during a scene involving Macheath in handcuffs, the zip went on his jeans. The first I knew of it was while I was waiting backstage, when Bob Manners, collapsing in unpolice-like giggles, informed me that the highwayman was wearing paisley knickers. I peered onstage from the wings, and sure enough, he was, and they were clearly on display.

Undercover of the action at the front of the stage, the chorus of tarts were engaged in an energetic argument about which of them was going to pin his jeans together with a large safety pin produced from one of their dresses. There seemed to be little enthusiasm for getting too close to Macheath's wedding tackle, and the gentleman in question was even less keen, watching the pin with a very nervous eye and enjoining them to be careful in tones that were clearly audible beyond the orchestra pit.

The point in the scene when Macheath had to rejoin the action was fast approaching. In the end he conducted the rest of his spirited defence in a loud voice and with his back to the audience, before scuttling offstage for a less risky costume fix than was offered by the tarts.

***

That summer saw Phil and me both working hard to save some money for our future together, so we embarked on the autumn term of our final year, rather more jaded than was ideal. Perhaps that's why the romance cooled a little. Or perhaps the novelty had worn off and we were taking each other for granted.

Bob seized his opportunity to offer more exciting diversions than were available to a penniless student. A trip to see a Stoppard play, a concert in the Festival Hall – both these came my way on occasions when Phil was tied up with an unavoidable visit home (his gran wasn't well), or a deadline for an important essay. Phil's good humour with Bob was starting to wear thin, and the joke was no longer funny, when a blast from the past stepped into this volatile mix.

Pete Lynch came back onto the scene in the least exciting way, but it blew my whole life out of the water. In those pre-mobile-phone days, if anyone wanted to get hold of anyone in the hall of residence, whoever was on the reception desk would pick up the phone and ask the caller who they wanted, then shout over the Tannoy for whoever it was to rush down the stairs and pick up the phone. The ensuing conversation would be listened to by everyone in reception or, if you were really unlucky and the volunteer receptionist was feeling wicked, it would be broadcast to the whole building over the Tannoy. On this occasion, I got the Tannoy shout, and galloped downstairs thinking it was Phil calling from his gran's. It wasn't.

A voice I vaguely recognised said, 'Hi, Elf, long time no see. Fancy a meal at Chez Francois tonight?'

This offer of French cuisine in Muswell Hill's answer to Le Gavroche was more than a little enticing, but I didn't know who I was talking to.

'Sounds good,' I said cautiously. 'But—'

'You don't know who I am, do you?' the voice cut in. 'It's Pete. Pete Lynch. I'm down here for a week's trial at,' and he named a big accountancy firm. 'So, how about it?'

'Why me?' I asked with more honesty than manners.

'I don't know that many people in London,' he said, 'so I thought of you and Phil, but I gather he's away at the moment. So how about you and I have a catch-up? Dinner's on me,' he added.

We agreed on 7.30, and I rushed off to change. My student wardrobe didn't offer a lot of choice. Outside of the normal daywear of jeans and jumpers, I had one Laura Ashley long dress (the one I'd worn as Lucy Lockit), a couple of minis which were beginning to be slightly old hat, and one dark purple dress that fitted tightly on top and swooped to a swirly skirt. That was the one I decided on and I added a lilac shawl at the last minute. It wasn't à la mode, but it was flattering. And I'd never been very worried about looking a bit different. I still thought of the big-skirted dress I'd inherited from my aunt with fondness.

I walked up to Chez Francois in the high street just after seven. Pete was already inside, waiting at the table with a glass of red wine in front of him. The maître d' greeted me effusively at the door with his usual mix of franglais and broken English and showed me to the table. I was grinning as I accepted Pete's kiss on the cheek and sat down.

'Something funny?' he asked me rather irritably and checked his image in the mirror behind me.

'No, nothing,' I said. 'It's good to see you, Pete. How's things with you?' It was a lucky question. Clearly, he liked talking about himself, as he embarked on a long explanation of his career so far in accountancy. I had no particular wish to explain that 'Francois' was actually 'Frank' and as cockney as Bow Bells, as had been very obvious on the one occasion I'd eaten there with a genuine Frenchman. When greeted with a torrent of fluent French, 'Francois' had hastily retreated to the kitchen with much arm waving and some excuse about a 'crise'. Later he'd explained that Pierre had obviously been a native of 'La France profonde' with an impenetrable accent to anyone from 'La Paree metropolitan'!

By the time our first course of snails (Pete) and prawns (me) had arrived, his good humour had returned, and he was questioning me closely about Phil and our lives together. As I watched him fiddling the snails out of their shells, I couldn't help wondering if he'd chosen them in a bid to look sophisticated rather than because he liked them.

'I never thought you and Phil would be an item,' he announced suddenly, giving up on the last snail and pushing his plate to one side. I finished my garlicky prawns before I answered.

'Why not?' I asked. 'We have a lot in common.'

'Really?' he said. 'Phil's a pretty ordinary sort. He's never going to be anything more exciting than a small-town solicitor, writing wills and conveyancing houses. While you, you could do anything.'

'That's not what you said when I joined the Potters,' I said, tactlessly. 'You didn't want to sing with a child.'

'Nor did I,' he said. 'But that was then, and this is now. You're not a child any longer, Elf.'

Our steaks arrived, accompanied by peas, fries and cauliflower cheese. The subject of Phil did not recur, as Peter deployed all the charm at his disposal. And it was very effective. He made me laugh, he engaged me in debate, and made me feel special. I had no idea, at the time, how much of the evening was a polished performance. By the time we had coffee and mints, I was feeling very well disposed to my old friend, and when he walked me back to the hall, I didn't demur at his demand of a goodnight kiss.

It was no peck on the cheek, but a full-on, full-body grapple. I emerged with my hair dishevelled and lipstick smudged. He laughed softly, wiped my remaining lipstick off with his thumb, then turned and walked away. I watched for a moment and saw him take out a large white hankie to wipe his mouth. He was talking no risks with lipstick on his face! As soon as he rejoined the high street, he held his arm up, flagged a taxi and got in. As far as I could see, he didn't turn round.

I made it through the front door, just before it was locked at 11pm. The resident on locking-up duty, a big lad named Derek, waved me in, then said, 'Phil's back. He's been looking for you.'

'Oh God,' I said, sounding guilty of a lot more than a night out with an old friend. 'I wasn't expecting him back until tomorrow.' And I shot up the stairs, along the girls' corridor, then down the back stairs in the hope of sneaking along to Phil's room without being spotted.

The only person in the boys' corridor was Gavin, without his glasses on, and I knew he wouldn't shop me even if he could see who I was, so I went along to Phil's door and tapped on it gently. He opened it to let me in, then closed it behind me hurriedly.

'How's your gran?' I asked. 'I wasn't expecting you back until tomorrow.'

'Obviously,' he said rather tartly.

'What do you mean by that?' I demanded. Bear in mind I'd been drinking wine all evening and wasn't entirely sober.

'I watched you coming home with Pete Lynch,' he said. 'Made quite a meal of your face, didn't he?' He turned me to face his mirror, and I saw that I had lipstick under my lower lip. It seemed Pete's manoeuvre with his thumb hadn't been very effective. Or, as I realised later, had perhaps been very effective, but not what I thought he'd intended. At the time, and fuelled with wine-inspired indignation, I swiped the back of my hand across my face, said something like, *Well if that's how you feel*, and marched off back to my own room.

We patched things up the following morning, as I battled my slight hangover, and everything went back to normal. Until a huge bunch of roses arrived in reception with a tag addressed to me with the words 'Until next time'.

That autumn, everything seemed to be bad-tempered. Phil was snappy and distracted by his degree studies. I had settled down to some concentrated work in my projects – one practical, one library – while also trying to keep up with the LOS and its demands. This year we were doing *HMS Pinafore*, and I was Buttercup. Between study and rehearsals, I didn't have a lot of spare time. Phil had dropped out of the orchestra owing to pressure of work, leaving me with a solo trek home on the Underground and buses after late nights. When Pete found out, he was furious and insisted on picking me up in his newly acquired car and running me back to the hall. I made a rather half-hearted demur and settled for enjoying the luxury of car rides instead of public transport. Before long he was picking me up after every rehearsal, and we'd stop somewhere for a drink on the way home. Phil had often turned in by the time I got home. He didn't ask why I was so late, and I didn't volunteer an explanation.

We went home for New Year, and it was a disaster. Phil had flu. My parents were worried about my grandad who, with hindsight, was developing dementia and kept going missing. On New Year's Day, he disappeared in the late afternoon. His neighbours called us to say he had gone out leaving the front door not only unlocked but wide open. The Three-Day Week effect didn't help. One of the scheduled power cuts hit at the same time, leaving us groping round in the dark, trying to find him. Another neighbour with an intelligent border collie, (is there any other sort? I hear you ask) came to help, and at the last minute Pete joined us as well. I spoke to Phil on the phone, but he was evidently not at all well, so I encouraged him to stay in bed.

After an hour or two, my parents threw in the towel and got the police involved. They came round remarkably promptly and took away details of my grandfather, his habits and acquaintances, as well as a relatively recent photo. Then with my mother under instruction to stay home and wait for a phone call, the rest of us went out again, torches in hand. It was after ten o'clock by now, cold and raining with a miserable sleet-filled air that did nothing for our optimism.

Pete was insistent that we should take another look round the allotments.

'Let's be absolutely certain he's not in any of the sheds,' he kept saying. 'We'd do that if he was a missing kitten. Why not do it for a vulnerable adult?'

'The police said they asked everyone to check their sheds,' I said, almost trotting to keep up with his determined stride.

'Huh.' Pete snorted. 'And what makes you think anyone does what the police say? I'm sure it's worth checking for ourselves.'

By the time we arrived at the allotments, everyone else had peeled off to carry on the search in the open fields near the town. So we were completely alone when we walked the path that ran down the centre. Most of the squares of garden, marked out by rickety fencing or in some cases with trellis propped up on old tyres, had at least one tumbledown shed. Some had a greenhouse as well.

We started with the plots nearest the road, I took the ones on the right, and Pete the ones on the left. By the time we were halfway across the field, I was growing discouraged.

'Pete,' I shouted. 'I think this is a waste of time. We should be helping up on the moor.'

'We're nearly there,' shouted Pete. 'We might as well finish now.'

I shone my torch in the direction of his shout and saw him move across the penultimate plot in the left-hand row, toward a very small shed in the corner. It was only half man height, and not much bigger than a small car in area. I think it had been used for chickens. I opened my mouth to say, *Don't be ridiculous*, then shut it again, sighed heavily and went on to the next shed on my side. It was locked. I banged on the door, listened for a moment, then found a window and shone my torch in. Nothing. I was just turning to call to Pete, when he shouted to me.

'Here. Come here, Elf. He's here.'

'What!' I almost dropped my torch, and ran over the field as fast as I could, given all the rough ground and half-grown vegetables in my way. The sleet had come back again, and the beam of light I was trying to use to illuminate my path, kept bouncing back at me from the air itself.

As I got closer, I saw Pete's torch was focussed on the body of a man, lying on some sacking in the tiny shed. At first, I thought it was a tramp. Then shockingly I realised the soiled and crumpled shape belonged to my grandad.

'I'll stay here with him,' said Pete. 'You go and get help.'

'No.' I was definite. 'You'll be much faster than me. I'll stay. You go.'

He was going to argue, but at that moment my grandad opened his eyes, looked into Pete's torch beam and screamed. I threw myself into the shed and put my arms round him.

'It's okay, Grandad,' I kept saying. 'It's okay now. We'll get you home.' Then I turned to Pete and said, 'Go on, hurry up. The sooner you go, the sooner you'll be back.'

He hesitated a moment longer, swore, turned round and ran back to the main road.

I was still holding my grandad and he was still moaning, then he looked at me properly and seemed to realise who I was.

'It's okay, Grandad. It's all going to be all right now. Pete will be back soon with help.'

He reacted to the name, shuddered, then said more or less clearly, 'He locked me in here.'

'No, Grandad,' I said. 'You've got confused. He just found you and let you out.'

'He locked me in,' he said again, and kept saying it. Contradicting him seemed to be distressing him, so after a bit I shut up and just concentrated on trying to warm him up by hugging him close.

When Pete eventually reappeared, it was with an ambulance plus a couple of police. My grandad was still mumbling about having been locked in, but his mumbles were getting less and less clear. The ambulance driver was emphatic that the priority was to get him into the hospital to be warmed up and checked over. They took him away, still mumbling. The police congratulated Pete, thanked everyone around them for their help, and headed for the station.

'What about my mum and dad?' I asked.

'They've already been told,' said Pete. 'They're on their way to the hospital. Come on, let me take you home.'

I didn't argue.

11

In the Dark

Grandad was taken to the North Staffs Royal Infirmary. Persuaded to make a diversion on our way home, Pete drove me there through streets darkened by more power cuts.

'I hope to God the hospital's okay,' I said.

'Hospitals are protected from the cuts,' said Pete. 'Along with a few other essential services.'

We rushed into the waiting room together, where we found my mum and dad. They greeted Pete with hugs and kisses, like a conquering hero. He got the full credit for finding Grandad from everyone except Grandad. It seemed Grandad was still accusing Pete of having locked him in the shed. There was a huge police sergeant, who insisted on sitting Pete and me down for a few questions. He'd have liked to see us alone, but my mother was having none of it. She barged in, almost knocking over the poor young constable at the door, and banged her handbag down on the table.

'What you need to understand,' she said firmly to the sergeant, 'is that my old dad has dementia. He often gets confused about things, which is why we got in a panic when we realised he'd wandered off again. He hasn't seen Pete here for some time, so it's not surprising he's in a muddle about when and where he saw him this evening. We're immensely grateful to Pete for finding him before he got hypothermia. Anyway, it must be nonsense,' she added, 'because Pete's sister spent the early part of the evening with him. She's just rung up, asking where he'd got to.'

The policeman looked up at that. 'Can you give me the young lady's name and address?' he asked and made a note of what Mum told him. Then he said, 'You won't mind me saying, I'm sure, that if the old gentleman has a habit of wandering off, perhaps you need to take better precautions.'

'We will,' promised my mother. 'We've already thought of that.'

At that point, the nurse came out and said we could see Grandad now, but only for a few minutes as he needed to rest. 'And only two at a time,' she said sternly.

'I'll wait here,' said Pete. 'He won't want to see me anyway.'

Mum hesitated, then said, 'I'm afraid you're right, Pete. Which is a pity, as he should be saying thank you. But you have thanks from the rest of us,' and she kissed him on the cheek.

'You go in with your mum, then get yourself off home,' said Dad. 'I'm sure Pete will take you. I'll go and see the old rogue after you come out, and then bring your mum home.'

The whole event occasioned a family conference the next day. Mum's sister Jenny and her husband came over from Leek, and everyone sat round the dining-room table. To my surprise, I was told to join them.

'This affects you, Elf,' said my dad. When I looked puzzled, he just said, 'There's something we need to explain.'

'The thing is,' said my mum, 'we need to decide what's going to happen to your grandad when he comes out of hospital. He clearly can't go on living alone. Moreover, things are going to get worse, not better, according to the doctors. So, the options are, either he lives with one of us, she looked at her sister, and we need to adapt our houses and hire carers to make sure we can keep him safe. Or he goes into a home.'

'Surely Grandad should be asked what he wants.' I got in first, just ahead of my aunt.

'He can't come to us,' she said. 'I can't afford to give up my job.'

My mother looked at me and chose to respond to my comment. 'I'm afraid we're past that point,' she said. 'The specialists at the hospital say he no longer has capacity, and we must decide for him. I have power of attorney jointly with your aunt Jenny, so we can make the decisions. And *I* think we should be looking for a good care home.'

'So do I,' said Aunt Jenny.

'Well, that's it then, isn't it,' I said. 'Poor Grandad. But it needs to be a good one. We don't want him ending up somewhere they abuse old people.'

'And that's where you come in,' said Aunt Jenny. 'As the inheritor of our father's estate, obviously you're affected by anything that uses up the capital on care home fees.'

'Me?' I said, amazed. 'Why me?'

'Because your grandad believed that spare cash should benefit the younger generation, not us,' said my mum, 'and you're the only one.' I looked at Aunt Jenny under my eyelashes and observed that she wasn't exactly enamoured of the arrangement. She noticed my gaze, and replied to the question I hadn't asked.

'It's my father's right to do what he wants with his money,' she said.

'And we have had gifts,' added my mum. 'We weren't entirely forgotten. But the point is, Elf, you need to understand that the more we spend on my father's care now, the less you'll inherit.'

'Of course you must spend it on him!' I was outraged. 'It's his money. He has a right to live in comfort, not in some squalid local-authority home. I can pay my own way,' I added. 'I don't need handouts.'

'You might be glad of a little something when you want to buy a house,' said my mum. 'But, all the same, I'm glad you reacted the way you did. It's what I expected of you. It's agreed then. We use the old family home to fund Dad's care for as long as it's needed.'

'Agreed,' said Aunt Jenny.

And that was that, until my father added, 'Just one thing, Elf, everyone, this stays in the family. There's no need to mention it outside this circle.'

'We'll have to tell your grandad's accountant and the solicitor,' my mother objected.

'Obviously,' my father agreed. 'But no one else. I hope we can trust the professionals to be discreet.' I said nothing, but did notice that the accountants were the company that Pete worked for. I shrugged mentally. Presumably it was a big company and there was no reason for Pete to get involved.

The following day, Phil and I took the train back to London. Pete had offered us a lift, but Phil had declined it. I thought he was mad, and said so, as he was still wobbly from the flu. But he was adamant. On the train, I filled him in on the details of the family meeting. He looked up sharply when I mentioned my bequest.

'Don't tell anyone about that,' he said. 'It's best kept within the family.'

'That's what Dad said,' I replied, rather defensively, and decided to keep to myself the fact that I'd also told Pete, when he rang up about the lift to London. My head had still been full of everything, and when he'd asked about the family get-together, somehow, it had leaked out. *It doesn't matter*, I told myself. *The company he works for already knows. And as for Phil – he will be family soon.* I knew I was making excuses to myself for my indiscretions. I decided not to say any more.

***

Back at uni, and after a week of rolling power cuts, we were beginning to get used to this bizarre way of living. Practicals and even some lectures were rescheduled to work around the interruptions in electricity supply. I got very efficient at putting mascara on by candlelight without singeing my eyelashes. Meals at the hall of residence were adjusted according to whether hot food was possible. We got used to filling flasks with hot water when we could, and huddling in duvets or blankets when the heating went off.

When I spoke to my mum at the end of the week, I asked after my grandad, now in a care home in Burslem. 'I assume he's doing better than the rest of us,' I said. 'I assume care homes are on the priority list.'

'Apparently not,' said Mum in a snappy sort of way. 'At least, not this one. It's something to do with it having a generator for emergency equipment, so it doesn't get priority supplies. It's a real pain, if you ask me. The staff are tearing their hair out. The generator only keeps some of the equipment going, so a lot of the home is in darkness when the electricity's off. They end up trying to get the residents off to bed early, and some of them aren't very cooperative, including your grandfather,' she added.

The following day, Friday, I had the first dress rehearsal for Pinafore, and I had rather assumed that Pete would give me a lift home as usual. I was a bit put out, when he rang to say that something had 'come up' and he wouldn't be around until Saturday.

'See you then,' he said.

'Sorry,' I said with some satisfaction. 'Phil and I are out on Saturday.' And I rang off.

But the news on Saturday derailed my plans. I got the Tannoy call at around 09.20, which was early for a weekend morning, but the reception volunteer said, 'I think it's urgent, Elf,' and pointed me at the telephone booth with a very serious face. I went in and picked up the dangling receiver.

'Hello,' I said.

'Elf, it's your mum,' said her voice. 'I'm sorry, Elf, but it's bad news. Your grandad died last night.'

'What?' I said, made stupid by shock. 'What d'you mean? I thought he'd got over his late-night wander at New Year. He wasn't ill, was he?'

'No, at least, not as far as we know,' she said. 'All I do know is that the care assistant went in this morning to wake him, and he was dead, face down in his bed.'

'How did that happen?' I asked. 'Didn't anyone check on him last night?'

'Apparently not. Because they had power cuts last night, so no one went in until this morning. Elf,' she gulped, and I could tell she was trying not to cry, 'the police are investigating.'

I was shocked and clung on to the receiver in my hand. 'Is that just because it's a sudden death, or because there's a problem?' I asked.

'We don't know. The lady at the home said they'd have to report it to the coroner anyway, but that the police had some concerns about the circumstances.'

I came out of the phone booth and headed for the stairs to the first floor and the boys' corridor, but Phil met me at the top of the stairs.

'I heard your name called,' he started, then stopped at the look on my face. 'Come in here,' he said, and ushered me into the residents' lounge, quiet and dark at that time of the day. He pushed me into a chair by the windows and sat opposite me, still holding my hands. 'Tell me,' he said.

'It's Grandad,' I said. 'He's dead, and it sounds like the police are treating it as suspicious.'

'What exactly have they said?' he asked.

'I don't know,' I cried, frustrated that I had so few details. 'It seems the care home found him dead in his bed this morning, but that's all I know.'

'Wait here,' he said, and ran downstairs. I stayed where I was, snivelling into my screwed-up hankie and wondered why it was hitting me so hard. The fact of his death was not so very surprising; we'd all known it might not be very long. I concluded it was the circumstances that were bothering me. The awful implication that he might have been mistreated in some way or neglected. I sat staring at the door, waiting for Phil to come back. He wasn't long.

When he did come back, he was carrying two mugs of tea and had a packet of biscuits stuffed in his pocket.

'These are from Angela,' he said, referring to one of our friends. 'I've just been on the phone, talking to your father. I asked should we come home, but he said not. He said to stay here, concentrate on our studies, and he'd keep us posted.'

'That sounds like Dad,' I said. 'What did he say about the police investigation?'

'Well, first of all, he said it was customary with an unexpected death like this, and you weren't to start climbing out of your pram about it. Second, he said the main focus of the investigation was had there been any negligence on the part of the care home, and that you could put your more lurid imaginings to bed. I'm quoting,' he added. I smiled a watery smile.

'I can tell you are,' I said.

'What's more, it seems the care home itself is also undertaking an investigation to see if it was at fault. Finally, there's to be an inquest, but that might be some weeks off.'

I blew my nose on the sodden hankie and straightened up. 'I shall go home for the inquest,' I declared. 'Otherwise, I'll do what Dad suggests, and get back to work. Thanks, Phil,' I added.

'Always got your back, Elf, you know that,' he said, and picked up the mugs to take them back to the kitchen.

Our plans for that Saturday got downgraded from a trip to Kew Gardens to a mooch around Hampstead and back home for a takeaway. I told Phil that Pete had suggested meeting up, but he wasn't keen, so I let it go.

The following Tuesday was the final rehearsal of Pinafore before the first night on the Wednesday. It was a disaster. My padding slipped – I was Buttercup remember, and in my early twenties I wasn't exactly buxom! The chorus of sisters and cousins and aunts got their, admittedly very similar, vocal entries muddled up and ground to an embarrassing halt. Then Captain Corcoran managed to suspend himself by his sword belt as he tripped lightly down the steps from the poop deck. On investigation, we found that his sword had gone through a hole in the stair rail, which should have been panelled but the stage crew hadn't got round to it. He'd then taken one step too many and found himself dangling a couple of feet above stage level, where he manfully delivered his recitative in a rather strangled gasp. At least that provided some light relief. Bob, who took the blame for the crucial lack of panelling, immediately set to correcting the problem. Pete was visible at the back of the auditorium, waiting to take me home, but I delayed a moment to chat to Bob. Addressing the back of his head as he hammered and stapled, I asked, 'Is there a way to find out about an investigation into a sudden death?'

'Depends on the circumstances,' he replied. 'And where it happened.' He put his staple gun down and turned round. 'What's bothering you, Elf? Is it that rather ruthless-looking spiv that's chauffeuring you around these days?' Ignoring the aspersions cast on Pete, I explained about my grandad.

'I just wondered if it was possible to find out what the thinking is? What the police think happened?'

'You can ask them,' he said. 'Otherwise, you have to wait for the inquest.'

'That's not very helpful,' I complained. 'And he's not a spiv.'

'Maybe not, but there's something about him,' said Bob. 'You're much better off sticking with Phil. Or me of course.'

'Now you're changing the subject. About my grandfather...'

'I've told you already,' he said. 'There's really nothing else you can do.'

Pinafore was a mild success. Apart from me starting a recitative a third too high on the first night, and having to improvise my way back to the key I should have been in – incidentally, the unfortunate Captain Corcoran's face when he thought he'd have to pick up from me at the higher pitch had to be seen to be believed. As I say, apart from that, everything went pretty well and our audiences were appreciative. Both Pete and Phil came to the last-night party, which was interesting. Pete attracted a lot of attention. His sportsman good looks would have been enough, but he was also in a very elevated mood, and was soon the centre of an attentive crowd, mostly female, hanging on his every word. Phil was, by contrast, moody and giving a good impression of a single sock in a pile of laundry. He hung around on the edge of the, slightly raucous, party, plainly wishing he was on his way home. At one point I found myself beside Bob and commented irritably on Phil's mood.

'Hardly surprising is it, given you and Pete,' replied Bob.

'What me and Pete?' I demanded of his retreating back. 'There is no me and Pete.'

'Could've fooled me,' he said, adding, 'and Phil,' as an afterthought.

Around one in the morning, we headed for home by shared taxi: Pete, Phil, a blonde girl I didn't know who seemed to have come to the party with someone else but was leaving it with Pete, and me. Phil and I were dropped off first, then the taxi took Pete and the blonde on to whatever he had planned for the rest of the night.

Phil and I had late passes for the hall, so let ourselves in and dropped the key into the box by the warden's office.

'Thank God that's over,' said Phil. 'I'm off to bed. See you in the morning, Elf?' I stared after him, gobsmacked, then as he showed no signs of turning round or waiting for a response, I took myself off to bed.

I was still fuming when I woke up in the morning, and judging by the face on him, Phil wasn't feeling any more emollient when he got up either. I sat down next to him in the canteen.

'What's the matter with you?' I asked. 'You were miserable last night, and you look even worse this morning.' If someone can be said to eat cornflakes aggressively, he managed it. 'You could have made a bit of an effort at the party,' I said. 'You knew most of the people there, and you knew it meant a lot to me, as my last production before I leave QMC.'

He put his spoon down with deliberation and looked at me for the first time. 'It didn't seem you needed me to make your evening complete,' he said. 'You already have Bob on a string, and Pete was getting all your attention, so what was I needed for? Window dressing?'

I gasped. 'That's so unfair,' I said, but he interrupted me before I could fairly get going.

'I love you, Elf, you know that,' he said in an undertone, 'but sometimes you can be a real bitch and it gives me the pip.'

He slung his half-eaten bowl of cornflakes onto the dirty-dishes trolley and stood up to leave. 'Perhaps you need to decide what you want,' he said. 'Pete, or me, or even Bob? Let me know when you've made your mind up.'

I was still seething when I got back to my room, breakfast-less, and found Pete sitting at his ease on my bed.

'Come out for breakfast?' he suggested. 'If you haven't eaten already.'

'No, I haven't eaten already,' I said.

'Phil coming?' asked Pete.

'No,' I said, and didn't enlarge on my reply.

12

Moving On

Pete took me for breakfast at the Muswell Hill Golden Egg. While not exactly haute cuisine, they served a darn good full English, and after the upsets of the morning, not to mention the alcohol content of the night before, a serious overdose of cholesterol was just what I needed. Better still, Pete continued to enjoy the elevated mood of the night before and was great fun to be around. After laughing at his jokes, and consuming copious quantities of toast and marmalade washed down by gallons of decent coffee, I plucked up the courage to ask him how his night had gone.

'Have a good time with the blonde?' I asked. 'Sorry to call her that, but you never told me her name.'

'You know a gentleman never tells,' he said with a wink, but then added in a rather ungentlemanly fashion, 'You don't need her name. It's not important.'

'That's a bit rude!' I exclaimed.

'Not really,' he said. 'She was fun for an evening, but you should know there's only one woman for me.'

I could feel my smile dying on my face, and whatever I was going to say died on my lips. I buried myself in my coffee mug again, and after a long pause managed, 'Don't be daft, Pete.'

He leaned over the table and took my mug from me and put it down. Then he took hold of both my hands in his.

'I'm definitely not daft, Elf. Not now anyway, although I concede I might have been when I was younger. I'm sure you know how I feel about you. Can I hope you're starting to see the real Phil now? And maybe growing out of your boy-meets-girl romance?'

I took my hands back and looked away. 'I think I'd perhaps better go back to the hall,' I said, then realised that I was looking through the restaurant plate glass window, straight at Phil. He turned away as I looked, walked a few strides, and got on the bus that was just about to pull away from the nearby bus stop. I stood and took a few steps toward the door, then realised the futility of rushing after someone who was speeding away on a double-decker. I stood in the middle of the restaurant, irresolute, and Pete stood up behind me and spoke over my shoulder.

'Looks like you've got a day off,' he said. 'My car's just down the street. Let's go to Cambridge.'

I gaped at him. 'What? Just like that?'

'Just like that,' he said. 'It'll only take an hour and a half. We'll be there in time for lunch, followed by a punt on the river and afternoon tea in Grantchester. What do you say?'

'What about Phil?' I said, feebly waving in the direction the bus had taken.

'What about Phil? He's gone out himself, hasn't he? Come on, Elf. Live a little. It'll be fun.'

'I'll need to change,' I said, waving at my black jeans and red jumper donned for a Sunday spent peacefully catching up with coursework and the TV.

'Rubbish. They're perfect for a boat trip on the Cam. You've got a jacket, haven't you? Yes.' He caught up the Puffa jacket from the back of my chair. 'Come on.' He seized me firmly by one arm, towed me down the street and round the corner to his car, where he thrust me firmly into the passenger seat. It seemed I had no choice. I decided to go with the flow.

***

We had a lovely day. The sun shone and even though the air was cold enough for me to see my breath, the exertion of propelling the boat through the icy waters of the Cam kept me warm enough for comfort. After the pub lunch that preceded our boat trip, I'd thought I'd be too stuffed to manage tea as well, but the exercise or the cold weather, or both, did their trick and we settled down to a late high tea in Grantchester, exactly as Pete had promised. He looked at me over the teapot, toasted cheese and stacked cakes with some satisfaction.

'There, that was fun, wasn't it, Elf?' he said. 'When shall we go out again?'

'I haven't said we will,' I said, but I knew, even as the words left my lips, that it was no more than a smokescreen. I would go out with Pete again, and I stopped myself from completing the thought. I didn't want to think about what that meant for Phil and me. We realised the waiter was hovering at our table.

'I don't want to hurry you,' he said, 'but we've got one of those dratted power cuts starting soon. So we'll be closing shortly.'

'No problem,' said Pete. 'Let me have the bill, and we'll be on our way.'

Outside in the village main street, he paused beside his car.

'Hurry up, Pete,' I said, rubbing my arms. 'It's cold out here now.' He took no notice, put the car keys back in his pocket, then reached out to me, pulled me close, and kissed me very thoroughly.

I tried to make some show of resistance but what I said was muffled by his lips, and my attempt to pull away was negated by his strong arms round me. I gave in and enjoyed the experience. When he did eventually let go, I was breathless and very turned on.

'See,' he said, 'we're meant to be together, Elf. Think what our life could be like.' Then he drove me back to Muswell Hill and dropped me outside the hall with a wave and a cheery toot on the horn.

Phil was waiting for me, just inside the door of the TV lounge, where he could keep an eye on the stairs. Whatever was on the TV was ignored as he leaped to his feet and intercepted me.

'What's going on, Elf?' he demanded. 'Where've you been?'

'Cambridge,' I said, attempting to carry on up the stairs.

'With Pete.' It was more a statement than a question. 'So where does that leave us?' he demanded, ignoring the small crowd backed up on the stairs, which was growing bigger even as we spoke.

'Let's not do this here,' I said.

'Yes, here,' he replied. 'Unless you've something to hide, of course.'

'I've nothing to hide,' I said, my voice growing louder. 'I'd point out that it was you who took off first. What was I supposed to do? Hang around until you got over your tantrum? I've had a lovely day out, and that's the end of it, unless you want to blow it up out of all proportion. Come on, Phil,' I said. 'Let's leave it for now, before one of us says something we'll regret. I'll see you in the morning.'

He wasn't listening and spoke over me. 'Don't tell me you haven't connected Pete's sudden interest in you with your new inheritance?' His voice was very close to a sneer. It just didn't sound like my Phil at all. I opened my mouth to deny having told Pete about the bequest from my grandad, then remembered it would be a lie. If anything, that made me madder, and I spoke without thinking.

'If that's how you feel, then maybe it's time we called it a day,' I said. 'We've had a good few years, but we don't seem to feel the same any more. Thanks for the good times, Phil, but this is the end.' I just had time to see his expression crumple, when our latest power cut arrived, and the lights went out. I turned away and went up to my room without another word, feeling as though I had just stamped on a puppy.

The following morning, a Monday, I looked for Phil. I wasn't comfortable leaving things between us like that, but when I ventured along the boys' corridor I was stopped by the senior resident, Felix. He was a tall gangling chap, studying Politics, Philosophy and Economics at King's College and, reputedly, aiming for a career in politics. Whatever he did, or volunteered for, was almost always aimed at burnishing his CV. On this occasion, however, he sounded genuinely concerned.

'You're too late, he's gone.'

'Gone where?' I asked.

'Gone home. At least that's where he said he was going. I hope to God he was. He's absolutely broken. I assume you know that.'

I disregarded the last comment. 'When did he leave?'

Felix perched his bony bum on the stair rail and looked at me over his glasses. 'Sparrow's fart this morning. Is it really all over between you two? Of all the relationships in this place, yours looked the strongest.'

'Perhaps that was the problem,' I muttered.

He said, 'You what?'

I said, 'Nothing,' and went down to reception, feeling in my pocket for some change.

One of the two public phone booths was empty, so I grabbed it while I could and rang home with my last few coins. 'Can you ring me back, Mum?' I asked. Then I hung around waiting for the phone to ring again, hoping that no one with an officious streak would come and throw me out for misuse of the public phone. The phone rang; I grabbed it before it managed more than one *brrnng*, and it was Mum.

'What's wrong, Elf?' she asked. 'You sound upset.'

'It's Phil,' I said. 'We had a bit of a bust-up last night and I told him we were over. I've just found out he shot off home this morning and I'm a bit worried about him. Is there any chance you can find out if he got home safely, and let me know?' There was a big sigh down the phone.

'That's a pity, Elf,' she said. 'I thought he was a keeper. But I always said you got together too young, so maybe it was inevitable. However, you don't sound as though you don't care.'

'I do care,' I protested. 'Of course I care. Just because I don't think I'm in love with him any longer, doesn't mean I don't care what happens to him. We've been best friends for a long time.'

'You're going to miss him,' she said with gloomy prediction. 'Of course I'll ask round for you. I have friends who live near his parents, and if all else fails, I can ring them, although I don't suppose either you or I will be flavour of the month in that quarter, once they find out you've dumped him.'

I went back to my room, supposedly to write an essay, but in reality waiting for my mum's return call. Lunchtime came and went, and I'd still heard nothing. I didn't dare go shopping for a sandwich in case I missed the call, so I made do with biscuits and coffee. Roundabout mid-afternoon, I finished my essay and ran out of biscuits. I searched all my pockets and had just found enough loose change for another call, when the Tannoy crackled and announced there was someone on the phone for me. I shot downstairs, nearly tripping and narrowly avoiding taking the last flight head first.

'Left-hand phone,' said the volunteer receptionist, and I dashed in to pick up the receiver.

'Hello,' I said.

'It's Mum. Phil got home, and according to *his* mum is staying up here for the rest of the week. She said to tell you she's sorry you've broken up and wishes you well. That's it.'

'Okay,' I said. Thanks, Mum. Bye.'

I was on my way to call at the bank for some cash before it closed, and to restock my biscuit supply, when I walked into Pete as I crossed the car park.

'I hear Phil's done a runner,' he said.

'Rubbish!' I said. 'It's true he's gone home though. We had a bit of a row last night when I got in.'

'So, he's history?' asked Pete, perching on the bonnet of his car. The picture of that encounter is still clear as crystal in my mind's eye. I remember I thought at the time that his smart trousers were going to get grubby from the salt and muck on the car, and I could hear a blackbird somewhere in the trees by the hall.

'He'll always be part of my history,' I replied. 'But it seems he's not part of my future.'

Pete stood up, clapped his hands together, then went round to the passenger door and held it open for me. 'Then let's start your future as we mean to go on,' he said. 'Hop in. We'll go for a drive and a meal.'

'I can't,' I said. 'I've got work to do.'

'Do it tomorrow,' he said. 'Come on, get a shift on. We may have the rest of our lives, but I haven't got all day.' I gave up and got in the car.

We ended up in a pub in Kings Langley. The Saracen's Head I think it was, in the main street, with just one bar and a lovely log fire. I sat by the fire while Pete brought our drinks over.

'Seems they don't usually do food on a Monday,' he said as he arrived at the table with two brimming glasses. 'I had to try a sob story, but it worked and they're rustling up some sandwiches and soup.'

'Oh, good,' I said. 'What sob story?'

'Doesn't matter,' he said, and took a swig of his beer. I looked at his regularly handsome features and thought that the sportsman was risking burial under a lot of weight, if he carried on like that. Then chastised myself for being mean. After all, it was me he was trying to cheer up. 'I always say,' he went on, 'that if you need cheering up, you need something to look forward to. So how about planning our wedding?'

I gasped, choked, and spat lager all over the table, my own legs and the floor. The barman, just delivering a tray of plates of sandwiches and two bowls of soup, recoiled, then with a pronounced grin placed the tray on the table with the words, 'That went well, mate!' And retreated to the bar. Even through my streaming eyes, I could see he was polishing glasses well within hearing distance of our conversation. This was more entertainment than he got most Mondays.

I seized the paper napkins off the tray and used them to mop myself up. When I'd stopped choking, I looked at Pete. I couldn't read his expression. It seemed to hover somewhere between amusement at my plight, irritation that his comment hadn't been received better, and embarrassment at being overheard by the barman. Reflecting later, years later, I realised the one reaction I hadn't seen was concern for me.

I took a careful sip of my drink to postpone the moment when I had to reply. Then I put my glass down very carefully, repositioned it a little, and picked up a sandwich in order to postpone my reply still further. As I bit into the sandwich – egg and cress, if you're wondering – I decided to see how long I could put it off. So, I solemnly ate the whole sandwich, then still without saying anything, picked up my spoon and started on the soup. Tomato, out of a tin. I ate with care and pernickety table manners, dipping the spoon away from me, and as I got toward the last few drops, tipping the bowl just slightly toward the centre of the table. At the end I dabbed my lips with one of the few remaining clean napkins, looked at Pete under my eyelashes, then picked up another sandwich. I noted, with considerable hidden amusement, that he looked fit to burst. This had become a competition between my delaying tactics and his unwillingness to speak next.

When I'd eaten all the sandwiches I could, without bursting, I leaned back, put the paper napkin on the plate, and finished my drink.

'That was very good, thank you, Pete,' I said. 'What next?' I noticed that his face was darkening and wondered if I'd pushed him too far, then he suddenly leaned back and laughed uproariously. The barman turned round, and so did a couple of locals leaning on the bar.

'What's so funny?' I hissed at him, but even through my irritation I could feel his laughter becoming infectious, and I was starting to grin despite myself.

Without replying, Pete turned to the bar and called, 'Have you got a bottle of champagne on ice? I think we have something to celebrate.' The barman looked puzzled, but reached under the bar, by no means averse to selling us an overpriced bottle of bubbly. Pete turned back to me.

'I'm right, aren't I, Elf?' he said. 'If the answer was going to be no, you'd have said something. You're only messing me about because the answer is going to be yes.'

'You are the most irritating and the least romantic man I ever met,' I said. I hesitated for just one second more – and that hesitation was genuine. *What was I letting myself in for?*

Then I said, 'The answer's yes. Bring it on, Pete.' I left it open whether I meant life, or the champagne. Pete assumed I meant the champagne and with a flourish opened the bottle brought by the barman. He poured two glasses, handed one to me and held his up in a toast.

'To us and the future,' he said. There was a cheer from the small group at the bar. Pete stood up and gave them a mock bow, then turned back to me and, bending over me, gave me a very long and thorough kiss. There was another cheer from the bar. Settling down again with his glass of bubbly, Pete picked up one of the few remaining sandwiches and said, 'So, where were we... Planning our wedding, I think.'

I looked at him through my bubbles. 'You really were serious then?'

'Of course I was. I told you that you were the only girl for me. I was just waiting for you to get Phil out of your system. Now, there's a piece of news I haven't told you. You know I've been doing a placement in the City...'

'Of course.' I nodded.

'Well I've landed a job there. I start next month. We can start house-hunting as soon as you graduate and get yourself a job. Where do you fancy living? North or south of the river?'

'You mean, we'll live in London?'

'Of course. Where else? You know the saying: He who is tired of London is tired of life.'

'I'd always assumed I'd go home when I graduated,' I said, trying to assimilate the sudden changes in my life.

'That was Phil. This is me,' said Pete firmly. 'We don't have to live in the middle of town. In fact, if we want to afford something decent, it's probably better we don't. We could look around the ends of the tube lines. Or somewhere a short train journey away – like Richmond.'

'Richmond would be even more expensive than London,' I scoffed, not quite realistically as it turned out. 'Croydon's probably more our mark. Look, let's take things one at a time. You mentioned a wedding, although I don't recall you asking me to marry you.'

'You will though, won't you, Elf?' It was a statement, not a question.

'I suppose I have to now,' I said, 'after you bought champagne in front of this little lot,' and I gestured at the group drinking at the bar. 'Although I must say, I had envisaged something more romantic.'

'We can do romantic on the honeymoon,' he said briskly. 'The first question is, wedding, large or small?'

'Small,' I said without stopping to think about it. Pete raised an eyebrow.

'Small it is,' he said. 'I thought that was where we might fall out. Glad we agree. Next question, this country or abroad?'

There I hesitated but came down firmly on home. 'My mother would never forgive me if we sneaked off,' I said.

'Okay, at home it is. See, it's easy,' he said, and raised his glass to me again. 'Next question. When? We could probably rush through a spring wedding if we really got a move on, or we could try for the summer, if we can get a venue.'

'So long as we can book the church,' I said, 'if we go for the summer, we could have a reception in my parents' garden. It's big enough for a small party.'

'How small were you thinking?' he asked, looking a bit startled.

'Oh, say about fifty,' I replied. 'I've never seen the sense in some massive do that's stuffed with ancient friends of the parents and takes all the money that could have been used in a deposit on a house.'

Pete opened his mouth, looked as though he was going to say something, then closed it again. After a pause he said, 'Sounds good to me. Fifty of the most important people in our lives, and if we want a party for other friends, we can have one later in London.' I thought, but didn't say, that didn't sound like saving money.

'When do we talk to my parents?' I asked.

'How about next weekend?' said Pete. 'No point hanging about if we want to get the church booked.'

'There's just one thing,' I said. 'My mum's going to think it's awfully quick after breaking up with Phil. In fact, everyone's going to think that. They're going to think we had something going on before I split with Phil. Perhaps we should wait a while.'

'No way,' said Pete, giving every impression of jumping in without thinking. Then he added, 'I mean, I've waited patiently for you, Elf. I'm not letting you get away now. We have nothing to be ashamed of. Let's just go for it and hang the gossips.'

13

MILESTONE 7: Watergate

My mother, however, fulfilled all my worst expectations. We'd phoned from the hall the night before to signal our intention to visit, so she had around eighteen hours to worry, and she seemed to have used them all. We rang Pete's mum too. She was divorced and lived on her own, in theory; but in practice there was usually a 'lodger' of some description. The latest version had lasted around seven months at the time of our announcement. He was about fifteen years younger than Pete's mum, seemed younger even than Pete, and whatever his attractions, it was clear his intelligence and his conversation were not among them.

Pete's mum shuffled the 'lodger' out to play soon after our arrival. At least that was what it felt like. She was polite enough to me, although I felt that I was found wanting in the make-up-and-clothes department, and we had nothing in common other than Pete. She expressed herself delighted with the idea of a summer wedding, and I could see hat designs floating in her mind even as we spoke. We left with her good wishes and moved on to the much bigger hurdle of my family, where we were due for lunch.

Pete had clearly put his mind toward making a good impression. He produced a huge bouquet of flowers for my mother from the boot of his car and a bottle of whisky for my father. I could see Mum's resolve softening behind the roses and freesias, but, unfortunately, it didn't soften much. We had barely got started on her signature lunch dish – homemade steak and kidney pie – when she launched her first missile.

'One thing puzzles me, Pete,' she said. I thought, *Aha,* and caught my father's eye. 'Why are you in such a rush? You know that Elf was in a relationship with Phil for years. Then it seems that, all in the same moment, she stops seeing him and she's engaged to you. If I didn't know my daughter better, it would look as though she'd been doing the dirty on Phil. But since I do know her, and I know she wouldn't do that, it must be you rushing her into something before she's had chance to turn round.'

I opened my mouth to chip in and my father shook his head slightly. *Leave it to Pete*, his eye was saying. I shut it again.

Pete swallowed a large mouthful of pie and put his fork down. 'The truth is,' he said, 'I've been waiting patiently for Elf for the last year, ever since I met her as a grown-up rather than as an idiot boy. Now I have my chance, I'm seizing it before someone else gets in.'

'You make my daughter sound like a bargain in a jumble sale,' complained my mother. 'Doesn't she get a chance to choose? She's barely got used to Phil not being around, and you're leaping in to take his place. I think she might benefit from standing on her own two feet for a while.'

'If you think Elf doesn't make her mind known, perhaps you don't know your daughter as well as you think,' replied Pete. Dad choked for a second and tried to hide a grin. Then he leaped into the conversation with a practical query about Pete's work, income and prospects.

When the arrival of a syrup sponge pudding and custard signalled the imminence of the end of the meal, the conversation turned to the wedding itself. My dad looked hugely relieved when he heard we wanted a small do, and my mum was pleased we were talking about a church wedding. The arguments began over the guest list.

'But we must ask Aunty Maud,' Mum protested.

'Why?' I asked. 'She's a hundred if she's a day, nutty as a fruitcake, and the last time she was here she stabbed Dad with her cake fork.'

'But she's family,' Mum replied.

'No, she's not even that,' I said. 'She's the cousin of an aged courtesy aunt. There's no relationship of either blood or marriage. Come on, Dad, speak up for me. You're the one who got a nasty flesh wound on her last visit.'

'Don't bring me into it,' said my dad, alarmed.

'I've got a suggestion,' said Pete. 'If we're talking about fifty guests in total, how about we say twenty-five for you, fifteen for my mum to choose, and ten of Elf's and my closest friends.'

'Won't your mum think that's a bit unfair?' I protested.

'I don't think so. I've a smaller family than you. We don't need to consider my father's side after all. And all the work of holding the party here will fall on you, so it seems fair to me.'

'Are you not going to invite your father?' My mother was shocked.

'No.' Pete was definite. 'No need. I've neither seen him nor heard from him since he left.'

My mother didn't look convinced, but I'm pretty sure my father kicked her under the table. He was all for a solution that let Mum invite her closest family even if it meant leaving Pete's missing father out of the picture.

At the end of lunch, Pete and my father went off to speak to the vicar about booking the church. Slightly to my horror, Mum and I settled down for a heart to heart.

'Are you sure, Elf?' she said, her face troubled. 'It all feels a bit rushed to me. You're not pregnant, are you?' she gasped as a sudden awful thought hit her. I was pleased it hadn't occurred to her earlier.

'No, I'm not pregnant,' I said. 'And yes, it is quick, but yes, I am sure. Sometimes you just know, don't you. It's like a mixture of chemistry and karma. The right person, and the right time.'

'You thought Phil was the right person for a long time,' she reminded me.

'Yes, but these last few months, it's been more habit than happiness.'

She was silent for a while, then said, 'Does he know about your inheritance from your grandad?'

'We haven't discussed it,' I said. Which was truth, but not the whole truth.

When Dad and Pete came back, they were triumphant. 'It's booked,' said Dad.

'Thursday, August the ninth', said Pete. 'That's okay isn't it, Elf? Enough time for you to find a dress?'

'I had thought of being married in a trouser suit,' I said just to wind him up, and nearly fell off my chair laughing at identical expressions of horror on his and my mum's face.

***

A month or so later, I went home on my own to go wedding-dress shopping with my mother. I arrived late on the Friday night and slept in my childhood bedroom, surrounded by my memorabilia, with Magic sleeping on my bed as she always used to. If I haven't mentioned her recently, it's because it was too painful. Obviously, I had to leave her with my mum while I was at university, and the vacations had been all too short for proper reunions, especially as they had been chopped up by field courses and the like. Now we were planning a home of our own, I was looking forward to having Magic with me all the time.

When I came down to breakfast, rubbing my eyes and yawning, I was snapped into sudden wakefulness by the unexpected presence of a burly man and a slightly less burly woman, both strangers, sitting in our living room and sipping cups of tea. My mum was there on the other side of the fireplace, looking tense and uncomfortable.

'This is my daughter, Aelfwyth,' she said, surprising me with the rare use of my full name. Then turning to me she added, 'This is Detective Inspector Lawton and Detective Constable Goodwin. They're here to talk about your grandfather.'

'Grandad?' I said stupidly and sat down next to my mum. 'What about Grandad? Is this the result of your investigation? Do you know what happened? Was the care home at fault?'

Mum shifted uncomfortably in her seat at the torrent of questions. 'If you'd shut up a moment, Elf, we might find out.'

'Sorry,' I said, and if my expression was grim, it was an accurate reflection of how I was feeling. 'So, what have you found?'

'That's the thing,' said DI Lawton. If a large policeman of the rugby-playing fraternity can be said to look uneasy, sitting drinking tea, he did. 'I'm sorry to say we haven't anything to report except a lot of unanswered questions and a hypothesis. As you know, sudden and unexpected deaths are always a matter for the coroner, and this one was referred to us for investigation. The care home has also carried out its own investigation. What conclusion the coroner will reach is a matter for them at the inquest. I'm here to report what we'll be saying at the inquest, so it doesn't come as a surprise.'

'Which is what?' I asked again.

'To start with, what we do know,' said DI Lawton, putting his teacup down on the hearth. I noticed Magic sneaked up behind his chair and quietly drank the dregs while he was speaking. 'We know that your grandfather was found dead, face down on his bed, by the care assistant carrying out their first round of the morning at seven-thirty, or thereabouts. They raised the alarm and attempted resuscitation, but he was already cold and had clearly been dead for some time. He was fully dressed and was lying on top of the covers, not under them. A doctor arrived shortly after, pronounced him dead at the scene and he was taken to the mortuary. A postmortem was carried out the following day; I'm sorry if this distresses you,' he interrupted himself, looking at my mum, but she waved a hand to indicate he should carry on.

'So, as I said, a postmortem was carried out the following day and found that he had died of asphyxiation. Apart from that, the doctor's report mentions that there were changes in the brain consistent with his diagnosis of dementia, that he had some symptoms of heart disease, and some superficial bruising on his back, and on one shin.

'One obvious question was, why hadn't there been any check on him the previous evening at bedtime? The care home has investigated, and we have interviewed their staff. It seems there was a power cut that evening and one or two of the other residents had got upset, causing a disturbance. In the confusion, it was assumed one of the care assistants had done the rounds of your grandfather's corridor. In fact, one of the assistants stated that they saw someone going up the stairs to the upper corridor, which was why they didn't do it themselves, but it was dark and they weren't able to say who it was.

'So, essentially, that's where our investigation rests. The theory at present is that your grandfather tripped or fainted and fell face down on the bed. And that, as he was a fairly heavy man, that resulted in his very unfortunate asphyxiation. I'm sorry we can't give you any better answer than that,' he said.

'What do you think the likely verdict will be at the inquest?' I asked.

'The conclusion, coroners don't reach verdicts,' he replied. 'A likely conclusion is death by misadventure. But, as I said, that is a matter for the coroner.'

111

'And when will the inquest be?'

'Three weeks today,' he replied.

It was a rather grim preface to wedding-dress shopping, and perhaps set the tone for the day. After a morning trying on successive collections of lace and fluff that looked and felt like lampshades, I was getting depressed, and my mum was getting irritable.

'What *do* you want, Elf?' she asked. 'We've tried white, cream and off-white in satin, silk, gauze, lace and everything in between. There can't be much more in the way of wedding dresses that you haven't tried.'

'I don't know,' I said rather helplessly, toying with my cod and chips lunch. 'I'll know it when I see it. I just know I don't want to look like a refugee from a soft-furnishings warehouse.'

After lunch, having exhausted all the obvious outlets, we started wandering the side streets for boutique shops.

'Perhaps I should look just for a long dress rather than a wedding dress,' I said. 'Or even that trouser suit.'

'Over my dead body,' muttered my mum, and marched off down the street ahead of me. I'd stopped by a charity shop, my eye caught by its window display. In among the teapots, jumpers and cushions that made up its staple wares, was a dress on a hanger.

'Mum,' I called, 'hang on a minute while I have a look in here.'

'You can't have a dress from a charity shop,' she said, aghast, then saw where I was looking.

'Wow,' she said, 'it *is* a lovely dress, but it's not a wedding dress and it probably won't fit either.' She was talking to empty air. I'd already gone into the shop.

'Yes, it is lovely,' the lady volunteer was saying, 'but you have to be pretty skinny to fit into it. You might do it,' she said, eyeing me up and down. 'It came from a rather grand lady who lives out of town. She said she'd been a bit of a flapper in her youth, and this dress had been one of her favourites.' I was holding the dress on its hanger up to the light from the shop window, and I could see why she would love it. It had a high round neck but left the shoulders bare. Obviously designed to fit closely to the body, it fell to the ground in sinuous curves.

'It has a fishtail skirt,' said the lady, warming to her task, and held it out. 'And look, it fastens with a lot of hooks and eyes like this,' – she demonstrated – 'so it fits perfectly with no pulling or gaping. If you're the right shape, of course,' she added. 'Why don't you try it on?'

'May I?' I didn't wait for an answer but took the dress into a small curtained changing room. After a few minutes the lady followed me in.

'You'll need help with the hooks and eyes,' she said, and fastened me up at the back. The dress fitted like a second skin, the fishtail skirt flicked out behind me and the mid-green sequins that covered the entirety of its surface sparkled and shimmered. I walked out into the main shop to look in a mirror and came face to face with my mum.

'Wow,' she said again. 'It could have been made for you, Elf. It's amazing. But you can't wear it as a wedding dress!'

'Why not?' I demanded. 'It's only recently wedding dresses have been white. It's perfect. It's just what I want.'

'But what about a veil?'

'No veil,' I said, and the shop lady echoed me.

'What you need with this dress,' she said, 'is a circlet of wildflowers, and you'll look like the spirit of nature. Wildflowers and barley,' she said with growing enthusiasm, and even my mother took fire.

Whipping out her purse as other shoppers pushed the door open with a tinkle of the doorbell, she asked, 'How much? I'll pay cash.'

We carried the dress home in triumph in a big box found by the friendly shop lady and called at the florist's on our way home to order the flowers and headdress. Shown the dress, the florist was equally enthused and was already sketching designs and scribbling lists before we left. When we got home, my father asked to see the dress, but my mum refused.

'It's a secret,' she declared, and winked at me. 'All you need to know is that it's haute couture and Elf will look absolutely stunning.'

'Of course she will,' said my dad. 'Tell me something I don't know.' And *he* winked at me. I hid the dress in my old wardrobe and went back to London.

When my big day dawned, I was torn between excitement and trepidation. I dressed in my old room, shaking hands making putting my earrings in difficult.

My father had demanded the right to contribute to my ensemble, so my mother had broken secrecy enough to say that the dress wouldn't suit a necklace (his original suggestion) but would look great with green earrings. He'd exclaimed, '*Green!*', given my mother a quizzical look that said as clearly as day that he knew she was up to something, then gone out and bought the most fabulous emerald earrings he could afford.

Once I'd managed the earrings, I came downstairs for my mum and my one bridesmaid, suitably attired in eau de nil satin, to quarrel over the correct placing of my wildflower and barley headdress. Then I picked up my posy of wildflowers, my bridesmaid took up Magic's new green lead, and my father was allowed into the room.

'Wow,' he said, 'just wow! That's so different, so stunning and so you. Well done, the both of you,' he said to my mum, smiling proudly in triumph and eau de nil lace coat dress, and to me. 'I'm so proud of you both. He bowed to me, held out his arm, and showed me to the waiting car.'

I timed my arrival at the church so that Pete was safely inside and waiting at the altar rail. His first sight of me was of me coming down the aisle on my father's arm, lit by a fortuitous beam of sunlight through the big stained-glass window.

His face was blank as I neared him, then he managed a smile for me and whispered, 'Very dramatic, Elf. I'll need to check for pointy ears.' Then he turned to the vicar at the altar rail. I smiled at my bridesmaids, the human and the canine, and handed my posy to Magic. We'd been practising this manoeuvre, and she took it from me, untroubled by stage-fright, and gave it to her human colleague. There was applause from that section of the congregation close enough to see what had transpired. When I turned back to Pete, he was rolling his eyes, but the smile on his face now looked genuine and I took it he was getting over his surprise. I smiled back, and the service began.

As with all these events, our first chance of a private word was in the car heading to my parents' house and the reception in the garden.

'That was a surprise,' said Pete as he leaned back and waved to well-wishers.

'The dress or Magic?' I asked.

'Both, but particularly the dress. You could have warned me,' he complained.

'That would have spoiled the surprise,' I said.

'The shock, you mean.' I turned to him with some alarm. But he was smiling again.

'Trust you, Elf,' he said. 'It's a stunning dress and you look amazing. Like a mermaid.' And he leaned over and kissed me, just as we arrived at my old home.

The reception followed the usual pattern: greetings, something fizzy, things to eat, speeches, more fizzy stuff, and then general circulating among our carefully chosen guests. Pete's mum, sporting an enormous hat, was there with the lodger, all togged up in rather ill-fitting hired tails. Most of our other male guests hadn't bothered with that detail but had stuck with their best lounge suits. The lodger didn't seem to know what to do with his top hat until, eventually, my dad took pity on him and parked it on the garden fence. It was still there the following morning.

Apart from congratulations – some on my wedding, most on my dress – one topic of conversation dominated: the not entirely unexpected, but unique, so far at least, resignation of the President of the USA, Richard Nixon. With his impeachment inevitable, it had only been a matter of time, said every voice, and today was the day he chose to jump before he was pushed. My wedding day: 9 August 1974.

14

The Next Phase

We started our married life in Pete's rented flat in Maida Vale, while we hunted for a house to buy. Shortly after our arrival we had our first row. On our return to London after our brief honeymoon in Devon, my first question was, 'When can we fetch Magic?'

Pete just looked at me blankly. 'What d'you mean? Fetch Magic? The dog's not coming here!'

'Of course she is,' I said. 'I was always taking her back once I finished at uni and left the hall of residence. It was understood.'

'Not by me, it wasn't,' he said. 'And anyway, she can't stay in the flat. It's not allowed.'

'But it's a basement flat,' I said. 'It has access to the garden, and she's an old, well-behaved dog; she won't bother anybody.'

'I tell you, it's not allowed,' he said and went off to work. I wasn't due to start in the civil service until the following week, so my first act that morning was to ring the landlord.

'No problem,' she said. 'If you wanted to import a whole kennel full, it would be different, but one elderly dog isn't

118

a problem. I have a dog myself. I can't imagine why Peter assumed it wasn't allowed. The lease specifically says "pets permitted with the permission of the landlord".' I knew that. I'd looked it up after Pete left for work.

When he got home that evening, I was flushed with success.

'It's all sorted,' I announced. 'There's no problem and you don't need to do anything. The landlord is fine about us having Magic here, and Mum has offered to bring her down at the weekend.'

'You what?' exclaimed Pete, and he looked furious for a moment, then left the room. I heard some banging and clattering before he reappeared in running kit.

'Are you going out now?' I asked.

'Yes. Won't be long,' he said. And left, just like that.

I put the casserole I'd prepared for supper back in the oven on a low heat and went back into the sitting room to do some thinking. Had I really not explained about Magic? Perhaps I hadn't. Perhaps she was such a part of my DNA that I'd assumed he understood. It was a miserable hour, but when Pete returned, he'd cheered up.

'Sorry about that,' he said. 'But it came as a bit of a shock. I'd assumed the dog would stay with your mother. But if it means so much to you, then fine, let her come.'

'Are you sure?' I said a trifle uncertainly. 'I thought you understood about Magic. How she's been a big part of my life since I rescued her. Phil—' I stopped, realising my mistake.

His sunny mood darkened, and he walked away from me.

'If you're about to say Phil understood, don't,' he said. 'Or I might change my mind and withdraw my permission.'

Permission! I was still getting my head around the concept as he left the room.

'Is supper ready?' he called from the kitchen. I changed what I had been going to say into 'Yes, in the oven,' and bit my tongue on the rest of the words piling up in my head. After all, I'd won my main point. Magic was coming to live with us.

Mum and Dad arrived around noon on Saturday, with an ecstatic Magic. After an energetic greeting, she sniffed her way round our flat, and then into the garden for a bit of an empty.

'You'll have to clear that up,' remarked Pete sniffily.

I said, 'Of course,' and went out with a little shovel acquired for the purpose. Mum unloaded a bag of dog food from the car, and Dad brought in Magic's bed.

'Where do you want this?' he asked.

'In the sitting room,' I said, and showed him a space carefully cleared by the sofa.

'My chair usually goes there,' muttered Pete.

'It's just here,' I pointed out, 'and no doubt when we find a new home it'll be moved again.'

'About that,' said Pete, and turned to my father. 'When do you think the house in Leek will be sold, so we can put a deposit on a new home?' Dad looked a bit gobsmacked and Mum, entering the room behind him, looked more than a bit put out.

'Let us fairly get in before you start talking business,' she said. 'Mine's a cup of tea, Pete, then we can sit down and have that chat.' I made a move toward the kitchen, but she caught me by the arm. 'I'm sure Pete knows where the kettle is,' she said. 'And if he doesn't, he'll never be younger to learn. Tell me about your new job, Elf.'

The three of us sat down, Magic on my lap, and had a bit of a catch-up, but I was twitchy about Pete being left to do the teas alone. When I made a move toward the kitchen, my mother shook her head at me.

'You're making a rod for your own back,' she predicted, just as Pete reappeared through the door with four mugs on a tray plus milk, sugar and a plate of chocolate biscuits.

Once everyone had tea and a biscuit, Mum took over the conversational reins.

'One thing we need to get straight,' she said. 'Since my father's death, his house has been let to a tenant, and the income from that has gone into a savings account for Elf. We haven't received probate yet, but that shouldn't be long. If she's now ready to buy a home of her own, or rather, if the two of you are now ready, then, of course, the house will need to be put on the market. But a sale won't happen overnight, and the tenant has to be given notice.'

'How long will that take?' asked Pete again.

'Probably the best part of a year all told,' said my dad. 'House sales take time, especially if there's a chain involved.'

'I see,' said Pete. 'Then the sooner the better, eh, Elf?'

'Yes, I suppose so,' I said. 'I assume I'll need to talk to the solicitor and then an estate agent.'

'I can help with that,' said Pete and my father simultaneously.

Then my father looked at my mother and added, 'Of course, Pete. I'll leave it to you.'

Mum and Dad stayed for lunch, then headed back to Stoke. I took Magic for a walk in the local park, Pete went for a run, then we all three went down to the local pub for a drink and supper. To my relief, Magic's behaviour was exemplary.

On the Sunday all three of us piled into Pete's car and made the drive out to Royston. Pete had made appointments for us to visit two properties. I knew no more than that. He said they were to be a surprise.

The first was a flat in the centre of town. I hated it. It was minimalist, flashy, soulless and wholly unsuitable for anyone with a dog. I tried not to be too dismissive in front of the owners but spoke plainly once back in the car with Pete.

'I can't imagine what you saw in that place,' I said. 'It's not at all *us*.'

'It's cheap,' he said.

'Do we have to go that cheap?' I asked. 'We'll have a substantial deposit once we have the money from my grandfather's house. At least half of the price of a decent three-bed on the edge of Royston.'

'That's all very well,' he said. 'But if we're relying on that money, we can't make a move until some progress is made with the house sale. And I didn't get the feeling your parents were pressing ahead with any enthusiasm. Maybe they like having the house rented out.'

'But it's going into savings for me,' I protested. 'I'm sure it's all above board.'

Pete grunted, then said, 'Well okay then, let's see the next one, since you hate the flat so much.'

We drove a few miles in silence, and Pete pulled up outside a modern detached house in a small development around a green space.

'This looks much better,' I said, feeling a lot more encouraged and got out of the car. Magic watched from the back seat as we walked up the path to the house. It was a new build, with sparkling clean carpets and a fitted kitchen with wood worktops. Upstairs were three bedrooms, one with an en-suite shower room, and a family bathroom with both a bath and a walk-in shower. The downstairs had a huge lounge, with a dining area opening off through an arch. The kitchen had an adjacent utility room, and a downstairs loo just off that. The front garden was open to the quiet road beyond, but the back garden was fully enclosed, with a large fruit tree in one far corner. There was even a garage.

'It's perfect,' I said. 'Why on earth did you show me that horrible flat when there was somewhere like this just around a few corners?'

'Because if we want this, we'll need to take out a loan,' replied Pete.

'Well, of course we will. We always knew the proceeds from a house in the Midlands wouldn't buy a house down here.'

'No. I mean we'll need to take out a bridging loan for the deposit. These houses are going fast. If we want this one, we'll need to make an offer now, and organise the finances quickly. We'll need a loan to cover us until your grandad's house sale goes through.'

'Okay,' I said slowly. I must admit I'd fallen for the house hook, line and sinker, and I've always been impulsive. 'Let's look at what that would cost, for, say, a six-month and a twelve-month loan. Then we can get the house on the market as soon as poss, and take it from there. In the meantime, I can take a look through what else is available in Royston.' I still had a vestige of sanity.

'I've already done that,' said Pete. 'There's nothing else so suitable. I'll see about a loan and making an offer, then we can sit down with the paperwork and make our decision.' We went back to the car and headed home.

The following week I started my new job. The slow commute to my office in Westminster meant that sometimes Pete got home first. Magic seemed to take fairly well to being left all day, and I walked her in the morning and evening. After a couple of days, Meg, the lady in the top-floor flat who worked from home, noticed the new arrangement, and asked if I would like her to let Magic out into the garden during the day and play with her a bit. I agreed with relief, and it seemed to work well to start with, but then I noticed Magic seemed a bit subdued.

'Do you think she's all right with Meg?' I asked Pete.

'Seems fine to me, although I told you at the time, I'm not keen on someone having our door key,' he replied.

At the weekend I made a point of watching Magic with Meg. Meg got the full body-wagging hello, so it seemed that was OK. Then Pete came into the garden, and Magic both snarled and slunk away behind me. Meg caught my eye for a moment but said nothing. Soon after she made her excuses and went back upstairs.

I took Magic out for a walk in the park, and did a lot of thinking. When I got back, Pete was working his way through a pile of paperwork.

'I've got the stuff for the loan,' he said. 'Let's get it sorted now, before we lose that house.' I opened my mouth to start the conversation about Magic, decided it wasn't the right moment, and sat down beside Pete. He'd organised all the papers, so the signature pages were uppermost. 'All you need to do, is sign here, here and here,' he pointed.

'Hang on a minute,' I said. 'I haven't read it through yet.'

'No need,' he said. 'I have. Do you think I'd put my name to it if I wasn't happy? I am an accountant remember!' He kissed me and handed me the pen. 'Why have a dog and do your own barking?' he asked. I gave in, and signed where he indicated, making a mental note I could read through it at my leisure.

'So, the next thing we need to do is put your grandad's house on the market,' he said. 'I think we should go up to Stoke next weekend and make sure that show's on the road too.'

'Okay,' I said. 'I'll ring Mum and tell her we're coming. I think they've given the tenant notice, so we can sort out the sales details with an estate agent, and Bob's your uncle.'

'They can start selling while the tenant's still there, provided they're cooperative,' agreed Pete. 'No need to wait.'

The following evening, I got home first, and before taking Magic for her walk, I had a look round for the loan paperwork. I couldn't find it, so when Magic and I got back from our wander along the tow path, I asked Pete for it.

'It's gone back to the bank,' he said. 'We'll get a copy in due course, don't worry.' Magic had slunk under the kitchen table, which reminded me of the other question I had for my husband.

'Is there any reason why Magic seems to be afraid of you?' I asked. 'Have you and her had a falling-out?' I tried to sound light-hearted, but I was worried about it and about Magic's behaviour.

'Only when she gets in my way,' he said. 'I can't be doing with her always under my feet. If she's minded to keep away, that's a plus from my point of view.' I didn't make any reply but made a mental note to try and get home earlier, just in case.

When we went to Stoke on Saturday, I was surprised by our welcome, or lack of. Mum was definitely a little frosty, and even Dad said he was surprised we were 'in such a rush' to sell. I tried to explain about the house we'd seen in Royston, and Mum thawed a bit, but Dad still seemed to be worried about something.

'How can you make an offer now, when the house here isn't even on the market yet?'

I opened my mouth to explain about the bridging loan, but Pete gave me a nudge with his foot and said, 'We don't need to sign on the dotted line just yet.'

The atmosphere was such that I was glad we'd said we'd have tea with Pete's mum. She made a huge fuss of Magic, even more than she did of us, to be frank, and laid out a sumptuous dog tea of sausage rolls and ham before we even got ours. After tea, when she and I were washing up, she said, 'I'm surprised Pete let you have a dog.'

'Really!' I said; it was my turn to be frosty. 'Actually, I've had Magic for years. She was always going to be with me.'

'He hates dogs,' said his mother. 'I thought you knew that. It's why I never had another dog after I lost my old border collie. He's my son, and I love him to bits,' she added, 'but I'd feel terrible if I didn't say this. He's not safe around dogs. Be careful about letting Magic spend time alone with him.'

'What do you mean?' I was astonished. But on the other hand, I remembered Magic's recent attitude to Pete.

'I was always worried he'd done something to my old chap,' she said. 'He died very suddenly—' She stopped abruptly as voices could be heard coming through the house to the kitchen. 'Thank you for helping with the dishes, Elf,' she said. 'And good luck with your new home.'

I was silent in the car on the way home. I found it hard to believe a mother would make an awful accusation like that against her own son. Pete looked across at me and smiled.

'Okay?' he said, and patted my knee.

'Okay,' I said, and put it out of my mind.

***

Three months later we moved into our new home. Three days after that, I found Magic dead in the kitchen when I came down in the morning.

Those of you who have pets, and have lost pets, will know how I felt. The shock was overwhelming. Yes, she was getting on in dog years, even assuming our guess of how old she had been when I first found her was accurate. But apart from slowing down a bit, she hadn't shown any signs of serious illness. She'd had a bit of a tummy upset when we moved house. I'd put it down to the stress of the move and the new home. Pete hadn't coped well with mess on our new kitchen floor, but apart from that, their relationship hadn't seemed any different. She left him alone and he left her alone. Now she was dead unexpectedly suddenly, and my sense of loss was all the worse because of the awful suspicion Pete's mother had seeded into my brain.

I hugged her cold and stiffening body to me and wept buckets. Pete was saying something, but I took no notice.

When I calmed down a little, I said, 'I think I'd better take her to the vets for a postmortem. I don't understand how it can have happened so suddenly, with no warning.'

'Don't be ridiculous,' said Pete. 'You can't get a postmortem for a dog.'

'Of course you can,' I argued. 'The vet will do one, if we ask.'

'And if we pay,' said Pete. 'Bad enough she cost an arm and a leg while she was alive. We don't need more bills now she's dead. Let's bury her in the garden and have done. I'll go and dig a hole.'

He took no further notice of me, but just walked away as though my voice was no louder than the whining of a gnat. And no more significant. I contemplated carrying her out to the car and just driving off, but when I looked round, the car keys weren't on their usual hook. I got up from my seat on the floor and did some searching, but I couldn't see them on the worktop or in the hall either. Looking through the kitchen window, I could see Pete digging vigorously in the corner of the garden, as far away as possible from the fruit tree and its widely extending roots. I picked Magic up in my arms and carried her out onto the patio, where I sat on the bench with her lying across my knees. Her eyes were half open, and I noticed that there were small bloody flecks in the whites. Then when I gently pulled her lips back from her teeth, her gums were blue. I sat thinking furiously and shaking. *Surely he couldn't have! Surely he wouldn't! Not only did he know how much she meant to me, he just wouldn't do anything so cruel. So unnecessary. His mother had to be wrong. She just had to be.*

Pete came over at that moment, his spade in his hand. 'I think it's big enough,' he said. 'I'm sorry, Elf, but she was quite old, you know. Best she went like this, than after a long illness. Not best for you, perhaps, but best for her.'

I had to acknowledge the truth of that.

'Here, let me carry her,' he said, and he picked her up carefully in his arms and carried her over the lawn. 'Why not bring her favourite toy to go with her?' he suggested. I picked the brightly coloured ball up from the lawn and brought it over. He'd put one of her blankets in the hole and placed her on it. As I watched, he pulled the rest of the blanket over her and taking the ball from me, he put it between her front paws. 'There,' he said.

I snapped a rose off the bush nearby and dropped it gently on her before I turned away.

'Go in the house, Elf,' he said, 'I'll finish here.' He waited until I'd walked away, then as I approached the house, I heard the first shovelful of earth go into the grave.

I was very subdued that evening. I'd rung my mum and told her what had happened. She'd commiserated and cried a little but expressed no surprise. I couldn't bring myself to ring Pete's mum. I was afraid of what she might say.

15

LOSS

Everything goes in threes they say, and so it was for us. Three years and three months after we moved into our first home in Royston, I found myself pregnant for the first time. This was a source of huge rejoicing for Pete. He was like a puppy, bouncing round me and desperate to tell everyone we knew about our glad tidings. I think he'd been worrying about our lack of news on that front. I hadn't done anything to avoid getting pregnant; it just didn't seem to happen. If I'm honest, even I had begun to wonder if there was something wrong, and – in all honesty – I wasn't that desperate to be pregnant. However, now I was, I was touched by Pete's enthusiasm and especially by the way it translated into a newly romantic approach to me.

Suddenly, nothing was too good for me, and I was the recipient of flowers, books on childbirth and endless rounds of gifts intended for the baby. Before I was even three months pregnant, he'd redecorated one of the bedrooms in pink and blue – covering all the possible bases – with pictures of cartoon elephants and ostriches and a mobile of sea creatures. Or they could have been dragons. It was hard to tell.

I had the conversation with my boss about maternity leave, then had another one with Pete, who was horrified I was planning to go back to work after the birth.

'There's no need,' he kept saying. 'I can keep us. We don't need your income nearly so much as the baby will need you. I want my wife at home with our baby. Hopefully there'll be more after Baby Uno,' which was what he called my still-tiny bump.

'Let's deal with one at a time,' I said, half amused, half horrified. 'It's me that has to have them, you know. I may not want more than one.'

'Of course we'll have more than one,' he pronounced, no less determined for the breezy tone he adopted. It seemed it wasn't going to be my decision. At least, not if Pete had anything to do with it.

Around a week later, I had my first ultrasound scan. Pete came with me, determined not to miss a single moment of our journey toward being what he called 'a proper family'. We went to Addenbrookes together, and after a long wait that had Pete muttering under his breath, we were called through for the scan. That was when we got the big surprise. The nurse at the scanner seemed to take a good while looking at the screen. I could only see part of it, and although Pete could see more, he didn't seem to be any more enlightened. After a pause, she muttered something about fetching her boss, and I was clutching Pete's hand nervously, convinced something was horribly wrong, when they came back. The two of them now studied the screen closely. ,

After a while, she looked up and smiled at me. 'I'd ask if you'd like to sit down, but you already are. Congratulations, Mr Lynch. You're about to become the father of twins.'

'Twins!' Pete exclaimed. I just gaped.

'Are you sure?' I managed.

'Yes. See here and here,' she pointed. 'Two heartbeats.'

'Boys or girls?' asked Pete eagerly.

'It's too soon to tell,' said the technician. Pete looked, disappointed, and the boss chipped in supportively.

'Twelve weeks is always a bit early, but especially when the babies are small, as these are.'

'Too small?' asked Pete, looking alarmed.

'No, just that there's two of them, so of course they're a bit smaller. Everything looks fine at the moment,' she stressed, reassuringly. 'Your midwife and your GP will have advice for you further down the line, but for now, just enjoy the news.'

Three days after that, I woke to severe cramps. I knew what was happening even before I saw the blood. I made it to the en-suite bathroom in a rush. Pete was already downstairs, getting ready for work. I tried to call him, but nothing came out but a groan that seemed to be pulled all the way from my guts to my lips. There was a rush from me, and when I looked into the toilet, I saw a lot of blood and a bigger lump of something pale. I stifled my tears in my next groan, and there was another heaving feeling from my insides and another rush. Now there were two pale lumps in the toilet, and any hope I'd had that one of my babies might survive died right there, with the foetuses Pete and I had briefly called into being. Pete was now banging on the bathroom door.

'Are you okay in there? Elf, is everything all right?'

I stifled another groan and managed to call his name. The door burst open, and with one look at me he was dialling 999 on his phone and calling for an ambulance.

'It's too late,' I gasped. 'They've gone. Oh, Pete, they've gone.'

He grabbed a bath towel, wrapped it round me then helped me off the toilet and through to the bedroom, where he threw the duvet back and lay me down on the bed. I tried to wad the towel under me, to limit the mess. I noticed he had carefully not looked in the toilet.

'Pete, tell them it's too late for the babies,' I said. 'You must have seen.'

'I'm not looking, and I'm not going to look.' His face was stubborn, as though the mere fact of not seeing would make it untrue, would undo the events of the past few minutes.

When the ambulance crew turned up about fifteen minutes later, they were kindness itself. One of them went to look in the bathroom, then had a conversation in an undertone with his colleague, before turning to me.

'If it's okay with you,' he said, 'I'm going to retrieve some of the...' he hesitated.

'My babies,' I interrupted. He flushed.

'Yes,' he said. 'I'm sorry. Your babies. Two reasons. You might want doctors to take a look to see if there is an obvious reason why they miscarried. And you might want a burial.'

Pete was not in agreement. 'What's in there can't be babies,' he said. 'It's a mess. I should just flush it away.'

'No!' My negative was explosive. 'No. They may be small, and they may have been at a very early stage, but they would have been babies. They would have been people. You can't just flush them away like they're nothing.' I looked at the ambulance driver again. 'Yes, please,' I said. 'I don't feel ready to look just now, but I'd like to know they're safe.'

He went away, then came back with a covered box, which he took into the bathroom. When he returned from his task, he looked at me and I beckoned him over. He drove me to the hospital with the sealed box on my lap.

Going into the obstetric ward was the hardest thing I'd ever done. I could hear babies crying and a woman shouting in labour. I saw another woman in a wheelchair like mine, but she had a newborn in her arms, wrapped in towels. She had a live baby, and I had a box with my dead twins inside.

Pete kept at arm's length, as though the fact of me holding the box meant I was somehow contaminated. But when I was taken in to see the doctor, the box was taken from me while he examined me. After, when he'd explained that one in four pregnancies end in a miscarriage, and that there was no reason why I shouldn't become pregnant again and go to term, he asked me gently if I wanted the hospital to dispose of the remains.

I said 'no, we'd make our own arrangements,' and Pete took me home in a taxi.

I'll draw a veil over the next few months. I surprised myself by how bereaved I felt. I cried, and when I wasn't crying outside, I was crying inside. The world seemed to be full of babies and happily pregnant women heaving their bulk around supermarkets and joking about backache and how they couldn't wait to be liberated from their bump.

Friends started off sympathetic but struggled to know what to say. Mostly they said, *It will all come right in the end*, and,

That next time I'll have a healthy baby. I wanted to scream that I was grieving the children I'd lost. Even another child wouldn't replace those that were dead. All I wanted them to say was that I was right to grieve, that it was natural and normal; but as time passed, more and more of them headed for the 'time to pull yourself together' and 'time to move on' camp. Even my mother dithered on the edge of those camps but didn't quite step over the line. One thing she did say was interesting: my grandmother had lost several babies after my mother had been born, and no one ever knew why.

'But, of course, medicine was different then,' she'd added hastily.

I didn't know why either. The doctors hadn't spent much time investigating. I was told that they would only investigate if I had three miscarriages in a row. Otherwise, my devastating experience was regarded as normal.

Pete's reaction wasn't. He started by pretending none of it had happened. No pregnancy, no loss. He threw himself into work, or so I thought at the time. Then things changed after the news of my grandmother's experience. At that point, it became my fault. With hindsight, I realised that he'd been looking for some way to blame me, so that there was no hint of fault or failure on his part. At the time, lost in my fog of misery, his barbed comments were just one more nail in my coffin.

Some days it was my genes that were at fault. I was from flawed stock, which he magnanimously allowed was not my fault, but somehow implied I had cheated him by marrying him. Other days, it was something I'd done. I hadn't been sufficiently careful, or I'd been careless of the valuable burden

I carried, or even, later, that I had never really wanted his children, so I'd ill-wished them.

By the time I emerged from the fog, soggy but still on my feet, the latter narrative predominated. From that time on, I found my activities, my hobbies, my eating and drinking, even my thinking, were monitored and controlled by Pete. And I didn't even notice.

16

MILESTONE 8: Women in Charge

The '70s were nearly over before I realised what was happening to me. For over four years I lived with the insidious and steady imposition of more and more restrictions. First, I couldn't sing any more, either in the folk club or in the choir. The first was the victim of pressure to conform with what Pete regarded as suitable behaviour for the wife of an up-and-coming executive. The second fell foul of Pete's demands that I spend more time in the home, in order to run the house as he considered appropriate and to entertain bosses and clients whenever necessary.

The next target was my work, especially after I was promoted and moved to a demanding job working closely with ministers. Pete *really* didn't like that. With hindsight, he'd done his best to torpedo my promotion in the first place, very nearly making me late for my interview by announcing that I couldn't use the car to get to the station because he was going to need it later in the day.

'But, Pete,' I protested, 'you knew I needed it this morning. It's been on the calendar for weeks.'

'This came up unexpectedly,' he said over his shoulder as he headed for his office upstairs – the office in the room which had briefly been the nursery and the focus of all our hopes.

'Can you run me there then?' I shouted up the stairs.

'Sorry,' came the reply, 'I have an important job to do first,' and the door slammed. I paused for a moment, irresolute, then reached for the phone and rang the local taxi company. Amazingly they *were* able to help. I raided the kitchen drawer for every last bit of cash I could find, and ran for the door when I saw the car approaching. Pete's voice trailed me down the drive, but for once I paid him no heed, and jumped into the cab.

'Station, love?' asked the fatherly-looking Sikh in the driving seat.

'Yes, please. I'm in a rush for the London train,' I explained, and he took off without delay.

I caught the train with seconds to spare. Most doors had already slammed shut when I jumped aboard, and of course there were no seats left. However, my panicky state did me a favour and a kind gentleman stood up and offered me his. I plonked myself down in it, and resolved to calm down so I was in the right frame of mind for the interview. It must have worked because I knocked it out of the park, and I already knew the job was mine before I got up to go.

So, I got promotion, and the grand job, and it did wonders for my self-esteem. It didn't hurt my bank balance either. When I started the new job, I had to fill in the personnel forms again, and I took the opportunity to have my salary paid into my personal account rather than our joint account. Pete noticed the change right away, of course, and demanded to know what I thought I was doing.

'I've set up a standing order,' I said. 'I'll be paying the same sum into our joint account as before, so no change there. You have a personal account as well,' I pointed out in justification.

'I need it for my other expenses, like the car,' he said. 'What do you need one for?'

'Perhaps I might want a car too,' I said. 'Especially if it's not going to be possible for me to use your car when I need it.'

'And how will we afford that?'

'I...' I put the stress on the first-person singular. '*I* will afford it. Just a little run around would be great.'

'There's no room in the garage,' said Pete.

'There's room on the drive,' I said.

Once I was well underway with the new job, I went shopping for a car. I asked Pete if he'd come with me, but he said he was away for a weekend conference, so I went on my own. I'd originally thought in terms of a Mini but ended up with a bright red second-hand Ford Cortina. That Sunday, looking at the loan agreement I'd just taken out, I had a sudden thought. *What's happened to the savings account Mum and Dad handed over to me?* I could have kicked myself. I knew we hadn't used all of it when we furnished the house, and possibly I hadn't needed the loan for the car, or at least, not so much of one. So, I went looking, first in Pete's desk, then in the safe we'd hidden in the airing cupboard.

I found the building society statements in the safe. I also found the paperwork from the bridging loan we'd taken out when we bought the house. That was two big surprises. First, the savings account was almost empty – not wholly a surprise. What did shock me was the steady trickle of money that had been leaving the account, month by month, into a bank account I knew nothing about. But the real sucker punch was the bridging loan. In fact, I sat down so hurriedly on the stairs, it was more of a collapse than anything else. The loan had not been paid off in full when we sold Grandad's house. More than half of what had been meant to be a short-term loan was still outstanding. And I had no idea where the money had gone.

When I got downstairs, I picked up the phone to ring Pete, then realised he was probably somewhere between the hotel and home. I put the phone down again and prepared myself to confront him when he got home.

I was expecting him around seven o'clock and got a meal ready, as I'd been trained to do. Seven-thirty passed, then eight o'clock, then nine, and still no Pete. I was on the verge of ringing round the hospitals when I heard his key in the door. By this time, I'd cleared supper away, put the unwanted casserole in the fridge, and was sitting in the living room, coiled tighter than a spring. I had just one table lamp on, the incriminating paperwork sitting in the pool of light. I waited in silence as footsteps went down the hall to the kitchen. I listened to the fridge door open and close, and the sound of someone pouring a drink. Then Pete came into the living room, glass in hand, and did a double take when he saw me sitting there. I think it was put on or, at the very least, exaggerated. It certainly didn't look genuine. His eyes narrowed as he took in the papers on the coffee table beside me, then he reached out and turned the main lights on.

'Why're you sitting in the dark?' he asked, and sat down on the sofa at right angles to me. He took a drink from his glass, then said, 'I assume you have a good reason for going through my private papers. You'd better have.' It sounded threatening, but for some reason, on this occasion I was quite calm. Perhaps because it didn't feel real.

'Well actually,' I said, 'they're my papers not yours. At least, they deal with my affairs.'

'Well *ectually*,' he mimicked me, putting on an unnaturally posh accent, 'you can mind your own bloody business and keep your ugly nose out of things that don't concern you.'

'They do concern me,' I said. 'Where's the money gone, Pete? There's a hole in my savings, and the bank loan hasn't been paid off.'

He got up suddenly and stood over me. Despite myself, I wilted into the back of the armchair in the face of his aggression. He leaned forward and took hold of the front of my blouse.

'Listen very carefully, Elf,' he said. 'Mind. Your. Own. Business.' He spaced the words out. Then he let go suddenly and stood back. 'I'm off to bed,' he announced. 'It's been a long day.' And he went upstairs without a backward glance.

I sat shaking for a while, then followed him up the stairs but not to our room. I spent that night in the spare room that looked over the back garden. I could see Magic's grave in the corner, and wished so much that she was there to keep me company.

I didn't get to sleep until the early hours then, of course, I overslept, especially as my alarm clock was next door, with

Pete. I was eventually awakened by Pete bringing me a cup of coffee.

He put it down on the bedside table, then said 'It's six-thirty, Elf. I imagine you'll want to be off to work soon.' He paused again by the bedroom door and, without turning, added, 'I'm sorry about last night. I didn't mean those things I said. I was tired and you took me by surprise. We can talk tonight when you get home.' He closed the door quietly behind him. I drank my coffee and wondered.

Work was a very necessary distraction that day, and it was after eight when I got home. I wasn't in much of a mood to cook a meal and was even less keen on the conversation I thought was pending. I went into the house with every nerve on the alert and dropped my car keys into the bowl on the hall table. Pete's keys were not there. It looked as though he was working late too.

When I went into the kitchen, the mugs and plates from breakfast were still on the table. Automatically I put them into the dishwasher, poured myself a glass of Lambrusco from the open bottle in the fridge, and took it into the sitting room. The loan and bank account papers were still exactly where I'd left them the night before. I sighed as I sipped and looked at my watch again. The later it got, the more fraught our eventual conversation seemed likely to be. I leaned forward to the TV remote, turned it on and flicked though the channels idly. Nothing grabbed me very much, so I turned it off again, put my glass down and went upstairs to change out of my office wear into jeans and a light jumper. The day had been warm, but the evening was cooling.

I waited until after midnight, and there was still no sign nor word from Pete. It seemed he'd chickened out of talking to me. My mind veered between fear he'd walked out and fear he'd been in an accident. Around one in the morning, apologising for the late hour, I rang his mother, asking if she had any idea where he might be. She hadn't, but she did offer to come and stay with me.

'He's an idiot, Elf, but then, a lot of men are,' she said. 'Are you sure you wouldn't like some company? He's bound to be okay and bound to turn up soon, but waiting can be hell, I know. I hate to say this,' she added, 'but might he be having an affair?'

I turned down her offer again, and rejected any thought of an affair. 'I'm sure he's not,' I said. 'I'd know if he was, I'm sure.'

I went to bed around three in the morning and slept very little. As there was no sign of Pete in the morning, I went to work again. What else was I to do?

While at work I tried ringing Pete at his office. He didn't answer the phone. When someone else did, I put the phone down. I wasn't going to wash our dirty linen in public.

That was Tuesday. By Thursday, with still no sign of Pete, I was starting to get angry. I spent my lunchtime visiting banks and building societies. I moved the depleted contents of my savings account into a new building society account and locked the passbook in my desk in the office. After a slightly tense conversation with the bank manager about the remaining part of the bridging loan, I paid it off using the contents of our joint bank accounts, both the savings account and the current account. Neither had much in them by the time I'd finished. I wasn't looking forward to Pete's reaction when he found out, but anger made me brave. That and the sneaking suspicion that he must have bank accounts I didn't know about, judging by the money that had gone from my savings.

On my way home, I popped into the community centre to cast my vote in the general election. As I was coming out, dodging the row of candidates and supporters asking which way I'd voted, I bumped into an acquaintance, a woman I often met on the train. We exchanged the time of day, and it was just as we parted that she dropped her bombshell.

'Aelfwyth,' she said. 'I don't know whether I should be saying this. My husband has told me I should keep quiet and mind my own business, but it doesn't seem right to me. So I'm sorry if I'm speaking out of turn.' She didn't look sorry. She looked as though she was enjoying her role, and I had a sudden realisation that I knew what she was going to say.

'I knew it wasn't you,' she was saying, and I realised I'd missed the beginning of her sentence, 'because she was blonde, and you'd never have dyed your hair that brassy colour.'

'Sorry,' I said, 'what was it you saw?'

'Your husband, Pete,' she said, as though I might have more than one. 'In the Black Oak with a brassy blonde. They definitely went upstairs together after their dinner. And when I asked at reception, the girl said he'd been there all week.'

I looked at her, then turned away to my car. I didn't know what to say, so I said nothing. I could hear her still flapping her chops in the background but took no notice. That night I went to bed early, but still didn't sleep. This time it was because I was planning.

The following day, Friday, Mrs Thatcher became our first woman prime minister, and I threw my husband out.

He had marched up the path with an unattractive bravado but came to a sudden halt when he spotted the suitcases on the doorstep. He tried his key in the lock, but the locksmith I'd called that morning had been commendably prompt. To pre-empt an assault on the back door, I stuck my head out of the bedroom window and addressed him from that safe distance.

'This is the end,' I said. 'Take the suitcases and go back to your fancy woman. The locks have been changed on all the doors, and I've got the police on speed dial, so don't try anything. My solicitor will be in touch about a longer-term arrangement.'

'The house is half mine,' he shouted. 'You won't get away with this!' Doors were starting to pop open down the street.

'If you want an audience, go on shouting,' I recommended. 'Otherwise, as I've said, my solicitor will be in touch.' And I closed the window. I was shaking when I sank down onto the bed, but all the same, a feeling of liberation was starting to flood my mind. I decided to raise a glass to Mrs Thatcher and myself, to both our newly expanded futures.

17

MILESTONE 9: Fairy Tales?

Of course, it wasn't as easy as that. I took the following week off work and spent it trying to get my affairs in order. Chasing bank and savings account statements was a first and difficult step, given that I'd left all that side of things to Pete. I cursed my stupidity now and said as much to my newly appointed solicitor.

She, Rebecca Sayers, leaned back in her chair, looked at me over steepled fingers and said, 'It seems to me it wasn't really your choice. Do you know how common financial abuse is in abusive relationships?'

I gasped as though she'd thrown a bucket of cold water over me, opened my mouth to say I hadn't been abused, then shut it again on a host of unwelcome recollections. She smiled a satisfied smile and pushed the plate of biscuits closer to me.

'I find chocolate is a great help when considering uncomfortable topics,' she said. 'I take it you hadn't thought about your married life in those terms?'

I shook my head, unable to speak temporarily, my mouth full of chocolate digestive.

'Enjoy your biscuit and listen to me for a moment,' she said. 'Everything you've said to me, and every bit of paper you've shown me, evidences a relationship where the husband exercised an unhealthy degree of control over his wife. You've talked about how Pete controlled what you ate, drank, and wore, the hobbies you had, the way you travelled to work, the house you bought with your inheritance, the furniture he chose, the bank accounts that held your savings,' she paused for breath. 'In fact, the only areas where you seem to have put your foot down were your dog and your career. And even the latter seems to have played second fiddle to the requirement that you entertain his clients.'

I had begun to think most of what she said, but hearing it listed with such clarity was salutary. Worse, I was having some awful thoughts about that one other area where I had stuck up for myself. *Was Magic's sudden death down to Pete wanting his own way too? Did I condemned her to an early demise by insisting on her move from Mum's, where she was safe, to me, where it seems likely she wasn't?*

I started to voice some of my misgivings, rather falteringly, and was cut short by Rebecca.

'I think you're expecting me to be shocked,' she said, 'but this wouldn't be the first time a family pet had been collateral damage in the war exercised by an abuser. It's too late of course, to find out whether your suspicions are correct. It's enough that your life with Pete was such that you can even entertain those suspicions. And if they are true,' she added briskly, 'then put out of your mind any thought that it was your fault. The only fault lies with Pete, not you.'

The first thing I did was put that house on the market. Then I started looking for something smaller, cheaper and more homely. I very rapidly discovered I couldn't afford anything I liked, and didn't like anything I could afford, not near Royston anyway. London was even more out of the question. I started driving round in ever increasing circles, looking for somewhere that was commutable and affordable. The trouble was, proximity to a station equalled high prices, almost without fail.

Eventually I struck lucky with a rather quirky house tucked in what had been a pub garden before the pub itself became a house too. I was only ten minutes' drive from a station and the train to Kings Cross. It was do-able, particularly if I could negotiate a day each week working from home. Then I really hit the jackpot. I was called into the boss's office and asked if I'd be willing to work out of Cambridge instead of London? *Would I?* I nearly bit his hand off, I was so enthusiastic.

While the solicitor beavered away in the background, sorting out my financial agreement with Pete, progressing my divorce papers and conveyancing my house sale and purchase, I concentrated on my new job and my special project in Cambridge.

I moved into my quirky cottage near St Ives in the spring of 1981. I'd thought I might be lonely, but not at all. Right from the start, I revelled in the unwonted freedom to do just what I wanted. I could choose the furniture I liked and arrange it how I liked, without reference to anyone else's taste or their concerns about how things might look to their bosses.

I browsed antique and junk shops, mainly in Suffolk. My sitting room was an eclectic mix of leather sofa from a department store, occasional tables from the Antiques Barn at Long Melford, and a chaise longue from the Cavendish antique centre. The chaise longue was a bit tatty, so re-covering it became an early project. The dining table was from Habitat and the chairs from another antique store in Clare. My desk came from there too, and the dark green leather captain's chair that went with it.

I felt strongly I needed to know the provenance of anything I was going to sleep in, so I kept two single beds from our house in Royston and bought a new double bed from John Lewis.

My cottage was only small. It had been renovated to some degree, and now had just two rooms downstairs. A big kitchen-diner took up half the space, and a sitting room the other half. Apart from a lean-to extension that housed a utility room and a loo, that was pretty much it. Upstairs were three rooms and a bathroom. One room was mine, one for guests, and the third became my study, with a fold-up bed in the corner for additional guests, if needed.

Once I'd settled in and arranged all my worldly goods, my car parked outside, I started the most important hunt of all: for a dog. Not to replace Magic, nothing could do that, but certainly a successor for Magic.

I let my fingers do the walking. Breeders and rescue centres, I tried them all. I was vetted by the RSPCA and found suitable, but they had nothing available. There seemed to be waiting lists for most of their dogs. The National Canine Defence League were the same. I was about to do the rounds of the smaller rehoming charities when, almost by chance, I spotted an advert in a local paper for a litter of terrier puppies on a farm not far away.

Their set-up appealed straight away. No sterile kennels or masses of overworked pregnant bitches here. The mother-to-be was a family pet and the father was owned by one of the sons. That led me to some penetrating questions about consanguinity, but I was reassured to learn that the sire had been imported from 'Oop North', as the son put it. No relation at all. The bitch and her sister lived in the kitchen, in a big sagging dog bed by the Aga, and I was shown where the litter would live when they arrived. I put my name down for a puppy and settled down to wait.

My first sight of my new best pal was a bit of a shock. I'd underestimated just how small a Jack Russell puppy would be at only a month old. Faced with a squirming mass of energy and curiosity, it was incredibly difficult to choose one from the five still unclaimed: two bitches and three dogs. In the end, one chose me. Climbing laboriously and unsteadily over my shins as I sat on the floor of the farm kitchen, one little lady fixed me with her button black eyes, and I was lost. That was how Lucky came into my life. Magic might have gone, but luck was now with me.

That month, while I waited for her to reach the important age of eight weeks, seemed to drag on for ever. I bored all my colleagues silly with talk about my new puppy, and I went shopping for a collar and lead, crate, dog bed and endless toys. Eventually the day dawned. The entire farming family of mum, dad and three sons lined up to say goodbye, and I drove home with Lucky sitting resplendently on the passenger seat.

I braced myself for complaints, crying and broken nights. Nothing. Not a peep out of Lucky, either on the journey home, during the first night nor on any subsequent night.

She faced every new experience with a calm, yet interested, expression, and seemed to fear nothing.

Strange dogs, strange humans, strange noises or experiences, she met everything with curiosity and a boundless enthusiasm, apparently convinced that the world and all its occupants would love her as much as I did. As her control over her bladder grew better, I even took her to work with me, and she spent many a happy hour under my desk, emerging occasionally when one of her favourite people visited, accepting their homage and an occasional biscuit with a regal air.

As time went by, and particularly when I realised I was eyeing up all sorts of random men as possible future partners, I started to dip my toe into the dating scene again.

It was after I caught myself chatting up the man who'd tiled my bathroom – perfectly nice chap, don't get me wrong, but we had absolutely nothing in common except a bathroom and he wasn't in the least interested in anything from me other than a paid bill – I realised that I should perhaps do some fishing in rather more promising waters. It wasn't easy after being off the scene for so long. And my experiences with Pete hadn't exactly set me up with much self-confidence. But I found Lucky was a great help, both as icebreaker and acid test.

I usually met new dates for the first time in a pub where I was well known and people looked out for me. If my date didn't make a genuine fuss of Lucky, or worse, if she took against them, then it was end of the line.

She only gave me the thumbs down on two chaps. One I was already winding up for the heave-ho, on the grounds that he had his hand on my knee within the first half hour of our meeting. That was enough, even without Lucky's growl of warning. I was warming to the second. His conversation was entertaining, he seemed to like the same sorts of books and plays as me, and he admired Lucky without being all over her. He asked my permission before offering her a treat from his plate of steak and chips – you'll note we'd got past the drinks-only stage and had a meal together – which I liked, but to my surprise, she refused the piece of steak and sat down under the table with her back to him. When he tried to stroke her, she growled, and I had to intervene, saying to leave her alone, she was in a bit of a mood that day. I went home alone, which hadn't been my plan, and was unsettled enough that I put him off when he rang seeking another date. I said I was busy, which was true, and would get in touch when I got back from a work trip to Scotland.

I planned to catch the train north at Peterborough, so I dropped Lucky off at the kennels on my way to the station. The lady in charge, Carol, was an old friend, and I knew Lucky'd get a heroine's welcome and a lot of extra attention while I was away. I was in a bit of a hurry and, concentrating on filling in the forms, I wasn't paying much attention to the background chatter until a name caught my ear.

'Didn't you meet him once?' asked Carol.

'Meet who?' I asked.

'This chap in the paper. Ian Compton. He's been charged with fraud.'

'He's what?' I seized the paper off the kitchen table. Sure enough. There was my ex-date, being hustled into the Crown Court in Huntingdon, accused of defrauding a widow of a substantial sum of money.

'Looks like you had a lucky escape,' said Carol.

'I did,' I agreed. 'In more ways than one,' and I kissed Lucky on the top of her brown head before handing her over to Carol.

***

A few months later, I had cause to thank Lucky again. The financial agreement with Pete had gone through surprisingly easily. At least, we'd reached agreement easily enough, a lot quicker than I was anticipating, anyway. But then it stalled. It seemed to take for ever for Pete to sign the papers, and my solicitor was plainly growing impatient. It seemed we weren't likely to make progress with the divorce until the money papers were signed, and suddenly everything seemed to be stuck in a muddy pit.

It was July. Lucky was now six months old and a feisty bundle of fun. A couple of mice and a frog in the garden had fallen victim to her terrier instinct. The latter occasioned a rather startling episode of frothing at the mouth, but no lasting harm had been done, not to Lucky, anyway. I expect the frog would beg to differ. It was when I was putting the sad remains into my dustbin, standing ready for collection by the side of the road, that I noticed a dark-coloured car parked a little further along. I might not have noticed it at all, except that it drove off while I was looking at it. The following day, when I brought my bin in, it was there again. After that, I started to notice it regularly. On two occasions I walked toward it to see who was sitting inside, but every time it drove off before I reached it. I started to feel a little uncomfortable and checked all the window locks in my little cottage.

On the 29 July, like a few thousand other people round the world, I settled down to watch what had been billed as the wedding of the century on TV. The romance of Prince Charles and Lady Diana was still being described as a fairy tale. Oddly, no one seemed to remember that most fairy tales have a more than macabre ending, and even with my unromantic history I was happy to watch all the pomp and circumstance with Lucky on my lap and a glass of something festive in my hand. Later in the afternoon I took Lucky for a walk by the river – no chance of her diving in; she would walk round even a puddle to avoid getting her paws wet – and picked up a Chinese takeaway for my supper. Lucky, as usual, got a share of my crispy duck. The following day was a normal working day, so we both went to bed early.

I was woken from a deep sleep in the early hours of the morning. My bedside clock was saying two-thirty when I rubbed the sleep out of my eyes and reached for my glasses. I couldn't make out what had disturbed me and was just going to write it off as a nightmare, when I realised there was a quiet rumble coming from Lucky's bed and a distinctive creak from the front door. I froze to the spot for the moment, then tiptoed across the floorboards to the window, which looked on to the road outside. Squinting sideways, I could just about see the front door, but it looked closed. Then I noticed the dark car was in place again along the street. The rumble from Lucky was getting louder when I tiptoed back to her, trying to avoid the creaky boards, and trying to shush her up too.

I listened for a moment, but now I couldn't hear anything but the normal noises of the night: wind in the trees outside, faint voices in the far distance, a car door slamming, also a long way off, and intermittently the *woo-hoo* of the local tawny owls. As I started to open the bedroom door, Lucky left her bed to join me. I felt that a surreptitious examination of my ground floor was not going to be very discreet with a growling Jack Russell at my heels, and I pushed her back a little, closing the bedroom door with her still inside. My first mistake.

I took the stairs to the living room very slowly, one hand on the banister. Dappled moonlight flooded the room and flickered as the wind blew the tree branches outside the window. Everything looked normal, the front door closed and locked. I checked the kitchen-diner next. There was less light in here. I hesitated, with my hand on the switch, made a sudden decision and flicked it on. The sudden glare blinded me for a moment, but it was quickly obvious this room too was empty of anything threatening. I turned the light off again, and paused a moment as I discovered my night-sight was now ruined. My second mistake.

Back upstairs to my bedroom, quite quickly this time, as I was now confident there was nothing to worry about. Lucky, quiet now, tried to get past me as I opened the bedroom door, but I shooed her inside, failing to notice anything odd about the darkness at the end of the landing. My third and fourth mistakes. I went back to bed.

Lucky had, I noticed, dragged her little bed over next to mine. She got into it, turned round twice and settled down with her head propped on the side. When I peered over the edge of the bed her mismatched ears, one brown, one white, were visible in the moonlight from the window above her. I couldn't be bothered to move her back to her usual place nearer the door, so I let my hand drop to stroke her ears and closed my eyes.

There was a loud bang that brought me to a sitting position without any conscious volition on my part as the door flew open hitting the chest of drawers behind it and bouncing back to slam shut again. But by that time the dark shape that had been standing at the end of the landing was straddling me on my bed, and I was flat on my back with a cushion pressed over my face.

I gasped for air to shout, then gasped again for air just to breathe. There was none. I could hear my heart pounding in my ears as my lungs laboured to fill and failed. I heaved my whole body but couldn't shift the weight on me. I clawed at the hands holding the cushion, but they seemed to be wearing gloves and I could make no impression. I was already failing, getting weaker, when Lucky intervened.

I couldn't hear much at first, what with the cushion covering my head, but became aware that the pressure was less, and that suddenly the cushion fell to one side. For a moment I could do nothing but draw in huge breaths with painful whoops, and it was a second or two before my ears caught up with what else was going on. There was a fearsome growling coming from Lucky that wouldn't have been out of place from a Rottweiler. As my eyes struggled to focus on the moonlight, I could see a dark shape on the floor by the bedroom door, shouting and struggling with an enraged terrier apparently engaged in ripping his balls off. For two seconds I was torn between cheering her on and worrying for her safety. At that moment, the figure succeeded in ripping her from his groin, at what cost I didn't know, and threw her across the room. Then he, I was assuming it was a he, wrenched the door open and dashed down the stairs for the front door.

Lucky, fulfilling her name, had landed partly on me and partly on the bed. She was shaken but quite willing to get back into the fight and she followed our fugitive down the stairs. I was next in line, rather more slowly as I was still breathless, and I seized an umbrella as I passed the doorway, as a rather inadequate weapon. By the time I got to the sitting room, Lucky was leaping up and down at the closed front door, barking her head off. The intruder had gone, and I could hear a car engine start up outside in the street. I sank down on the sofa, picked the phone up and dialled 999.

18

Follow-up

The police arrived after about fifteen minutes. While I waited, I cuddled Lucky, examined her as carefully as I could for any injuries, and sipped a glass of brandy. I felt I'd earned it. I decided to book a vet appointment for the following morning, to get Lucky checked over, but as far as I could see, she seemed to be intact. She covered my face with licky kisses, several times in fact, then settled down in my lap.

When the police did arrive, it was mob-handed. Two cars with blue flashing lights shattered the peace of our normally quiet street, followed by an ambulance and a van labelled forensic something. I opened the door to the first two police coming up the garden path, Lucky still tucked under my arm. She muttered a bit but didn't seem to regard these apparitions as a threat. I noticed my neighbour's lights going on and a face or two at a window, and realised I was still in my jimjams.

'Come in,' I said, and preceded them inside rather hurriedly, grabbing up something to pull on over the PJs as I passed the coat hooks by the door.

The first, uniformed, policeman held out his warrant card.

'I'm Sergeant James,' he said, 'and this is Constable Fenwick.' The woman slightly behind him held out her card too, in distinctly unmanicured fingers. I was to learn, quite swiftly, that she was an incorrigible nail-chewer.

'You reported an assault. We understand the assailant has left the premises. Is that correct?'

'Yes,' I said.

'Then the next most important question is, are you injured? I know you told our operator you were okay, but things can catch up with you later. I'd feel a lot better if you were checked over by the experts, then we can sit down, and you can tell us what happened. As you can see,' – he nodded over his shoulder at the green-clad ambulance crew already hot on his heels – 'we've come with back-up.' He smiled in a way that I think was meant to be reassuring. 'So, if you just go with them and get checked over, we can secure the crime scene here. Then we'll have a word.'

'I don't think I need medics,' I started to say, 'but a vet might be handy.'

'A vet?' That was the constable. 'Is the little dog hurt?'

'I don't know. I don't think so, but I'd like to be sure.'

'Well, for now,' she said, 'just you go and get checked over by the team here, and I'll hang on to the little dog until you're done.' She reached out for Lucky, who, to my surprise, went to her without demur. As I went to the ambulance, still protesting slightly, Sergeant James and a couple of colleagues in coveralls went into my house.

About ten minutes later, after a blood pressure check and a general going-over, I was met at my front door by the sergeant.

'You can come into the kitchen,' he said. 'We've finished in there for now. Constable Fenwick will make you a cup of tea and we'll have a preliminary chat.'

'Lucky?' I asked.

'Being spoiled rotten by Fenwick, don't worry,' he said.

In the kitchen, the three of us sat down at the table, Lucky now on my lap.

'Let me explain what's been happening and what's going to happen next,' he said. 'You gave our operator a remarkably detailed account of why you rang. Well done! Not many callers are as clear as you. So, while you were with the ambulance team, the forensic team have done some preliminary work in the house – taking samples, fingerprints, etc. We'll need your prints for exclusionary purposes by the way, but we can do that down at the station.

'Now, as I said, we know a lot from your phone call, but I'd like to go over it with you again, to start preparing a statement. And I should warn you, the inspector will probably have some questions for you too, so you are going to feel you're saying it all over and over again. But the fact is, that repetitions often bring out new facts, so I promise you it is worth it.'

I interrupted at this point. 'My concern is that while you do all this,' – I waved an arm around the blue-lit scene – 'he's getting away. Can't we short-circuit some of the process and catch up with him before it's too late?'

'With who?' asked Sergeant James.

'My soon to be ex-husband.'

'You saw him, did you?' he asked.

'Well, no, but—'

'Or you are able to identify him as the assailant in some other way?'

'No, but—'

'Then I'm afraid we do need to go through the process of collecting evidence,' he replied. 'Don't worry, an ex-husband is definitely going to be up there with the key suspects, but you said on the phone call that you hadn't seen your attacker and weren't able to identify him. It seems that's still true. Or have you now remembered something that would identify him?'

'No, but—'

'Okay. Let's start at the beginning. Tell me about your evening, up to the point you went to bed.'

I described what I'd been doing, unable to rid myself of the suspicion that he was assuming I'd gone to bed drunk and dreamed everything. On that I was doing him a disservice, but tiredness and stress were catching up with me.

I explained how I'd gone to bed, been woken by a noise, then gone downstairs to investigate. I described the attack, which gave me the shivers to do it, and I hugged Lucky closer while Constable Fenwick poured me another mug of tea.

'So,' I concluded, 'thanks to Lucky, all you need to do is check my ex over for a dog bite in a very personal place, and bingo, you've got him.'

Fenwick looked up from her notes. 'Sounds as though anybody bitten may have gone to a hospital,' she said. 'We can check the hospitals too.'

'Correct,' said the sergeant, whose eyes appeared to be watering. He looked at his watch. 'It's close to two o'clock now,' he said. 'Have you somewhere you can go for the rest of the night? We can pick this up later in the morning.'

'Not round here,' I said. 'Can't I just go to bed? In my spare room?'

'I wouldn't recommend it,' he replied. 'We're going to be here for a bit, and we might disturb you. How about Constable Fenwick here helps you pack a small bag, then we'll drop you off at a hotel for the rest of the night and see you at the station at, say, ten?'

'I need to take Lucky with me,' I said hurriedly.

They looked at each other, then James said, 'I'm sure we can arrange that.' Which is how Lucky and I, plus an overnight bag, came to spend what was left of the night at the Holiday Lodge on the edge of town.

***

At 10.00 sharp the next morning, we were picked up from the hotel and taken to the police station in Cambridge. Lucky sat on my knee all the way there, her nose sticking out of the partly open window, and clearly enjoying the whole experience. There was some muttering and pulled faces when my companion was spotted, but eventually we were shown to an interview suite. Lucky and I sat there alone for a while, until an officer I hadn't met before came in with a bowl of water for Lucky and the offer of tea or coffee for me. The coffee arrived simultaneously with the inspector and sidekick.

I wasn't impressed by either. Inspector Grant looked overdue for retirement and only barely awake. It was plain he hadn't read the papers in front of him, which represented Sergeant James' account of our conversation the night before.

The sidekick, apparently a newly promoted DS, was eager, excited and transparently wet behind the ears. My heart sank.

After more than two hours, I felt they hadn't learned any more than I'd already told the initial responders: that all I'd seen was the dark shape of a man, probably wearing a balaclava, as I hadn't seen his face. That he hadn't spoken except to shout when Lucky bit him, and that I couldn't identify him by voice, smell or appearance, but was still convinced in my heart of hearts that it had been Pete. Who else would have a motive?

However, *I* learned two things from *them*. No one had reported to a local hospital with a dog bite in the groin. And Pete was out of the country.

'How do you know?' I asked.

'He checked in to board the ferry to the Hook of Holland the day before, and he's on CCTV footage from the port. We'll show it to you shortly, so you can satisfy yourself it's kosher,' said Inspector Grant with a yawn.

They did, and it was. I sat back in my chair, baffled.

'Perhaps he came back,' I suggested.

'We've checked,' they replied. 'He's not been on any ferry or flight back. And he's still at his hotel in Amsterdam.'

I paused to take that in. I didn't, at the time, reflect that they seemed to have achieved a lot in a very short space of time and wonder how accurate their information was. Nor how thorough their investigations.

'What happens next?' I demanded.

'We're checking cameras and so on for anybody near your house last night,' he replied. 'But unfortunately, your area is not well covered by CCTV.'

'Fingerprints?' I asked.

'Only a few found, and it's likely they're all yours. It seems whoever it was wore gloves.'

'Is that it?' I asked, disbelieving my own ears.

'We'll keep looking,' they assured me, 'but it seems likely it was a robbery that went wrong. You may have to resign yourself to us never finding out who did it. But we'll send someone home with you to go over your security,' Grant added cheerfully. 'Your front door is hopeless. You can open it with a credit card. You need a deadlock and bolts at the least.'

I'd already reached that conclusion myself. As for the rest, I was flabbergasted. I went home with Lucky and a crime number, and that seemed to be that from Grant's point of view.

In the circumstances, I was glad I'd kept to myself my other thought: that my grandfather had died, suffocated, at a time that had proved very beneficial to Pete. Perhaps that hadn't been the accident it seemed.

19

Where Next?

I thought I'd coped well with the attack. I went home to Staffordshire for a long weekend, where both Lucky and I were cosseted by my mother. If the parallel with what had happened to Grandad occurred to her, she didn't say anything. I nearly broached the topic several times, and several times I saw her open her mouth then close it again without speaking. I didn't call on Pete's mother.

Back at work, the few people I told about the events of 29 July fussed around me a little, but stopped when it was clear the fussing wasn't welcome. I buried my mind in my work and my head in the sand, only pulling it out when I heard from the police. This dwindled quite sharply, and stopped altogether in October when, I discovered, Inspector Grant retired.

I tried to follow up with the teenage detective sergeant, but it was clear he had dismissed it as a case of burglary gone wrong, and was spending his time on the much more exciting, and potentially career progressing, cases of murder that had cropped up in Cambridgeshire: one involving the body of a nurse found in the Cam, and the other a stabbing at a folk festival. I read about both in the papers, and while sympathetic to the grieving relatives, I must admit to envying the amount of attention accorded the cases by the police. It seemed one had to be dead before an assault was taken seriously.

After giving it some anxious thought, I rang a few old friends and eventually found what I was looking for: a contact number for Bob the Bobby, now Sergeant Robert Manners, married and father of three. The beginning of the conversation was a little awkward, but it warmed up when I explained I was divorcing the man he'd always referred to as 'the Spiv'. It cooled again sharply when I outlined my problems with the local police.

'In short,' I said, 'it seems a little odd to me that they gave up so quickly. Okay, they don't believe me about Pete, but the assault is a fact, and they don't seem very bothered about finding out who did it!'

There was a long pause, then a deep sigh. 'I'm sorry, Elf, I really don't think I can help. Different police forces do things differently, and any questions from me would be as welcome as a tick on a tit. If they've decided it's a cold case, it's because they don't have enough evidence to take it further.'

'But what about Pete's alibi?' I argued. 'They say he definitely wasn't in the country, but they never seemed to me to look at it very hard. One statement from an unnamed woman in a Dutch hotel and a quick check of the ports, and they say he's in the clear.'

'That's the one thing that does look a bit odd to me,' admitted Bob. 'To check all the possible ports in one night is next to impossible. But I doubt you'll get anywhere unless you have new evidence.' I stored that piece of information away for future thought and rang off.

My divorce went through, with my solicitor handling all contacts with Pete and his solicitor. I was expecting more hassle over the financial arrangements, but in the end, he settled for what even I could regard as reasonable.

The truth was that, even spared a meeting with him, I was a nervous wreck. I was sleeping badly, my heartbeat shot up to unheard of heights every time I spotted a dark car in the road outside my cottage, and as for an alert from Lucky! They would bring me to my feet so fast I felt dizzy and had to sit down again.

My colleagues started to look at me a little oddly, and in some cases I realised they were covering for me. When I had a panic attack – sparked off by a sudden bang from a door – in the middle of a meeting I was chairing, I knew something had to change. I had a word with my boss's PA to make an appointment for a chat, and it was while I was sitting in his outer office, half listening to her on the telephone while I waited for his preceding meeting to conclude, that I picked up a copy of papers on an internal circulation that was lying on the table in front of me. As the name on the top of the circulation list, my boss had already seen it. My name was about a third of the way down, and I wouldn't normally see it until a few days later. It was just luck that I picked it up, and even luckier that the top paper had a heading that caught my eye. When I went in to see the boss, I had a suggestion to make.

I barely let him get a civil greeting out before I jumped in with my speech.

'I think you know I had a bad experience recently,' I said. 'And we both know that it's affecting my work.' I waved the paper I'd picked up from his outer office. 'So I have a solution to suggest. There's a job advertised here, for someone at my grade to move to Cornwall. I'd like the job.' Then I sat back and looked at him.

'You're right on both your first counts,' he said slowly. 'But wrong if you thought I was about to tick you off. We all realise you had a terrible time, and we're sympathetic. I was going to suggest some time off, and perhaps some support from the health team.'

I suppressed a shudder at the thought of time on my hands, and said, 'I don't want time off. At least, no more than might be needed to effect a move. But I *would* like this transfer to Cornwall. That would give me the break I need, and the job looks interesting too.'

'You could do it standing on your head,' he replied. 'But until now I'd have said your next move would be on promotion. If you move that far from London, you're putting your prospects on hold, you do realise that?'

I hesitated for only a moment. I'd hoped for promotion but hadn't realised it had been within my grasp. I considered the possibility briefly, then replied, 'I'd really like the move to Cornwall.'

He reached for his phone there and then. 'I'll have a word with the Director General,' he said, 'and get back to you. Go on. Scoot. Leave this with me.'

By the end of the day, I had a new job. At least, all the formal processes had yet to be worked through by the HR team, but my current DG and my new one had agreed it between them, which pretty much made it a done deal.

'I told him he'd be lucky to have you,' said my boss, 'and the sooner you can take up your new job, the better for them. I'm afraid I put my foot down about needing you for another month, but after that you start in Falmouth at the new Marine Science Research Lab, as their deputy director responsible for admin and operations. As it's a compulsory move, you get the appropriate removal package, including guaranteed house sale, removals and the costs of a visit or two to look around. HR will brief you.' He waved away my thanks. And I went home with a much lighter heart.

Somehow, the fact of my imminent departure greatly relieved my fears. I spent that last month bringing my successor up to speed at work and arranging for my cottage to go on the market. The 'guaranteed house sale' arrangement meant that, with three professional valuations under my belt, I had the middle valuation available as a government loan to buy my new home whether or not my old cottage had actually sold.

The week before starting my new job, I took a long weekend to go house-hunting, and tripped over my new home while trying to find a completely different property in the narrow lanes of the Cornish countryside. I never did find the house I'd got an appointment to view, but as I stood in a field gateway studying my map, I realised there was a 'For Sale' sign just down the road. I took the risk of leaving my car where it was for a moment and walked down as far as the sign. It was sticking out of a stone wall near the entrance to a small yard. To one side, I could see an old stone barn. In front of me was a traditional Cornish cottage, white-painted and slate-roofed.

It had a small garden in front, and as I looked, an elderly lady stood up from the flowerbed she'd been weeding and asked, 'Can I help you? Are you lost?'

'I am actually,' I said. 'But I stopped because of your 'For Sale' sign. How would I make an appointment to view?'

'Well come you in, me lover,' she replied. 'I'm not doing anything.'

'I have my dog with me,' I said. 'Is that okay?'

'That's fine,' she said. 'I'll have the kettle on dreckly, then you have a good look round.'

I fetched my car, and its slightly indignant occupant, and turned in at the gateway to park in the small yard. Lucky got out with a stretch and a wiggle of her tail.

'Well, he's a proper job, no doubt 'bout that,' said the lady, emerging from her back door.

Lucky went to her as I said, 'She's a she!' and followed them both in.

The cottage was in some ways quite similar to the one in St Ives, although several centuries older. At some point the lean-to running the full length of the cottage had been converted into a long, narrow kitchen, while the remaining two rooms seemed to work as sitting room and dining room. The narrow, very narrow, stairs ran up from the front hall to access two bedrooms and a bathroom. The walls were solid stone and very thick, with windowsills broad enough to sit in. The view from the front was over another garden, with fields beyond leading down toward the Lizard.

'That paddock goes with the cottage,' said the lady, coming in from the kitchen behind me. 'It's only an acre, but...'

I turned to survey the stairs. 'How do you get anything up those?' I asked.

'Through the coffin hatch,' she said, and pointed at the ceiling. Between the joists above my head, I could, sure enough, see a hatch to the room above.

By the time tea had been taken and Lucky had demolished several digestive biscuits, we had reached an accord, and I set off for Helston and the estate agents handling the sale. As a cash buyer, they greeted me with open arms and, if anything, were even more enthusiastic when they learned I was taking up a job locally and wasn't just looking for a holiday home.

'That's good,' the manager enthused. 'It's sad when incomers snap up all these old places then don't live in them. But you'll be fine there. Provided you don't mind your nearest neighbour being half a mile away.'

'No problem,' I assured her. 'It'll suit me fine.'

We completed the paperwork, and I went off to notify the HR team that I would be needing their cash.

In reality, the sale of my St Ives home went through quickly too, so I didn't need that interest free loan for long. The old lady I'd met, Mrs Pascoe, was moving in with family so was happy to move swiftly. Her family, when I met them on a visit to do some measuring up, were also happy.

'We've been worrying about her, living on her own with no near neighbours,' her son confided. 'It was fine when she was younger, but she had a fall last month and it wasn't the first.'

In fact, everything went smoothly, until it came to booking a removal company. Mrs Pascoe had advised me to use a local firm – local to her, she meant – because of the difficult access. She wasn't joking. The first two companies I approached turned it down out of hand when they saw the lane, the turning into the drive and the coffin-hatch arrangement. In the end, I found myself using the same company Mrs Pascoe had employed to move her out. They weren't bothered by the lane, explaining that they'd warn the neighbours it would be blocked for an hour or two while they emptied their van, and the coffin hatch was practically an old friend for them.

My newly acquired PA at the Marine Science Research Lab found me a dog-friendly B&B, where I stayed until I could move into my new home, which the pragmatic Pascoes had named White Lodge many years before. I decided to stick with the old name, so Lucky and I moved into White Lodge on 1 November 1981.

2O

1982–84 New Job: New Life

The original description was, in essence, to run the new laboratory in a sort of Laboratory Secretary role. As my old boss had said, I could, in all modesty, do that standing on my head. It didn't take long to knock the new establishment into shape and embed appropriate processes. Getting the culture right took a bit longer, but the young scientists and specialists were all knowledgeable and enthusiastic. It wasn't difficult to engage that enthusiasm in delivering a quality service to the various agencies and businesses looking for our help.

After a few months I started looking round for other tasks to put my hand to, and by virtue of saying yes to any experience that could teach me something, I soon found myself involved in all sorts of projects, from measuring river pollution to devising a quality system for roll-out around all the department's research units.

One task that wasn't new was one I was asked to take on quite early in my tenure. I had previously, much earlier in my career, been secretary to a statutory government committee. Now I was asked to take on another, which had run into difficulties when the chairman had resigned with ill health and the deputy had, to be blunt, made a cock of it. By the time a new Chair was appointed, the deputy had seriously peed off every other government department involved and most of the independent experts. The existing secretary had been signed off with a stress-related problem, and the new Chair was demanding some help in getting things back on track. Enter me, apparently assumed to be a new, slightly plumper, version of Superwoman.

I approached our first meeting very tentatively. The new Chair was about fifteen years younger than the last, and full of energy. Sir Harry Llewelyn was medium height, medium build with a broad face and an even broader grin. He was also full of charm and charisma, which, while helpful from the point of view of re-engaging with the discontented committee members, was the cause of some suspicion, especially in me. However, I was won over very rapidly, and within the first meeting had switched from watchful caution to enthusiastic advocate.

He combined an in-depth knowledge of his subject with an unparalleled, in my experience, capacity for communication. I'd never come across the combination before in an academic, and the experience was salutary. I discovered I could safely, with minimum briefing, field him to answer questions from any area within the committee's purview. He sucked in data from members like a sponge and dolloped it out again in the direction of reporters, interviewers, TV and radio in bite-size, quotable chunks that even the right-leaning red tops couldn't misconstrue. As a communicator on behalf of government, he was heaven. As a man, he was entertaining and personable. He was also, unfortunately, married and around seventeen years older than me.

With those two facts in mind, I settled down to enjoy working alongside him, and enjoying his company on those relatively rare social occasions that followed a meeting or an official visit.

From time to time, he would invite me to attend a lecture he was giving, sometimes at the university, more often as part of a conference or other special event. Gradually, the invitation included dinner after the lecture – at first to an official dinner, later as his guest in a restaurant. I was dazzled with hero worship and blinded by admiration. Inevitably, I fell in love.

If you're assuming this was part of a cunning, predatory ploy by the chairman, you'd be wrong. At least, you might be right as to his original motives, but wrong as to how it played out because, by the time, much later, he got round to asking if I would spend a night with him after a conference, he had fallen in love with me too.

I can feel your cynicism from here, all these years later, but I promise you, it *was* love, and it was one of the happiest times of my life. For the first time since I broke things off with Phil, I felt valued and cherished. He challenged me intellectually, and it drove me to achieve more than I would have thought possible, professionally. He introduced me to all sorts of new experiences, from fly fishing to sailing. We never stopped talking and laughing. The one problem was, of course, that he wasn't free. He had a wife and children, and I knew there was no possibility of his leaving them, even if he had found little fulfilment in his marriage for some years.

We were discreet at work in the committee. I've no idea if anyone guessed our special relationship. I don't think so. That we got on well was obvious and that we met occasionally in related areas, such as conferences, was also known. But I don't think anyone knew or guessed about our emotional connection or our physical link. One potential giveaway was Lucky, as she took to greeting him like a long-lost friend whenever they were in the same room. But he brushed that off with a comment about dogs always liking him.

About two years into our liaison, his wife was diagnosed with breast cancer. For the duration of her treatment, I saw much less of him than usual, and that little only in the office or the margins of committee meetings. I missed him desperately, even though we spoke on the phone almost every day and tried very hard to push away the thought that if something 'went wrong', he'd be free to marry me. That the thought could even pass through my head disgusted me, and I'd be rather terse when we next spoke, out of guilt and shame. He was a bit the same with me, and I wondered if this was going to be the rock on which our relationship foundered. Ironic if so, that it could survive a well wife, but not a sick one.

Months down the line, and she got the all-clear. We celebrated with a quiet dinner at my cottage, Lucky going wild with excitement to have her friend back. I was more circumspect, and he was awkward. It was only after dinner and some stilted conversation that we settled by the fire with a glass of brandy each, and he seemed to relax.

'I have a confession to make,' he said, holding his glass up and looking at the fire through the tawny liquid. 'It's not a pretty one.'

I held my breath and squeezed the stem of my glass so tightly it nearly snapped. *What was coming next?*

'But I can't carry on while hiding this,' he went on. 'When Mairi was ill, when she was being treated, I found myself thinking how much easier everything would be if she died.' He looked at me, sitting silent beside the fire. 'I didn't wish her dead, at least I don't think so, but it frightens me I could even have the thought.'

'Why does it frighten you?' I asked, almost admitting my thoughts in a similar vein, but waiting to see how he answered the more important question first.

'Because it shows just how important you are to me. You know I've had affairs before,' he added. 'I've never hidden that. But you're different, and that scares me. I thought I could carry on having a family and a mistress, but I'm not sure I can any more. I think we may need to make other arrangements.'

I swallowed painfully. 'Are you saying you want this to end?' I asked.

'No.' He put his brandy down by the hearth and turned to me. The flames flickered in his dark eyes, and Lucky rolled over with a groan, waving her silly little legs in the air. He smiled involuntarily and rubbed her tummy, then looked back at me. A log slipped and a shower of sparks flew up the chimney. I could smell the wood smoke, and knew even then, that smell would bring this moment back to me for ever. 'I'm saying the opposite, I think. I'm saying that I never want this to end. That I never want to be apart from you again, if you'll have me.'

'Your wife...' I asked. 'What about your wife?'

'I'm not going to say anything until I'm sure she's definitely well, and I'll make sure she never wants for anything.'

'Except you,' I said.

'I'm not sure I'm so very important to her,' he replied, turning back to the fire. 'Not any more. Not as important as I think I am to you. Am I right?'

I held my hand out. 'You're right,' I said. 'But I don't think we can build happiness on someone else's misery. Provided I have you, I can stay in the shadows. If need be.'

'No, I don't think you can,' he contradicted me. 'I don't think I can hide how I feel any longer.' He took my hand and kneeled on the hearth rug, next to Lucky. 'Please, Elf, will you marry me when we can?'

'Yes, I will,' I said and, to my own astonishment, burst into tears. He pulled me down beside him and Lucky licked them off my face.

'Don't be daft,' he said. 'Be happy.'

21

MILESTONE 10: Testing to Destruction

So there we were, engaged to be engaged. Back then in 1984, I, at least, assumed that this would be a short phase, followed by a possibly painful break from his wife, a time of adjustment, and then we would proceed with our new life. But the weeks, months and even years dragged on with no change. First, she had some ups and downs with scares which proved to be groundless, then she became depressed and temperamental, alternating between throwing tantrums and, occasionally, crockery, and draping herself all over him while weeping that she couldn't understand why he stood by her.

Nor could I, to be blunt. Well, yes, of course I could really. I could see the difficulty of leaving her while she was in that state, and I tried to be sympathetic, but as time wore on, I became more and more certain that this was calculated emotional blackmail. That she had, somehow, got wind of our relationship and was deploying every weapon at her disposal to hang on to him. Into the middle of this volatile mess landed another complication.

One February evening, which had been characterised, yet again, by a slightly tetchy exchange on the subject of unreasonable demands – hers, not mine – Harry suddenly said, 'I've been meaning to ask you, Elf, have you an enemy?'

I stopped mid-gulp of my wine, choked slightly – I can still remember the taste of wine at the back of my throat – and asked, 'Why would you say that?'

'Because I've been getting some anonymous letters. I ignored the first few, but they've been coming for some time, and they're getting more frequent and nastier.'

'What do they say?' I asked, my suspicions flying immediately to his wife.

'Mostly, they ask if I really know you, and do I realise you're probably out for my money.' He grinned at me and leaned over for a handful of peanuts. 'Which we both know is rubbish,' he added. 'I haven't got any.' My mind was still running on bitter, neglected wife, when he went on, 'The most recent say you took money off your ex-husband, emptying your joint bank accounts before he could get his share.' He chewed the nuts, swallowed, and said, 'But what really got me going is that the last letter named a restaurant we visited recently. I assume that means you have a stalker, and that frightens me, which is why I've mentioned it.'

I put my glass down on the coffee table very carefully and picked Lucky up for a hug. That didn't sound like trouble from his wife. It sounded like trouble from my past.

'What's the matter, Elf?' he asked. 'I'm sorry. I didn't want to scare you, but I started thinking that perhaps you needed to be on your guard.'

I found my voice. 'It sounds like Pete, my ex-husband,' I said.

'The one who was controlling? Yes, that fits, if he knows where you are,' he said.

'It wouldn't be hard for him to find out. I've not exactly been hidden away. But there's stuff I haven't told you about Pete.'

It took a long time to explain everything that had gone on, from my suspicions about how Magic came to die so suddenly, to the assault on me that the police had written off as a failed burglary, and even my worries about how my grandad had died. The fire was on the verge of flickering out by the time I finished, and the room was growing cold. There was a long silence, then he got to his feet and reached for the log basket which was, of course, empty.

'I'll fill this and let Lucky out. Be back in a minute.' And he left the room.

He doesn't believe me, I thought, and wondered what in earth I should do next. *I've tried running away, all the way to Cornwall. If that hasn't worked, what is left?*

He came back with the log basket and piled up the fire. To start with all we got was smoke that eddied in the draught from the still open door. Then a few flames slid along the new fuel. Lucky came back in, gave a shake to rid herself of the rain on her fur, and he closed the door before coming back to sit by me.

'Sorry,' he said. 'I needed to think for a moment. I find it easier to revert to the scientific approach, so let's look at this that way. Hypothesis number one, you're a fantasist and none of this actually happened. That doesn't fit what I know of you, and doesn't fit readily checkable facts, so we'll forget that one.

'Hypothesis number two, the basic facts are correct, but your conclusions are incorrect.

'Hypothesis number three, you're right, all the way down the line.

'Okay, what *are* the facts? Your grandfather died of suffocation, his death was not investigated thoroughly, and you received a valuable inheritance just in time to benefit you and Pete. But we note that Pete helped himself to a substantial share without your permission or knowledge.

'The dog Pete didn't like died suddenly and unexpectedly, possibly of suffocation, shortly after you married.

'In the midst of your divorce proceedings, but before your financial agreement is signed off – incidentally, was it also before you made a new will?'

I nodded.

'As I say, before financial arrangements are settled, an attempt is made to suffocate you. The police think it was a robbery gone wrong, but nothing is stolen.

'I'm no criminologist,' he went on, 'but from what you read in the papers, people who kill are often creatures of habit. The method they use tends not to vary. And there does seem to have been a lot of suffocation in your life, if I can put it that way.'

There was a long silence, broken only by Lucky scratching. At last, he said, 'I think we have a problem, Elf. What do you want me to do about it? Do we go to the police again?'

'It didn't get me very far before,' I said.

'No, I can see that. There *is* one thing that's new, though. The poison pen letters. I haven't kept them all, but I do have quite a few locked in my desk. I think I should report them to the police. Sending threatening anonymous letters is illegal in itself. At the very least, an investigation might scare him off.'

'It hasn't got me very far before,' I repeated. I was dubious about involving the police again. 'It's unlikely to solve anything now.'

'It's worth a try,' he said. 'Rightly or wrongly, I'm in a better position to make a fuss than you were.'

'What about the publicity?' I asked.

'Unlikely to be any, and if there is, perhaps we just take it on the chin. Perhaps we've been quiet for long enough. One thing puzzles me, though. Why is he so obsessed with getting even with you? From where I'm sitting, I'd expect him to be irritated, resentful, angry even. But not homicidal. Any idea, Elf?'

'I really don't know,' I said. 'Believe me, I've thought about it lots over the years, but all I have are theories, not answers. He set enormous store on success, and nothing was ever his fault. That was obvious when we lost the twins, as I told you. I think he hated to be the one that was left. If *he'd* left *me*, that would have been different. As it was, *I* left, *I* got most of my inheritance back, *I* had a good solicitor who agreed a decent financial package, *I* had a new life, a new home, even a new dog that, adding injury to insult, bit him. So, you tell me ... is it jealousy? Or is he just plain barking?'

I suddenly realised I felt warm, and it wasn't just the resurgence of the newly fuelled fire. I wasn't on my own now.

Someone was at least *trying* to look after me. 'Thank you,' I said.

'You don't need to thank me,' he replied. 'You never need to thank me. I love you, although I'm well aware I don't say it often enough.' He kissed the top of my head and stared into the fire again. 'If the police don't get a grip this time,' he said, 'we may need to think of something else. I need to keep you safe, Elf.'

'What sort of something else?' I asked.

'Perhaps a move abroad. I'm often offered jobs in the US or Europe. We could go a long, long way and never have to worry about him again.'

We reported the poison pen letters to the police the next day. They took all the letters and envelopes that we had in our possession and interviewed us both. They were discreet about it, and I was left unsure whether to be pleased or disappointed about that. In some ways, I would have welcomed coming out of the closet, even if we hadn't chosen the timing.

Then a silence fell – not greatly to my surprise, but much to my lover's disappointment, who had expected more action. He got impatient and started to pursue possible new jobs. I discovered he'd meant what he said on that front, and wondered, if he did take a new job, whether it wouldn't just be me running away. Then the Soviets decided to test one of their power stations to destruction, and everything changed.

Monday 28 April 1986, and some workers at a Swedish power station got the fright of their lives when the radiation detectors on the perimeter recorded higher than normal radiation levels. Thinking they had a leak to contend with, they got a second fright when they found that the radiation, far from coming from their plant, was coming *in* over their perimeter. Tuesday 29 April, and with US satellites turned to focus on the Ukraine, it was plain where the problem was coming from: a major explosion and subsequent fires at the Chernobyl nuclear power plant near Pripyat which, it became clear, had happened days earlier on 26 April but not been declared by the Soviet authorities, and were still burning out of control.

By the bank holiday weekend at the beginning of May – I've said before that all emergencies happen on bank holidays and we should build that assumption into our emergency planning – the clouds of radioactive caesium had drifted west across Sweden and Germany and arrived over the UK just in time for heavy downpours to wash the radioactivity out of the clouds and onto Scotland, Cumbria and Wales.

Cue phone call to me and a politely expressed invitation, which was not an invitation at all, to go to London and assist in the development and implementation of the emergency control measures.

I left Lucky with a friend in Helston and took the train from Truro to Paddington with not much more than a hurriedly packed overnight bag.

At this distance in time some of the detail is a little hazy, but I do remember very clearly the confusion caused by the different reactions around European governments. Among the lists of foods whose consumption was banned were leafy vegetables, milk and some meats, but *which* were banned *where* varied enormously, and if the French government's reaction was anything to go by, the radioactive cloud had taken a sharp right turn as it approached their border such that no contamination whatsoever fell on French soils!

In the UK, the prevailing wisdom was that we didn't need to worry too much about iodine in milk because the half-life was only a matter of days. A much greater problem was the radioactive caesium with its half-life of thirty years.

In the finest example of Sod's Law I have ever seen, the soils on which the radioactive rain fell were precisely those least capable of rendering the caesium biologically unavailable. On mineral-heavy soils, such as the clay soils of Cambridgeshire – so heavy that the saying is, if you stick to it, it will stick to you – the caesium is rapidly locked away and becomes unavailable to plants. On the peat-based soils of Cumbria and parts of Wales, that doesn't happen. The caesium moves into plant structures, is grazed by animals, excreted by them back onto the peaty soils and back into the plants. Round and round it goes, like an evil carousel. Hence our problem with radioactive sheep and the many jokes about sheep glowing in the dark.

The first problem was to find out just how badly the sheep were affected. Our first sampling method involved killing the sheep, which left the shepherds understandably unhappy, especially if the sheep were found to be only slightly affected, as they were still dead! I don't expect the sheep were too chuffed either. Later, an enterprising technology firm developed a method of testing sheep with a hand-held device held against the live sheep's rump. I remember one reporter at a press conference asking what a sheep's rump was, and the very heavy foot that came down on mine as I opened my mouth to give a four-letter reply.

Sorry to bang on about this, but I wanted to give a flavour of the hectic nature of my working life at this time, as we struggled to get our heads around the science, establish where and what the problem was, and develop both methods to manage it and the legislation to enable us to implement said methods. For a week or more, I was up to my eyes in it all, and barely had chance to get back to my hotel room to sleep and change, let alone keep up with what was happening in Cornwall.

Once the emergency orders were approved by Parliament, we had control over the radioactive sheep. Then we had to implement a monitoring process, so we'd know when their radioactivity dropped below 1000 becquerels per kilo, plus a means of identifying those that failed, in order to keep them out of the food chain until they were safe to eat. After all that, I felt I had, at last, got chance for a breather and an opportunity to take stock.

It was the first time I was able to ring home for more than a hello and how are you. It was only after I'd been rabbiting on for what I thought was a few minutes but was probably half an hour – see above to get a flavour! – that I realised the contribution from the other end was a bit perfunctory.

I stopped in the middle of a vivid description of the reaction of some Cumbrian shepherds to being told their sheep were going to be painted apricot, and asked, 'What's the matter?'

There was a bit of a silence, then he said, 'I'm afraid I've got some bad news, Elf. Your house has been broken into.' Now I was silent too.

'When?' I said at last. 'And what damage has been done?'

'Last week. Friday to be precise. And the damage isn't too bad. But some of your paintings have been slashed, and the photos of you and Lucky were taken outside and burned. I've had a clean-up team in, so you're not met with all the mess. That's after the police came, of course.'

'And what do the police say?' If I was unnaturally calm, it was because I was finding it difficult to process.

'They say it doesn't look like a burglary, that it looks personal. But they also said whoever did it was wearing gloves, and the forensic team haven't turned anything up yet.'

'How did he get in?'

'You're assuming it was Pete?'

'Who else?' I asked. 'How did he get in?'

'Smashed a window at the front, away from the road. It's such an isolated spot no one noticed for at least a day. I found the mess when I popped in at the weekend to check everything was okay. And I'd been past on Thursday, so I knew it must have happened either Friday or late Thursday night.'

'Elf, I don't think you can carry on living there alone. It's not safe. You're too isolated, and if anything does happen, there's no CCTV or anything.'

'Not that that would protect me,' I remarked. 'It might just help catch whoever did it but forgive me if I don't find that very reassuring!'

'There may be a deterrent effect,' he argued, 'but I get your point. Either way, I think we need to make some changes.' I was silent again for a few moments.

'Elf, you're not cross with me, are you?' he asked. 'I didn't want to bother you with it all, when you were so busy.'

'I'm not cross, no, at least not with you,' I said. 'But I'm bloody furious with Pete, and I resent having to run away. Again!'

'Yes, I can see that.' Another pause, this time from his side, then he added, 'You need to think of it as a strategic retreat, not a defeat. We need space and time where you're safe, so we can work out how to get this maniac off our backs for good. There is one other thing I should mention,' he added. 'You had an old writing desk in the bottom of your wardrobe. You know, that thing that unfolds into a writing slope and has space for writing paper and so on.'

'Yes,' I said, with a horrible feeling I knew what was coming next.

'That was something else that was damaged. Whoever it was ripped it in two. And it's empty now. I think you told me once you kept my cards and letters in it. Well, they've gone.'

'As long as I still have you,' I said, trying to put a brave face on, and rang off.

Later I rang back but caught him just before he was going into a lecture. 'I'll be quick,' I said. 'Just to say, I'll be on the late train from Paddington to Truro.'

'I'll pick you up at Truro,' he said. 'Love you.' And was gone.

The train journey was interminable. As we pulled into Truro I searched the platform eagerly for the familiar face, but it wasn't there. I went out to the front of the station, checked the car park and the streets near, but nothing. Then I waited increasingly impatiently, sometimes sitting at the front of the station, other times marching up and down. After an hour I was starting to give up, and after another half an hour, I found a late taxi to take me, not home, but to my friend, Mary, who was housing Lucky.

'I'm so sorry to disturb you so late,' I said, explaining about the non-appearance of my lift and the break-in that made me reluctant to return home alone in the early hours.

'Of course you must stay here,' she said. 'You know where everything is. Forgive me if I go straight back to bed, I've got a full day tomorrow. See you in the morning.' Yawning, she slippered off, while Lucky and I went to the spare room.

I wasn't particularly worried about Harry's non-appearance at the station. It had happened before, when something unexpected had blown up in the family, and I knew he'd be in touch as soon as he could. Home was where he'd find me, so home I'd go, as soon as I could get a taxi in the morning. Despite, or perhaps because of, the stressful journey, I slept heavily and late, only waking when Mary brought me a mug of coffee just before she went out.

'Sorry to love you and leave you,' she said, 'but I'm going to a craft fair today and I need to get a shift on.' Mary made hand-thrown pottery, rather well, and often sold at craft fairs.

'By the way,' she stuck her head back round the bedroom door, 'isn't Professor Harry Llewelyn one of yours?'

'Yes,' I said, clutching my coffee very tightly. 'He's chairman of our committee. Why?'

'It's just been on the news,' she said. 'I'm afraid you're going to need a new chairman. He was killed in a road accident last night.'

22

Disaster

I don't know how I got rid of Mary without letting on just how hard I was hit. I think she put my monosyllabic reaction down to shock at losing a good chairman. She may have guessed there was more to it than that, but after looking at me rather hard, she went off to work.

Without any sense of what I was doing, I got up and pulled some clothes on at random, mostly what I'd been wearing the day before, but it hardly mattered now. Then I sat down with Lucky on my lap and started trawling the news channels. I couldn't find much: just a couple of snippets. It seemed he'd lost control coming down the steep hill in Penryn and ended up nose down in someone's garden. It didn't sound like Harry. Yes, he liked driving fast – he had a Porsche for God's sake! But he wasn't reckless, and he knew those roads like his own garden path.

Should I go to the police with what I know? Should I go home and take stock? Should I ring his wife with my condolences, or the office about action I need to take to replace him as chair?

I defaulted to my safe space and rang for a taxi to take me home. I could think what to do next when I got there.

In my distress, I'd forgotten what Harry had told me about my house being burgled, so it was a second shock when the taxi pulled into my yard and I saw the remains of crime scene tape blowing round my garden.

'Are you sure this is okay, my lover?' asked the taxi driver, looking worried. 'Should you be here on your own?'

'Yes, it's fine,' I said. 'I'm not really alone.' And I gestured to Lucky. He looked dubious, but said no more, getting my small case out of the boot of his car and carrying it up to my front door. Then he sat in his car until he saw me open the door and go in, before driving off with a friendly toot.

Inside, it was much as Harry had described it, but someone had obviously been in and done some clearing up. I remembered Harry saying he'd had a professional cleaning company in. There were a couple of large, sturdy cardboard boxes with broken glass and crockery inside. The damaged paintings he'd mentioned were stacked neatly against a wall. I couldn't summon up the energy to look through them just yet. Someone had slashed the seats of the leather chairs in the sitting room, and someone else had patched the slashes with gaffer tape. The all-pervasive smell was of strong disinfectant, which reminded me that Harry hadn't wanted to go into details about the nastier elements of the attack on my home. Judging by the smell and the scrubbed look of my carpets, there'd been quite a mess to clear up. My bed was stripped of all bedding, and I couldn't find the usual duvet or pillows, so I concluded they'd also been collateral damage. Luckily the attacks hadn't encompassed my airing cupboard. Or the attacker had been disturbed before he reached it.

I took out some spare bedding and made up my bed for the night to come, then sat down on one of the damaged leather chairs with Lucky in my lap and before me, on the coffee table, the two halves of what had been my writing box. I would need to see about some food for Lucky soon, but for now, it was time to consider the letters that had disappeared from my writing box, and their likely involvement in the 'accident' that had killed Harry.

The letters had been Harry's to me. Whether he'd kept mine to him, I didn't know for sure. If he had, I hoped they were somewhere his new widow wouldn't readily find them. No point now torturing her with what might have been, would have been, if Harry had survived a little longer.

My torture, by contrast, was with me with every breath I took, and every snap of a synapse in my beleaguered brain. Through the blank sense of despair and loss, the thought hammering away at the front of my mind, was that if those letters hadn't existed, or if they hadn't been found and there was no paper trail linking Harry and me romantically, then this so-called accident would never have happened. Both he and all my hopes would still be alive. Because I was totally convinced, with a certainty that outstripped everything, that the burglar had been Pete, and that the accident would prove to be no accident at all.

The big stumbling block was that I had no status in this case. News of any police investigation of his death would go to his widow, not me. She would be the one with the family support team on hand. She would get the heads-up if they found anything suspicious. She would be kept abreast of developments.

But I was pretty safe in assuming that she knew nothing about the poison pen letters Harry had received. That she knew little or nothing about me, and nothing about Pete. And would, therefore, be incapable of pointing the police in the right direction.

So, the only course of action I could take, would be to talk to them myself. To go to them with what I knew, and what I suspected, and hope they didn't take me to be a fantasist.

That decision made, I bestirred myself to get a mug of coffee, then sat down again with Lucky, to consider where I went from here. I considered three options, in traditional civil-service style.

1. Stay put and reinforce the locks and security generally.

2. Stay put and get a friend or lodger to move in.

3. Move out somewhere. No idea where.

I dismissed No. 2 out of hand because it felt like I'd be putting someone else at risk. No. 3 I parked for future consideration after a chat to my boss about career options. Which left No. 1.

No time like the present. I reached for the phone and in quick succession rang a locksmith to come and fit new locks on all the doors, a computer expert to advise on CCTV and a security firm. Then I rang the police station in Truro and asked to speak to the senior officer dealing with the recent death of Professor Harry Llewelyn. They tried to put me off with helplines and the front desk, but I refused to speak to anyone lower than an inspector. Partly, this was an opening move in me finding out whether they were taking Harry's death seriously and investigating it further. After a lot of waiting around, I was told the case was being handled from Exeter and Inspector Graves would ring me back later in the day.

I waited with ever increasing impatience for the phone to ring. When it did, it was the security company, promising to send someone round the following day. By the time it rang again, the locksmith had arrived, and I was outside the front door with him, discussing options. I galloped in as fast as I could, but even so nearly missed the call.

'Detective Inspector Graves,' said the rather mellow Cornish voice on the end of the line. 'I'm told you have some information you want to share with me about the recent death of Professor Llewelyn.'

'That's right,' I said. 'Just to establish my credentials a little, I'm the secretary to the government committee that was chaired by Professor Llewelyn and I worked with him for some years.' I hesitated over sharing more, but decided to keep the personal stuff for later. 'Can you tell me what your role is in relation to Professor Llewelyn? Were you, for example, involved in investigating the complaint he made about poison pen letters?' I asked.

'Yes, I was,' replied DI Graves, with a new note in his voice. 'Am I right in assuming that you are the lady who is the subject of many of the letters?'

If it was a guess, it was a good one. I knew Harry had redacted my name from the letters he had shown the police. I made a swift decision.

'Yes, I am,' I said. 'And I think Harry's death was connected to the letters, or at least to the writer of the letters.'

There was a long silence, then DI Graves said, 'I think we'd better meet. Where are you now?'

'At my home near Helston,' I replied. 'I could come to the station if that would help?'

'I take it you mean Truro. How soon can you get there?' he asked.

And I said, 'Give me an hour, and I'll be there.'

'Make it two, and ask for me,' he replied, and rang off.

I had the usual hassle parking in Truro and had to walk quite a long way to the police station, Lucky at my heels.

I asked for Inspector Graves at the front desk. They were clearly expecting me, but not Lucky. I was parked on a chair in the reception area while someone went to find Inspector Graves. That seemed to take an inordinately long time, but all became clear when a young man in plain clothes dashed in from the street and planted a warrant card on the front desk.

'Has my interviewee arrived?' he asked the officer behind the desk. The desk officer indicated me, sitting in the corner, and the young man came over, out of breath and hair on end.

'Sorry I'm late,' he said. 'Traffic from Exeter was terrible. Come on through.' The desk officer started to say something about 'the little dog' but was brushed aside as we were waved into an interview room.

'Coffee or tea?' asked DI Graves. 'And water for the little dog?'

'Coffee, please,' I said. 'And yes, a bowl of water would be good.' I doubted she'd drink much, but I wanted to see the officer's face when sent to fetch refreshments for Lucky.

While we waited, I took the opportunity to assess the man in front of me. Probably around early thirties I guessed. He'd smoothed his sandy hair down and straightened his jacket when he sat down. His shirt collar was open at the neck, and he wore cords with scuffed leather brogues. In fact, he looked very like an academic, or at least my experience of them. All he needed to complete the image was leather patches on his jacket elbows.

'Will I do?' he asked with a smile, and I realised my scrutiny had not gone unnoticed.

'That depends on whether you take me seriously,' I said as the coffee and water arrived.

'And that depends on what you've got to tell me,' he replied. 'So let's get started. From what you said on the phone, you seem to think there was something we should be investigating about Professor Llewelyn's death. Why do you think that?'

'Don't you always investigate sudden deaths,' I countered. Then added, 'You already said you were aware of the poison pen letters. So, I think you know, or guess, that I was in a relationship with Harry Llewelyn.'

'Yes,' he said. 'But not yet why you think there was something odd about his death.'

I took a deep breath and tried to order my thoughts. I might only have one chance at this.

'Okay, in summary, this is what I wanted to tell you. I have been Harry's mistress for some years. Before that I was married to a man who turned out to be abusive and controlling. I have good reason to think he killed my dog, and that he attacked me in my Cambridgeshire home before our divorce was finalised.'

I hesitated, wondering whether to say anything about my grandfather, and decided against it for the moment.

'A few months ago, Harry started to get the poison pen letters you know about, and a few days ago, while I was working in London, my home was burgled and some personal letters from Harry to me were stolen. Soon after that, Harry has a car accident and is killed outright. I think,' I said, very aware that I sounded like a conspiracy theorist, 'that my ex-husband vandalised my cottage, stole the letters, and with the link to Harry established, took revenge on the new man in my life.' I stopped and waited for a reaction. DI Graves looked at me for a long, and silent, moment.

'I think you know that all sounds very far-fetched,' he said.

I nodded. This wasn't going well after all.

'Except for one thing,' he added. 'I have a report from the garage that recovered Professor Llewelyn's Porsche 911. It states that the brake pipes had been cut.'

I heaved a huge sigh, and realised I'd been clutching the edge of the table with whitened fingers. Lucky looked up at me and pushed my knee with her head.

'You believe me?' I asked.

'I won't go quite as far as that yet,' he said. 'Tell me first why you're so sure your ex-husband is involved.' There was another pause, then he added, 'Don't censor what you're going to tell me. Leave that to me. I think you were going to say something a few moments ago, then thought the better of it.'

I took another deep breath, patted Lucky, for luck, then said, 'Because of a pattern in a long chain of events. My grandfather suffocated to death in mysterious circumstances. I think my previous dog was suffocated too. And during the attack on me a couple of years ago, my assailant tried to hold a cushion over my face, until Lucky here bit him in the balls.' DI Graves winced as he made a note. 'I think my ex has never forgiven me for getting away, and especially for managing to hang on to an inheritance he'd tried to steal from me. I think the poison pen letters and the attack on Harry are revenge on us both, but especially on me.' I blinked back tears. 'He couldn't have found a better way to destroy me,' I said, and choked up.

DI Graves reached behind him, picked up a box of tissues and handed it to me.

'Were these events investigated by the police?' he asked.

'There was some sort of coroner's enquiry into my grandfather's death, but it concluded it was death by misadventure. My dog? No, she didn't get a postmortem, but I noticed broken blood vessels in her eyes which made me think of suffocation. The attack on me – yes, but it went nowhere. They said they couldn't find any fingerprints at the scene that couldn't be accounted for. They thought Pete's alibi stacked up, then dismissed it as a robbery gone wrong and dropped any further investigations.'

'In these circumstances, I always ask myself, who benefits?' he said. 'Let's assume for a moment that you're correct and all these events were suspicious. Who benefitted?'

I started to tick things off on my fingers. 'My grandfather? I benefitted because I inherited his house. Pete benefitted because he married me and took control of all our finances. And I found out, when we split, that the bridging loan he insisted we take out had only been partly paid off when we completed the sale of my grandfather's house. Some of that money went missing.

'My dog, Magic? Pete again, because he hated her and hadn't wanted her to live with us. The attack on me happened while the paperwork on our divorce was being completed. At that point we were still technically married, and I hadn't yet changed my will. He'd have got the lot.'

' "He" being Pete again?'

'Yes.'

'As for Harry...' my voice trailed away, and I gulped. 'I think that was plain revenge, and therefore my fault.'

'Whatever it was, it wasn't your fault,' contradicted Graves, 'unless you cut the brake pipes yourself.'

'No.' I managed a watery grin. 'And I've got an alibi. I was in meetings in London, with loads of witnesses.'

'There you are then.' He tapped his pen on the desk for a while, then looked up.

'How thorough would you say the previous police investigations were?'

'Not at all,' I said straight away. 'The one in Stoke never seemed to take my grandfather's death seriously. He was old and frail, and it was assumed death was to be expected. The robbery at my Cambridge home was investigated by a detective on the verge of retirement who couldn't care less.'

'There's hope then,' he said, placing his pen on the table with a clatter. 'We've more forensic material now from the Porsche, and I'd like them to come and have another look round your cottage too. Then we'll see what may still be in the evidence stores in Stoke and Cambridge and take it from there.' He stood up. 'No time like the present,' he said. 'I'll get the SOCOs out to you asap.'

'One more thing,' I said. 'How much does his wife, I mean widow, need to know?'

'For the moment,' he said, stuffing papers back into his bag, 'just that we're investigating it as a suspicious death. If we find evidence of a link to you, then she'll need to be told.'

23

Investigations

DI Graves had promised to keep me abreast of developments, but for over a week there was nothing but silence. It took a few days to sort out my new security arrangements, and I very rapidly discovered that a private security company was an expensive option. I had to settle for an alarm that would alert them to a need to respond, recognising that it would take them the best part of twenty minutes to reach me, by which time anything could have happened. My friendly neighbourhood locksmith came up with another solution, which involved fitting an extra strong door to my bedroom and equipping it with secure locks, to create a safe room for me and Lucky. That was all very well I reflected, but wouldn't be much of a solution if someone set the house on fire. However, it was better than nothing.

I went back to work and found myself delegated to deal both with the need to appoint a new Chair, and with the departmental response to the upcoming obsequies for Harry. Drafting a press release on the sudden death of my secret lover was a surreal experience.

As for the other arrangements, I was torn between thankfulness that I had an official reason to attend his funeral, and the fear that I'd break down in public. As it happened, I wasn't given the chance.

A couple of days after returning to work, with silence still from DI Graves, I steeled myself to ring Harry's widow, Lady Llewelyn. Someone else answered the phone and when I explained who I was and why I was ringing, I was put through after a short delay.

'Yes,' a sharp voice snapped.

I explained again who I was, and that I was ringing to ask if she wanted me to mention the funeral arrangements to Harry's (I was careful to refer to him as 'the Professor') colleagues on the committee.

'I'm amazed you have the effrontery to ring me,' the voice said. I immediately felt that the speech was scripted, but waited to see what else would be said. 'I know who you are and what you are,' she went on. 'You're not welcome anywhere near the funeral or the thanksgiving service. I would like you pay me the respect of staying away.'

'I gather the police have spoken to you about the poison pen letters,' I said, making a guess. 'If so, then you'll know I was close to Harry. I appreciate that you have good reason to resent me, but this is about Harry, not us. Can't you put your dislike on one side just for an hour or two?' I was wasting my breath, as I well knew.

'You are not welcome at the funeral,' she repeated. 'Don't force me to have you thrown out, because have no doubt, I will. It's bad enough—' She stopped suddenly and slammed the phone down.

I sighed and looked down at the newspaper announcement in front of me that listed the details of the thanksgiving service and the subsequent proceedings at the cemetery. I passed the former on to all the committee members and noted the latter in my diary. I wondered what was 'bad enough'.

Two phone calls in the following hour resolved some of my queries. The first was from Harry's solicitor. In carefully modulated tones of sympathy, overlaid by a slight tinge of prurient curiosity, he informed me that Harry had left me a small bequest and a letter. The 'small' bequest turned out to be £15,000, which in 1986 was a substantial sum.

'How would you like me to send you the letter?' he asked. 'Recorded delivery?'

I asked if I could call in to collect it, and that was agreed.

The second call was much more important. It was from DI Graves.

'Sorry I haven't got back to you before,' he said, 'but I was waiting until I had something worth reporting.'

'Letting me know that Lady Llewelyn had been told about the letters would have been worth a call,' I said with some feeling.

'Ah, yes, I hoped I'd speak to you first,' he said. 'Sorry about that. But I have got some other news. Are you anywhere near Truro?'

'Yes, I'm in the office today,' I said.

'Then can we meet? How about...' and he named a cafe near the cathedral. 'It should be quiet now.'

'Can do,' I said, 'if they'll let Lucky in. I'm too scared to leave her at home at the moment.'

'I'll wave my warrant card and have a word,' he said. 'See you there in half an hour.' That suited me. It gave me chance to pick up *that letter* on my way.

The cafe tables by the windows were busy, but the ones at the back were empty except for the now familiar figure of DI Graves. Also sitting at the table was another man – older and broader, and with less hair. He looked like a boxer going to seed, even to the bent nose.

'This is Detective Sergeant Enys.' Graves introduced him. I said hello and sat down with Lucky under the table. Three coffees arrived, even as I took my seat, and Graves jumped straight in.

'We've got something,' he said. 'The reason I've been quiet for so long is because I've been waiting for information from four different sources: the forensic team who crawled over your cottage, the data from the Professor's car and from the two cold cases, in Cambridge and Stoke.' He paused and I couldn't stop myself from jumping in.

'So, what've you got?' I demanded.

'Fingerprints.' If it was meant to sound impressive, it didn't.

'Only now? After all this time?' I asked.

'To be strictly accurate, what we've got is two fingerprints and two partials, but improved techniques mean we can identify the partials with much more confidence. One of the partials is on the underside of one of the Porsche's wheel arches, where a hand might go while the brake pipe was being cut. The other is on the hinge of your writing slope. In that case, we think a plastic glove got torn on the broken edge of the box. Both of them match, beyond reasonable doubt in my opinion at least, the fingerprint that was taken from your ex-husband, for exclusionary purposes, during the investigation of your assault in Cambridgeshire.'

'And the second fingerprint?' I asked. I'd been keeping count.

'The second was taken from a bedside table in the care home where your grandfather was living. Did your ex-husband ever visit him there?'

'Not to my knowledge,' I said, growing excited. 'Have we got him then? Is it enough?'

'It's enough to make him a person of interest in the Harry Llewelyn case,' he replied. 'But it's not enough to tie him to your grandfather's death. Dave here,' – he nodded at DS Enys – 'has been trawling the evidence, but that's all we've got at the moment.'

DS Enys cleared his throat and added, 'Give it a few years, and we might have more science to help, but that's our lot for the moment.'

'More science?' I asked, still trying to get my head round it all.

'DNA,' said DS Enys, obviously more of an intellectual than he looked. That would teach me to judge by appearances. 'But don't worry, we've got enough to bring him in for a chat. And to do some checking of where he was on the key dates and times.'

'Anyway, that's it for now,' concluded Graves. 'I'll let you know if we find anything else. And if we're to take this further, we'll need a formal statement from you. Can you come to the station now?'

'Can you give me a few minutes to clear up something? Then I'll join you there,' I replied.

'Okay, let's say, in half an hour. Are you going to the thanksgiving service?' he asked as he stood to leave.

'No, it's been made plain I would not be welcome,' I said, and kept quiet about my other plans.

After they'd gone, I sat still at the table for a few moments, then pulled the unopened letter out of my bag. I couldn't restrain my curiosity any longer.

Dear Elf,

If you're reading this, then I'm dead, probably unexpectedly.

I wrote this after I flew to China in 1985, because it occurred to me that mistresses, even beloved ones, have no rights in the event of a sudden death, and that Mairi was unlikely to be kind. I hope you'll never need to read this; that by the time I die we will have been married for years. But in case things don't work out as I'd like...

I just wanted you to know that you have been the light that lightened my darkness. For years there has not been much in my marriage other than duty and business. And for years, as I've never hidden from you, I made do with relationships that did little more than scratch an itch. I hope I was kind, but I wasn't in love. Then I met you and everything changed.

The last few years have been the happiest of my life. I've laughed more and loved more in these years than in all the rest of my life. I'm sorry now that I put duty before love. I'm sorry I probably didn't tell you often enough just how much you mean to me, and now it's too late.

I think I know well enough how you feel about me to know that you will be sad. But, Elf, please don't grieve too long. Look for another man who will give you all the love and care that I wanted to give you. You deserve it.

Goodbye, my beloved. Until we meet again.

Your Harry.

PS I've left you a tiny gift in my will. I couldn't leave too much without provoking Mairi into malice, but I hope you'll spend it on something that makes you happy.

After a moment I folded the letter carefully and replaced it in my bag. Then I picked up Lucky's lead, wiped away my tears and stood up. Time to make my statement and nail that bastard Pete, once and for all.

24

A Statement and a Farewell

Back I went to the familiar Truro interview room, this time with DI Graves and his sidekick Sergeant Enys to make notes. Between them they took me, item by item, through my fears about my grandfather's and Magic's deaths and the money that had gone missing, the attack on me in St Ives, what I knew about the poison pen letters, the burglary at my house and the 'accident' that had killed Harry. At the end, as I could see from their disappointed faces, we weren't much further forward.

'It doesn't amount to much,' said Graves at last, after reading through Sergeant Enys' notes. 'The only hard evidence we have is still the fingerprints.'

'And the ANPR,' interrupted Enys. Graves scowled at him, and I got the impression he wasn't supposed to have said that.

'You have him in Cornwall,' I said. It wasn't a question. 'He's been caught on camera in Cornwall. Isn't that enough, together with the fingerprints?'

'I'll be having another conversation with the CPS, but I doubt it's enough to charge him. We don't have many cameras and while this puts him in Cornwall, it doesn't pin him down to any of the key locations. We'll bring him in for questioning, but unless he gives something away, and on past performance that doesn't seem likely...' He shrugged.

'Where does that leave me?' I demanded.

'If it all goes the way I expect,' he said, 'then to be blunt, I think your best bet is an injunction. The partial print we found on your writing desk might be good enough for that. I doubt it will stand up for a charge of burglary, and even less so for murder.'

I picked Lucky up from her place under the table and looked at them in silence for a long moment.

'That really is the best I can hope for?' I asked. I wasn't expecting an answer, and I didn't get one. I stood up. 'Thank you for trying,' I said.

Sergeant Enys jumped to his feet too. 'I'll show you out,' he said, opening the door.

We walked the corridor in silence, but he stopped me with a hand on my arm when we reached the front door.

'I know you're disappointed—' he said.

'I'm terrified—' I interrupted, but he interrupted me in his turn.

'—and bitter, I get that,' he said. 'Personally, I think you've had a rough deal too. But you need to know the DI has stuck his neck out for you and the bosses aren't happy. There've been mutterings about unjustified use of resources. He went with a hunch, and he's done his best to find evidence to back it up.

Unfortunately, it just isn't there. Your ex has been too street smart.

'He's sticking his neck out some more just bringing him in for questioning, and bluntly, if he doesn't wind it in soon, he's going to get bounced back to uniform.' He ruffled the fur on Lucky's head and added, 'Also, I think there's another agenda being pushed here. It feels like there's a lot of resentment in certain quarters about cocky young detectives criticising their elders and betters. So, please do take his advice about an injunction, and if we can help your solicitor with evidence to justify one, believe me we'll do what we can.'

He held out his hand. I put Lucky down, shook the proffered hand. Then I went round the corner, back to the offices I'd visited earlier in the day, and asked to see Harry's solicitor.

The girl on reception interrupted buffing her nails long enough to tell me he was about to leave. Looking up at my expression, she amended whatever else she was going to say, and reached for the phone.

'Mr Penrose can spare you a few minutes,' she said after a brief exchange, and pointed to the door behind me.

He was indeed already stuffing papers into a battered briefcase when I opened the door.

'Well hello,' he said. 'I wasn't expecting to see you. Is there something we missed? I understood you'd picked up the letter earlier.'

'I did, and no, this isn't to do with Harry's will,' I said. 'But I do have a problem. I don't know any other solicitors in Cornwall, but if you were good enough for Harry, that's good enough for me.'

He stifled a laugh and sat down again. 'Blunt, but honest,' he said. 'I like that. How can I help?'

'I need an injunction to keep my ex-husband away from me,' I said, and explained the circumstances.

He heaved a huge sigh and leaned back in his worn leather chair. It was a good match for his briefcase, I thought. My second thought was that behind the smooth county-solicitor image, tidy in dark suit and short hair, there seemed to be an acute brain. It showed in the flashing of his bright little eyes.

'Why aren't the police taking action?' he asked. 'If they put him away for the murder of Harry Llewelyn, your problem is surely solved.'

'I've been told he's unlikely to be charged, and, going on past experience, that doesn't surprise me,' I replied. 'Not enough hard evidence. But I thought the burden of proof was different for an injunction. Am I wrong?'

'No, you're right in that the civil standard of proof applies. In other words, that the court must be satisfied on the balance of probabilities, rather than beyond reasonable doubt.' He leaned forward again and picked up the phone. 'Carol, can you ring my wife and tell her I'm going to be late,' he said. Swopping the phone for a pen, he looked at me again. 'Let's put a witness statement together and I'll take it from there. I think this is worth a try.'

When I left Penrose, Penrose and Penrose, wondering which Penrose was *my* Mr Penrose, Lucky and I turned left to walk past the police station to my car.

Two steps down the road, I stopped short and stepped behind the inadequate shelter of a streetlight. Going up the steps into the police station was a man I knew. It was Pete, a little thicker round the waist, a little thinner in the hair than when I last met him, but unmistakably Pete. My heart was beating faster than usual, and something must have alerted Lucky because she looked up at me, her head on one side, and gave a little *Wuff*.

'Shhh,' I said, and looked back at Pete again, but thankfully he was just disappearing into the station, followed by a man I assumed to be his solicitor. As far as I could see, he hadn't looked round. 'Come on,' I said to Lucky. 'At least we can go home knowing he's out of the way for a few hours.' Even so, I went back to my car the long way round. I didn't want to risk walking past the police station, not while he was there.

The next few days were busy, catching up with work that wasn't Chernobyl-related, keeping on top of queries from Mr Penrose, and supervising handymen (and some not so handy) making security improvements to my home. One of the more difficult work tasks was fending off enquiries from committee members who were puzzled that I wasn't taking part in, let alone attending, Harry's service of thanksgiving.

After three or four days, the level of enquiries started to diminish, and I couldn't decide whether that was because everyone who wanted to ask had already done so, or whether the rumour mill had belatedly joined up the dots. I found I really didn't care. If Lady Llewelyn had, by her animosity, drawn attention to things she would have preferred to remain hidden, then that was her lookout.

I thought long and hard about her strictures, regarding my attendance at the thanksgiving and the funeral, and decided I would comply with her order to stay away from the former, but that nothing would stop me saying goodbye to Harry in my own way. I made my arrangements accordingly.

So, while the great and the good sat down in Truro Cathedral to celebrate a life in science with mediaeval polyphony and Victorian hymns, I parked my car in Falmouth and took the ferry to Flushing. From there I joined the coastal path, knowing that the service would proceed at a traditionally stately pace, and in due course arrived at the tree-surrounded parish cemetery of Mylor.

I'd taken the precaution of asking the funeral directors which plot was to be Harry's. It was near one of the paths. I looked around for a suitable vantage point and found one between some trees on the perimeter. Then I spread the rug from my small rucksack and settled down to wait, half hidden by long grass.

I spent the time remembering Harry, the journeys we'd made together, the meetings we'd scheduled, delivered and reviewed afterward, the laughter we'd shared – such a lot of that – and the plans we'd made. I was so lost in my reverie that I only realised the funeral party had arrived when the sound of voices, raised in yet another hymn, impinged on my ears. I shifted slightly on my rug, so that I could see better.

A robed priest, presumably the vicar, was commanding proceedings, assisted by two black-garbed men I assumed to be from the funeral directors. The widow, elegantly clad in dramatic black, stood at the head of the grave, her back to me. I heaved a sigh, realising I'd guessed correctly. Harry was going to be buried facing the sea. There was a small group of family gathered close to the widow, and a tiny choir, just eight singers, at the opposite end of the grave and therefore facing me. I kneeled, both because it seemed appropriate and because it kept me well hidden by foliage, and I waited.

The service of committal was short; earth was scattered, then the weeping widow was escorted away by a tall man in black. After a short pause, a man with a spade walked over and, under the supervision of the funeral director, set to work to fill in the grave. It didn't take long. Their final act was to place the formal flower arrangements from the funeral on the mound, and then they left, shovel on shoulders and chatting quietly.

After a heartbeat or two, I stood up, rather stiff, folded my rug and replaced it in my rucksack. Then I walked down to Harry's grave, the long grass dragging at my ankles.

At the graveside I bent down twice. Once to stroke the earth at his head, as though I could stroke his hair back from his brow as I had so often before. The second time at his feet, where I buried the special token I'd brought with me. Then I stood for a few long moments with the wind lifting my hair just as it did the tree branches around me, and Harry's voice sounding in my ears.

The light that lightened my darkness. I'd had those six words engraved on the slice of amethyst I'd just buried with my lover. Then I turned to face toward the coast and repeated his last words to me in the letter.

'Goodbye, my love. Until we meet again.' And I went home.

25

Keeping Calm and Carrying On

The next few weeks were a bit of a blur. The powers that be interviewed for a new committee chairman and appointed a Professor Clare Romilly. She was smart and personable, and soon had all the members wrapped round her little finger. I heaved a sigh of relief that the committee was in good hands and started to look for a new job in a different part of the country. My boss was aware of my issues and kept his ear to the ground too.

It was a huge stroke of luck that I got two important phone calls on the same day. The first was from Sergeant Enys.

'You didn't hear this from me,' he said, 'but you may not need that injunction after all. I spoke to Mr Lynch's office this morning, just to tie up some loose ends, and they told me he's transferred to a new job in the States. He started last week.'

'Wasn't he prohibited from leaving the country?' I asked.

'While the investigation was live, yes, but that prohibition was lifted last week. He must have left almost immediately. I thought you'd want to know.'

I thanked him and rang Mr Penrose.

'It's good news for you if it's a long-term move,' he said. 'Let me check with his employer before we get too carried away and cancel the application for an injunction. You might still want to proceed.'

The second phone call was from my boss. 'Can you pop down the corridor for a chat?' he said. 'There's something I want to talk to you about.'

The something turned out to be a job in Norfolk. The role of Controller of Plant Variety Rights was about to be advertised internally and he was willing to recommend me, if I was interested.

'It's right up your street,' he enthused. 'Science-based, and with an industry service element as well. You'd be good at it. It used to be based in Cambridge,' – I shuddered slightly. *Too close to St Ives and old memories.* – 'but the whole team are moving on to a new location at the science park near Norwich. Obviously, I can't guarantee anything, but I'll give you a good recommendation and I think you'll be in with a chance. A good chance.'

'Can I think about it?' I asked.

'Of course, but don't take too long.'

I went home that evening, walked Lucky on one of my favourite cliff paths and admired the view. Then I went home to my, now super secure, cottage and looked around. I'd loved living here, and I'd loved Harry here. But it was time to move on and make a fresh start. The following morning, I put my application in.

***

It took a whole year before I was able to make the move back to East Anglia. My Cornish adventure was over, the old threads were severed, and it was time to start a new life in Norfolk.

I took my time to find the right home for Lucky and me. I had leave due, so I spent a couple of weeks staying in a holiday home on the east coast and acquainting myself with a whole new county. Even though I'd lived in Cambridgeshire, Norfolk had been a closed book. I knew it only as a county on the edge of everywhere but on the way to nowhere, with no motorways and only one major city. Now I spent many happy days exploring the richness of its wild environment, the wealth of its culture and the variety of its history, from Romans to the Royal Family.

When it came to selecting a location, I was spoiled for choice between city and village, country and coast, river and lakeside. I was horribly tempted by one riverside cottage with a mooring for a small boat, but caution prevailed as friends ganged up to point out the practical and insurance problems which might result from high water levels. I ended up in a village big enough to have a pub and a shop, while small enough to have a community. I joined a dog agility club and a choir, volunteered in the local branch of Coastwatch and generally made myself at home.

After another year or so, I began to consider venturing on to the dating scene again, but my immediate options were not very promising. Most of the men I knew were married. Of those that remained, it was obvious why they weren't, or they were too young by a decade or so. I toyed with the idea of the local paper's lonely hearts column, but not for long. I wasn't quite as desperate as that. At that time, online dating wasn't yet a thing.

It was during one of the choir practices that someone sitting near me mentioned they were going to a folk club and named a pub in Norwich. At that point we were called to order by the conductor and obliged to get down to work on the anthem we were studying – a rather lovely piece by Tallis. When we finished the rehearsal and we all headed out of the church to our respective cars, I asked about the folk club.

'Want to come?' asked the alto I was quizzing, and her husband, one of the scarce tenors, chipped in, 'We can give you a lift if you like.'

I accepted gratefully. It sounded like a fun night out.

It turned out to be one of those nights when a professional folk band was eked out by locals taking a turn. The first half was the amateurs, and I was thoroughly enjoying the singalongs to the first duo, when the tenor hissed in my ear, 'If you like joining in, you'll enjoy the next pair too.'

'Let me get us all a drink then,' I said, and battled my way to the bar for another round of pints. I was halfway back to our table with the glasses when the next duo took to the small stage. I was watching my footing rather than the stage, trying hard not to spill more beer than absolutely necessary, so the sounds took me by surprise. Especially the flute. It instantly transported me back a couple of decades, and as soon as I'd got the beers safely on the table, I turned to the performers. One of them I knew rather well. Older but little changed, it was Phil.

We were sitting at a table near the stage. As luck would have it, my seat was nearest to the performers, but facing the table. For the first part of their set, I stayed facing my friends with my back to the stage and sipped my beer from a glass that quavered in my nervous hand. By the time of their second song – 'Shoals of Herring' – I had calmed down enough to turn my chair round and join in the choruses. Their next piece was another sea shanty – 'The Wellerman', I think it was – and again I, along with almost everyone else there, joined in on the chorus.

After that, there was a small hiatus while Phil whispered in his partner's ear. She looked surprised, then nodded. Phil struck a familiar tune, and I suddenly knew he'd not only spotted me, but also recognised me. It was 'Scarborough Fair'. When it got to the Canticle, Phil looked straight at me and nodded. I was late on the entry and my voice wobbled at the start, then grew stronger, and I finished the song with them, as I had done with Phil so many times, but so many years before. At the end there was a lot of kind applause, especially from my thunderstruck table. Phil and the girl took their bows; he waved to me to share in the applause, then they left the stage through the door at the back. I turned back to my friends, my face, judging by the heat I felt, a bright pink.

I quite simply didn't know what to do next. I hadn't spoken to Phil for over twenty years. We hadn't parted on the best of terms. I buried my face in my glass, or tried to, but found it to be mysteriously empty.

A voice above my head said, 'Let me get you another, Elf.' A familiar hand reached over my shoulder, and Phil took my glass from me. I made some excuse or other to my friends from the choir and followed him to the bar.

'Is it still lager?' asked Phil.

I nodded.

When he'd been served, he led me to the side of the room where there was, miraculously, an empty table. He waited until I sat down, put the glass in front of me, and seated himself opposite. He took a long draught of his bitter, put his glass down with a hand I was pleased to observe wasn't wholly steady, and asked, 'How are you, Elf? How long have you been in Norfolk?'

26

Catching Up

Considering the circumstances, it's not surprising the conversation was a bit stilted. I tried to explain what I'd been doing and how I'd ended up in East Anglia again, but the effort of self-editing the tricky bits made me sound like a parrot with a verbal tic. After a few moments, when I'd already ground to a halt twice on the twin reefs of the assault in St Ives and the death of Harry, Phil interrupted.

'Would it help if I told you I've already heard some of your story?' he said. 'Only from the other side. And I didn't believe a word of it,' he added hurriedly.

'You mean, you've been speaking with Pete?'

'Not directly. I don't exactly enjoy his company. But I found myself in the same room at a do in Stoke a year or so ago, and I overheard enough of his conversation to make me curious. So I admit, I went over after he'd moved on, and asked the group he'd been talking to, what he'd been saying.'

I used a sip of my pint to create a small delay, before I asked, 'And what *had* he been saying?' Phil looked at me for a moment, then looked down at the table, where his finger was tracing patterns in spilled beer.

'Mainly, that you were a greedy bitch who'd taken him for everything he had, then tried to get him arrested on a trumped-up charge of assault.'

It shouldn't have come as a surprise, but even so I gasped. I was so angry that I couldn't say a word.

'I told you,' he said, 'I didn't believe a word of it. And I told them the same. The evening got a bit tense,' he added with a grin that faded rapidly as he took in how I was looking. 'Elf, I know you,' he said. 'And I know Pete. I knew then and I know now who to believe.'

'It's a long story,' I said. 'And this isn't the right place to tell it.' I was interrupted by the arrival behind me of the woman who'd been singing with Phil on the stage.

'I'm off now,' she said over my shoulder. 'I'll see you later? Pleased to meet you,' she said to me, and she was gone.

'Your wife?' I asked.

'My daughter,' he said. 'Good job she didn't hear what you just said. I'd never hear the last of it.'

'Your wife doesn't sing with you then?' I was blatantly fishing for information.

'Nor anything else. We parted a long time ago,' he replied. 'Come on, Elf, let's go somewhere quieter, and you can tell me the long story. If you'd like to,' he added more uncertainly.

'Just let me say goodbye to my friends and I'll be with you,' I said. 'My car's outside.'

'You can leave it there,' he said. 'There's an Indian restaurant a short walk away. Let's get a bite to eat. If you don't mind missing the rest of the evening,' he added as an afterthought.

'Sorry, I didn't mean to mess up your arrangements. I guess I'm just excited at meeting you again. If you'd rather...'

'Stop burbling, Phil, and I'll meet you outside in five minutes,' I said with a smile.

I made swift apologies to my fellow choir members, who greeted my explanation with knowing looks, then took a few minutes to tidy up in the ladies' loo.

When I looked at myself in the mirror it was with double vision. I seemed to see a younger, hopeful me, overlain by the older, tired, and cynical version. I tried a smile and tucked some hair behind my ear, then went out to meet Phil.

***

The Tastes of Spice was only two streets away, and it was as quiet as Phil had promised.

'It'll get busier when the folk evening's over,' he said. 'But we should have a quiet hour or so.'

He was greeted by the staff as though he was recognised, and we were shown to a table in the corner, by the window on to the street. Drinks and poppadoms arrived swiftly, then the waiting staff left us in peace while our main meal was prepared.

'So, what's the real story, Elf?' he asked.

'You first,' I said. 'With a grown-up daughter, I'd say you've been pretty busy yourself. Is she the only one?'

'No, I have a son too,' he said. 'Andy's at Reading studying agriculture. Ffion studied music in London and is now a teacher.'

As he didn't seem inclined to go on, I asked, 'And your wife?'

'Blunt as ever, Elf,' said Phil, but he didn't seem to mind. 'If it wasn't for the kids I'd say the marriage was a mistake from the start. A case of marry in haste and repent at leisure. It's not an unusual or an exciting story. We divorced when the children were still young, and it's only in the last few years I've been able to reconnect again. But that's enough about me for the moment. Stop playing for time and come on, Elf, give.'

'Pete was another mistake,' I said slowly. 'One I'm sure you saw coming, but I didn't.' At that moment we were interrupted by the arrival of curries, breads and rice. By the time the flurry of activity had died down, I'd had chance to decide how to approach this conversation. I delayed a few moments more while I tasted the food on my plate, noted it was as good as Phil had promised, then put my fork down so I could concentrate on Phil's reactions.

'Phil, I've told this story several times, to the police and to a very important person in my life. I've only been believed twice, once by the police in Cornwall and once by that person, Harry.' Phil was watching me intently, his face impassive. 'I know to most people it comes across as outrageous, outlandish even, but I promise you I haven't taken leave of my senses.' I took a deep breath. 'Pete was controlling and vindictive and stole some of my money. That much I can evidence. I have also come to believe that he killed my dog and my grandfather and had a hand in the accident that killed Harry. The police believe me about the accident,' I added, 'but don't have enough evidence to prosecute.'

Now Phil stopped eating as well. A waiter came over to ask if there was a problem and Phil waved him away. There was a silence.

'I don't know what to say,' he said at last. 'The assault he complained you accused him of? That really happened?'

'I told you, people don't believe me,' I said.

'I didn't say that. In a weird way, I don't want to believe you because I don't want to think Pete could do all that, but in my heart I do. And in a funny way, Pete's complaints primed me for some of this. Out of the two of you, I know who to believe.'

I looked at him for a moment, and then picked up my fork with a ridiculous sense of relief. 'We'd better eat something,' I said, 'or the chef will be having palpitations.'

Phil picked up his fork, then put it down again. 'Where is he now?' he asked.

'As far as I know, he's in the States and likely to stay there for the long term.'

'Thank God for that.' He picked his fork up again and started eating in earnest. 'But we'd better cross the USA off our list of holiday destinations,' he said.

'Are we going on holiday then?' I enquired.

'Oh, I think so, don't you?' he replied. 'In due course. Let's get acquainted again first, shall we?'

By the time we left the restaurant, it was starting to fill up with customers from the folk music evening. Phil was greeted by name several times, and there was a degree of interest in my presence by his side.

'It'll be all over Folk Norfolk by tomorrow,' he said. 'That I have a new lady, I mean.'

'It's a common occurrence, is it?' I asked, teasing. We'd reached my car.

'Not unknown but not common,' he said. 'I am really happy to have met you again, Elf. Quite ridiculously happy, in fact.'

He leaned forward and planted a gentle kiss on my cheek. 'See you soon, I hope?'

'I hope so too,' I said. 'But it might be tricky.' He looked panicked for a moment, then I added, 'I don't have your phone number and you don't have mine.' He struck his head with his open palm, melodramatically.

'I thought I was in trouble there for a moment. How stupid I am.' He whipped out his wallet and handed over a business card. 'Both my phone numbers are on that. Call me soon, Elf? Promise?'

'I promise,' I said, and put the card safely in my pocket, making a mental note I was going to copy the number down soonest. It would be awful if I lost the card. 'Do you want mine?'

'I'll have it when you ring me,' he said. 'I'm worried it might feel like I'm rushing you, so this is my way of giving you some space. Putting the decision in your court. Just ring me soon, please.' He waved and got into his car, a dark Mercedes just across the car park.

I drove home with a smile on my face, let Lucky out for her empty in the back garden, then sat down at the kitchen table and thought, *Why not? To hell with caution*. And I rang the carphone number on the card. Phil picked up within two rings.

'Elf?' he said.

'I just wanted to say how much I appreciated you giving me your numbers and leaving it to me,' I said. 'I'm not used to that sort of consideration. You have *my* number now.'

'So I do,' he said. 'How do you fancy dinner tomorrow? There's a village pub in Fleggburgh that has a really good chef. We could carry on catching up.'

'I'd love that,' I said. 'It's a date.'

I put the phone down with a strong feeling of satisfaction and looked at Lucky, busy attending to a persistent itch. 'I've someone for you to meet, Lucky,' I said. 'And I think it's going to go well.' She yawned.

27

MILESTONE 11: Fall of a Wall

The next few months were among the happiest in my life. We ate out, went to the theatre, sang folk at a range of venues, and I got to know Phil's wholly delightful children. To my relief, they seemed to take to me. I asked Phil once if they knew how badly I'd treated him, but he brushed it aside.

'That's not how I remember it, Elf, and anyway, shit happens. What counts is now and the future. And that's looking bright for me. I hope you feel the same?'

It wasn't really a question. This time around, I don't think he needed reassurance. He knew full well how happy I was.

We lived in our own little bubble, Phil, me, Ffion, Andy, and Lucky of course, who thought Phil was the absolute bee's knees, greeting him with mad circles of delight whenever she saw him. Apart from work, very little impinged on our self-satisfaction, until we sat down one evening after a long walk, and rather randomly turned the television on to see the news wholly taken up by events in Berlin.

Huge crowds of East Berliners were flooding through to the Western side and being met by champagne celebrations. As time wore on, the reporting began to focus on young men with hammers and chisels knocking bits off the wall. By the time we went to bed, new crossing places seemed to be emerging. Trying to make sense out of what had happened was difficult. Some commentators were saying one thing and others something entirely different, such that Phil was moved to comment that the cock-up vs conspiracy theorists would be having a ball.

One reason I remember this so clearly, is that Phil's other response was to fetch a bottle of champagne from the kitchen for ourselves.

'Isn't it a bit late in the evening to be opening a bottle?' I demurred.

'That depends on your answer to my next question,' he said. 'Men are notoriously bad at remembering anniversaries, so I thought this would be a good way of prompting me.'

'What anniversary?' I asked. Believe it or not, I was still puzzled.

'This one,' he said, and got on his knees on the floor by the sofa. 'Elf, I've done this before, but this time, I think we've got our timing right. Will you please marry me?'

I looked at the slightly shop-soiled version of Phil kneeling at my side, and knew my vintage matched his perfectly.

'After all that's passed, you really do want this, do you?' I asked.

'I really do want this, you silly mare,' he said. 'Why do you think I'm holding this incredibly uncomfortable, but traditional position?'

'Then yes, I'd love to,' I said. 'Now get up before you stick there for good.'

'That's a relief,' he said, making it back onto the sofa and giving me a resounding kiss. 'How soon can we do it?'

'Ah,' I said. 'Well that takes me to one of my conditions.'

'Which is?' He looked slightly alarmed.

'That we have a quiet wedding with a minimum of guests. Perhaps Andy and Ffion and my parents, but no more. We've both done the big performance version, let's do it just for us this time.'

'Agreed,' he said with a note of relief. 'What's the second?'

'That we find a whole new home of our own, not just live in mine or yours. Let's have a fresh start in somewhere that's truly us.'

'Done and done,' he said, and clinked his glass on mine. The silent celebrations on the muted TV were still going on.

'To mark the day, how about a bit of Berlin Wall in your engagement ring?'

'Not on your nelly,' I said. 'You're not getting away with concrete in my ring, you cheapskate.'

'That's good,' he said, 'because I wanted you to have my grandmother's ring, if you would,' and pulled from his pocket a battered box containing a ring with a central ruby stone shouldered with small diamonds.

'Perfect,' I said as he pushed it onto my finger. Lucky muscled in between us to see what was going on, licked the ring then lost interest and sighed heavily.

***

We married in April 1990 in Barbados. I used my bequest from Harry, which I'd kept in a special savings account for a special day, to pay for my parents to fly out with us and enjoy their one and only long-haul holiday. In view of what he'd said in his final letter, I felt he would have approved. Exactly as we'd discussed, Phil brought Andy and Ffion, and the wedding couldn't have been more different than either of our past experiences.

We all holidayed together for five days, then the day came when I got into my floaty pale green dress and pulled cream sandals on my feet.

Ffion, dressed in cream, helped me with my hair, and looked stunning herself. She gave my mother a hand too. Mum had been dissuaded from going the mother-of-the-bride route in something hot and uncomfortable, and was also, at my request, dressed in cream but, in her case, with a huge shady sun hat waving in the gentle breeze. The two men wore cream chinos with, in Andy's case, a white shirt, and in Phil's, a pale green version. Then we all walked together onto the beach for the ceremony within the sound of the waves, and the wedding breakfast that followed in a grape-hung arbour close by.

Andy kept us entertained with an account of the trip round the island the rest of them had enjoyed the day before. From his account, the driver-cum-guide had been a character and a half! According to him, his previous guests had been a group of Americans, some of whom were, shall we say, ample in size. He had apparently run his experienced tour-guide eye over the group, then suggested that most of them get in the back of his Land Rover, while 'the fat one comes in front with me'. The ensuing hysterics on the part of the lady in question had totally bemused him, and it had apparently been left to the hotel manager to try to explain where he'd gone wrong. Judging by some of the driver's comments to us the next day, the manager hadn't had much success.

The rest of the party went home after our wedding, while we stayed on for a further five days.

28

MILESTONE 12: Death of a Princess

When I look back at my diaries and my memories, I find the next seven years flew by in a haze of happiness. We found our dream home in a small Norfolk town. It was one of a Georgian terrace and looked exactly like a child's drawing of a house, with a door in the centre and windows to either side. Tucked away in a quiet street, it was out of the way of the visiting tourists, but only a short walk to the shops, while in the opposite direction we soon reached open fields and places to walk Lucky. We had a tiny front garden that was little more than a place to park tubs full of flowers, but the back garden was huge and went on for what felt like miles, starting with a terrace and flowerbeds near the house and ending with an orchard at the far end. Lucky loved it.

As with most dream homes, some things about it were a bit of a nightmare! I could write an entire manual on bodged plumbing. And as for the wiring! Our friendly electrician took one look at it, pronounced it to be 'shot' and recommended rewiring the whole house without delay. As we'd already experienced the unfortunate consequences of water dripping from a light fitting and the disturbing sparks that flew from the hinges of the oven door, we took his recommendation seriously. It was a good job we did, as he showed us when he disinterred a nail from the fuse-box where it had apparently been doing duty as a highly illegal fuse!

But you're not here to read a DIY manual and there are few things more boring than an uninterrupted account of bliss, so I'm going to skip to August 1997.

By this time, Lucky was a venerable sixteen years old and begging to slow down a little. She still greeted me every morning and after every absence, long or short, with a little dance of joy. But the dance was getting shorter and less exuberant. Various trips to the vet followed, and she was given medications for her arthritis. At least, she'd been prescribed them. Getting them into her was another challenge altogether. In theory they were palatable and could be chewed, but not in the opinion of a determined and wily Jack Russell. Generally, it took several spoonfuls of jam or peanut butter before a single pill would pass her lips.

Then the morning came when she didn't greet me at the kitchen door. When I found her on her bed, she could produce little more than a slight wag of her tail and a flutter of her eyelids.

I sat down with her on the floor calling, 'Phil, come quick.' But by the time he came into the kitchen, Lucky had sighed her last and was lying still in my arms. It felt as though she'd waited for me to come downstairs so she could say goodbye.

That done, she let go. He got down beside me and put his arms around us both.

'I'm so sorry, Elf,' he said. 'So very sorry. She's been with you so long, she's part of you, and part of me too.'

Behind me, the TV, which I'd turned on automatically when I entered the kitchen, was babbling about something. I didn't pay it any attention. My focus was on the small brown and white body in my arms that had contained so much love, joy and loyalty.

'Do you want me to call the vet?' asked Phil against a background of solemn voices and dark ties.

'No, thank you. No point,' I said. 'There's nothing they can do now, and they did warn me she mightn't have much longer.' There were slow, silent tears pouring down my face and wetting her fur.

'You hadn't told me that,' said Phil, slightly accusingly.

'There wasn't anything to be done, and I didn't want to upset you. They said her heart wasn't as strong as it had been, but that's hardly surprising given her age. Let's arrange for her to go to the pet crematorium after the weekend, and then we can think about where to put her ashes.'

'If that's what you want,' he said, then, at last, took in what the TV was saying. 'Good Lord,' he said. 'Princess Di's dead. In a car crash in Paris. This morning.'

'Poor woman,' I said distractedly, then with more feeling, 'Poor boys.' But in truth my mind was much more on my lost puppy than on the Royal Family.

Less than a week later, along with much of the rest of the country, and maybe even the world, we watched Diana being laid to rest with a grand ceremony in Westminster Abbey and a simpler one at her family home of Althorp. Then we took Lucky's ashes to her favourite walk on the east Norfolk coast and scattered them in the dunes behind the beach.

Even with Phil holding my hand, that was one of my loneliest walks. I'd never again see that perky tail bobbing front of me, or that mischievous face peering round a gorse bush, self-evidently debating whether she was going to choose to do what I'd asked or go her own way. I still had pockets full of training treats and black plastic bags. I still looked down automatically every time I stood up from a chair to make sure she wasn't under my feet. And the evening custom of cheese straws and sherry just wasn't the same, without two bright button eyes fixed on me to see when she was going to get her share. A shadow walked at my heels everywhere I went, and it was breaking my heart.

29

MILESTONE 13: 9/11

The next four years were full of incident. Both Phil and I got promoted and found ourselves unexpectedly affluent. Ffion got married in a rather splendid ceremony at Norwich Cathedral. Andy got married in a registry office, and divorced again soon after. He came to live with us for a short while, but soon got itchy feet and went travelling the world. What he was living on we didn't exactly know. One minute he seemed to be a beach bum. The next he was selling real estate. We made up our minds not to worry, and just kept in touch as best we could. Thank God for the improving reach of the internet.

Around six months after we lost Lucky, we got our names down with a rescue charity to rehome a dog. In fact, we ended up with two: another Jack Russell named Toby and a mostly spaniel named Whizz. They were from the same kennels and had bonded during the moments they were allowed to play together, so when we were asked if we'd take both to avoid breaking a little dog's heart, it was a no-brainer. As far as anyone knew, they were around two years old and a bit wild, but not all aggressive and they soon learned what we meant by 'Here', 'Sit' and 'Stay'.

When the office was quiet, I used to take them to work with me, so they were sitting under my desk on that Tuesday when I got a call from Phil around 2pm saying, 'Put the news on your desktop. Now!'

Puzzled, I did, and watched open-mouthed the smoke pouring from one of the World Trade Centre towers where a plane had apparently flown into it. As I sat watching, another plane did the same thing to the adjacent tower, right in front of my disbelieving eyes. I scrabbled for the phone again, without taking my eyes from the screen.

'You saw that?' asked Phil. 'What the hell is going on?'

'It has to be terrorism!' I said. 'Once might be an accident, but twice! Definitely not! There's that book by Tom Clancy – where a plane flies into the Capitol or somewhere. Hope to God he didn't give them the idea.'

'Hang on, they're saying something about more planes,' said Phil. 'I'll ring you back later.'

I put the phone down and paid attention to the screen in front of me. Less than fifteen minutes later, the towers just disappeared. I couldn't believe my eyes. They'd just gone. In the space of minutes. The camera cut to images of terrified people running through billowing clouds of grey dust. Then back again, while the news reported a further attack on the Pentagon.

My mind was awash with fragments of thought, about the victims in the towers, and the firefighters who'd been on their way up the stairs to try and effect a rescue. So much carnage. So much hurt.

By this time every desktop in the building was showing the same images and no work was being done at all. I went with the flow and sent everyone home early.

Phil arrived home soon after me and the dogs, clutching an armful of evening newspapers.

'They don't say much more than we've all seen,' he said. 'But the images are shocking.'

We watched the news intermittently all evening, then went to bed to rise to more of the same. Just before he went to work the next morning, Phil voiced the thought at the back of my mind.

'Pete works in New York, doesn't he?' he said. 'Wonder if he's been affected.' I wondered too.

We got our answer, in part, a couple of weeks later. Phil, through his contacts with City firms, had managed to get sight of a list of New York based staff who were still missing.

'He's on that list, Elf,' he said to me that evening over supper.

'But let's be clear, that's not a list of bodies that have been identified?'

'Not yet, no,' said Phil. 'Word is that very few bodies came out of that disaster in one piece. I don't want to go into graphic details, Elf, but the reality is that most of the identifications will be made by DNA, not by someone recognising features. The work of identification is still going on and it might take weeks.'

'What happens then?' I asked.

'Apparently, the rule is that any citizen who dies abroad gets an inquest here in the UK, so eventually that's what will happen.'

I sat in silence for a while, watching Toby and Whizz playing one of their wrestling games.

'So we may never know for sure,' I said.

'Possibly not, but they are being very thorough. I think there's a good chance we'll know by the time of the inquest.'

The following day I was due to attend an international meeting in Geneva on plant breeders' rights. The meeting itself was routine. What occurred when I paid a visit to the ladies' restroom was not. I was followed in by a lady from the US delegation, and while I was washing my hands and checking that my ever-recalcitrant hair had not completely abandoned tidiness, she came up to me.

'Excuse me,' she said. 'But I'd like to give you this.' She proffered a small badge still wrapped in clear plastic. I took it from her, a little confused, and looked at it. It carried the Stars and Stripes and the Union flag, crossed at the base. I looked up at her with a question in my eyes.

'It's just a small token, to say how much we appreciate what Prime Minister Blair said, and the support of Great Britain,' she said.

I had a vague recollection of Tony Blair pledging that Britain would stand 'full square alongside the US' in the battle against terrorism. I had no idea, until then, how threatened the US had felt and how glad they were of support. My eyes were wet when I left the restroom with the badge on my lapel.

I rang Phil just before I got on the plane home but didn't get an answer. That wasn't unusual and I thought nothing of it, until I drove home from Stansted to a street filled with blue flashing lights.

30

Aftermath

To make sense of what had led up to the blue lights, I'm dependent on Phil and Andy's accounts.

I should have said that, a few days before, Andy had turned up from one of his jaunts, bronzed and long-haired and generally looking like the hero from a Norse saga. We'd enjoyed his tales of life in Sri Lanka, where it seemed he'd been employed in turn as waiter, restaurant manager and, subsequently, hotel manager.

'Can't keep a good man down,' he'd said with considerable complacency. 'I've told you before, Dad, I always find work.'

'How about finding a career?' Phil had asked without much hope, then had been surprised by the answer.

'I'm coming round to the idea,' said Andy. 'I think it might perhaps be time to think a bit more long term. But on my terms, of course. I have some ideas I'm thinking through. Is it okay if I bunk down here for a bit, while I look around?'

'Of course it is,' I said. 'No problem. What sort of thing do you have in mind?'

Andy looked slightly embarrassed. 'You'll think I'm dotty,' he said, 'but I got interested in cooking while I was at the last hotel. I'm thinking it might be fun to train as a chef.'

'Lots of hard work, and long hours,' warned Phil.

'Yes, I know. I have worked as a chef before,' he reminded us. 'But my plan would be to look for a partner and open a little place serving fusion cuisine. I have a bit put by. But I need to polish my skills first.' We drank a toast to his new venture, and then I went off on my travels to Geneva.

That evening, Phil got home from work at his usual time, walked the dogs, and got himself some supper. By bedtime there was still no sign of Andy so, leaving the door on the latch, he settled the dogs in their crate and went upstairs to bed. He claimed later it was the middle of the night when his sleep was disturbed, but in fact it must have been not much after midnight.

Disentangling the stories, it seems he'd gone into a very deep sleep very quickly, from which he was wakened by sounds downstairs. He'd just decided that it must be Andy coming home late, when the dogs kicked off a racket to raise the dead, barking and howling and, judging by the rattling noises, hurling themselves at their cage door.

At first Phil turned over, assuming that the problem was Andy and he could sort it. Then, as the noise went on, he thought he'd better go down and see exactly what the problem was.

He got as far as the top of the stairs, when he saw a dark shape move across the front hall toward the sitting room, and smelled petrol.

The next thing he knew, there was a bang and a sheet of flame leaped up the stairs toward him. For a split second he contemplated jumping through it, but sanity thankfully prevailed and he retreated back along the landing to our bedroom. Fear for the dogs filled him with horror as he listened to the barking, now reaching new levels of panic and rage.

Those noises ringing in his ears, he ran through the bedroom, flung the window open and scrambled through it onto the roof of the conservatory below. From there it was easy enough to reach the ground, and his first thought still being the dogs, he ran round the side of the house to the kitchen window. He was about to smash it open, when a neighbour caught him by the arm.

'Don't do it, Phil,' he shouted in his ear. 'It's too well alight. The fire brigade are on their way.'

'The dogs,' Phil shouted. 'I must get to the dogs.'

'They're safe,' the neighbour shouted in his turn. 'Your son has them.'

Turning, Phil saw Andy covered in soot, with Toby in his arms and Whizz on the end of an improvised lead, which he later found to be Andy's belt.

Pushing them all firmly before him, the neighbour got them away from the house and into the middle of the road, just as the first of the fire brigade engines arrived. The police weren't far behind.

The next few moments passed in a bit of a blur. When he got his head together, Phil found himself sitting in the back of a police car with Toby in his lap, Andy alongside him and Whizz in the footwell. The officer in the passenger seat was turned to face them, his notebook at the ready.

'What happened here?' he asked.

'I saw a man in my hall,' said Phil, 'smelled petrol, then the fire started. I think it was an arson attack. I got out through a bedroom window and came round to rescue the dogs, but Andy had already got them out.'

'And you?' said the policeman to Andy. 'What did you see?'

'Just a car driving off, as I walked up the road. I remember a glow in the windows as I was about to put my key in the door, but I thought it must be from the living-room fire. Then the windows to my right suddenly shattered with the heat and I realised there was a problem. I ran round to the back door, heard the dogs making a racket in the kitchen and saw my father sliding over the conservatory roof. Since I knew he was safe, I went for the dogs. There's no one else home, you see.'

'Did you get a number for the car?'

'No way. I had no reason to think it was a problem at that point,' said Andy. 'I only noticed it because you don't see many cars in this street at that time of night.'

'And you, sir?' said the policeman, turning back to Phil. 'Can you describe the man you saw?'

'Sorry, no. He was just a dark shape in the hall.'

'But you're sure it was a man?'

'Yes. I don't know why. No, I do. It was the height and the silhouette that looked male. But that's all I can say.'

By the time I got home, the fire was out, and the investigation team were in place. When I came round the corner to the blue flashing lights, I stood on the brakes in horror and the car skidded to a halt as I started to take in the scene before me.

When I leaped out of the car, I caught my foot in the seatbelt and fell into Phil's arms, my nostrils filled with the smells of smoke and ash.

It took some argument before I was allowed past the tape. The ground floor at the front of the house appeared to be burned out, with the centre of the fire having begun in the hall, then spread to the sitting room and dining room to either side. I stood in the street with tears in my eyes, partly at the destruction but mainly because what I loved most, Phil, Andy and the dogs, had been saved. Behind me, Phil was talking to the policeman on duty. He'd left the dogs with Andy and Ffion at Ffion's home in Norwich.

I was still standing there when Phil came up and put an arm around me.

'They say it looks worse than it is,' he said. 'We're going to need a new floor and to redecorate throughout, but the structure is still sound. It seems the quantity of accelerant was quite small, and the fire brigade got on top of the flames very quickly.'

'But who did this? And why? There's only one person who's ever had it in for me like this, and even he never went this far. And he's dead. He *is* dead, isn't he? I don't understand, Phil. What've we done to deserve this sort of hate?' I shuddered uncontrollably.

'Why don't we leave it to the police?' suggested Phil.

'Like I did when I was attacked. Like I did when Harry was killed. Much good they've done me.'

'Mrs Waters?' Another voice spoke behind me. 'We'd like you both to come down to the station, please.'

'So you can accuse us of arson? Of burning our own house?' I was angry and bitter. And scared.

'We need to talk to you, and we have some CCTV footage we'd like you to see.' The young detective stayed calm even in the face of my anger. 'I'm Detective Sergeant Henning. My boss DCI Margaret Tayler wants a word.'

We were taken to the police station in Norwich, just up the road from the marketplace, and shown to a room on the first floor. A motherly-looking DCI Tayler showed us into an interview room and offered us coffee. Slightly mollified by her approach, I was still in no mood to be softened up and sat down in the chair with a bit of a thump before putting my forearms on the table and glaring at her.

'Before you say anything,' I said, 'I've been here before, and I have no confidence at all in your ability to bring anyone to justice.'

She blinked, but said quite mildly, 'How about I bring you up to speed first, then you deliver your judgement?' She didn't wait for my reaction but pressed straight on.

'First, we've checked CCTV in the area around you. It's lucky that some of the shops just round the corner from you have security cameras, and even luckier that they are angled into the road. After your son Andy' – I didn't bother to correct her as regarded our relationship – 'mentioned seeing a dark car drive off just after the fire started, we did some checking, as I say.' She twisted her laptop toward me and showed me the screen.

Despite my determination to be sceptical, I leaned forward to watch. A dark car drove down the shadowy street on the screen and she suddenly paused the picture.

'Look!' She stabbed a finger. 'It's blurry but the image shows the registration number. We've had that image enhanced and we have the details of the owner.'

'And who is it?'

'That's where it gets interesting. It's a hired car. The man who hired it yesterday at Stansted Airport had flown in from the US. He showed his passport when he hired the car and they photocopied it, so we have a lot of details.' She did something to the laptop and the image on the screen changed to a photocopy of a passport. 'What's even more interesting, is—'

I interrupted. 'But surely you don't have anything directly linking this car to the fire.'

'No, we don't. But as I was about to say, this car driver is interesting because, according to the information we have, he died on September the 11th in New York.' She sat back and regarded me. 'In the circumstances, that makes this man a person of interest. It seems he travelled from New York to Stansted on someone else's passport, hired a car, drove to North Norfolk, parked near your house and shortly after that, your house bursts into flames.'

I sat looking at her with my mouth open.

Phil asked, 'Have you found any connection between this man and us? And where is he now?'

'In answer to your first question, the name on the passport belongs to your wife's ex-husband's senior manager, if that doesn't sound too much like a French exercise! And that man has been positively identified by belongings and DNA as one of the victims of the 9/11 atrocity. The ex-husband, on the other hand, although he's disappeared, has *not* been identified among the victims. I spoke to the company's London office this morning, and although they were reluctant to speak ill of the supposed dead, they did tell me that Peter Lynch had been about to be "let go" as they put it, for reasons they didn't wish to be too clear about but probably involved fraud or, at the least, misappropriation of funds.

'My guess is that Lynch had been sacked earlier in the day, or even the day before, and therefore wasn't in the office on the day the terrorists struck. Lucky for him twice over, because not only did he escape the destruction, but in all the confusion he had the perfect opportunity to steal a passport belonging to someone he knew for sure would be dead.

'As to where he is now. That, I'm afraid, we don't know. That's the next task.'

31

Next Steps

I looked Margaret straight in the eye.

'You realise that we're none of us safe until he's caught? I *know* he was involved in the so-called accident that killed Sir Harry Llewelyn and in the attack on me a few years before. I also think he killed my grandfather. He's a serial killer and a maniac.'

She looked me straight back. 'Yes, I have all that on file,' she said. 'The detective who investigated in Cornwall was very thorough and he made it clear where his suspicions lay. I'd say that if he had the science available then, that we have now, he might have been able to take his case to court. I appreciate why you feel let down by the police. In part, you are right to feel that way. But, in my opinion, DI Graves and Sergeant Enys did their best. Now it's down to me, and believe me, you'll get nothing less than my best too.

'As to where he is now, we've alerted all police in Norfolk and adjacent counties to the car registration number and his identity. The ports, airports and railway police are on the alert too. Believe me, we'll get him. It's only a question of time.'

'And if he's not run? If he's lurking somewhere around here, waiting for another chance?'

'Then he'll make it even easier for us to catch him. We will get him, I promise you.'

We went back to Ffion's home in Norwich with a police car following and promise of regular passes by squad cars. When we went in, we found a family liaison officer already ensconced in the kitchen, drinking tea and playing with the two dogs. Ffion was taking this invasion of her home remarkably calmly.

'Andy's gone to stay with a friend in London, to relieve some of the pressure here,' she said, putting the kettle back on for yet more tea. 'I've taken the phone off the hook because the media are already on to the story and being a pain in the neck.'

'How do they know where we are?' I asked, alarmed. 'If they can find us, so can he!'

'Seems Dad's office passed someone on, innocently assuming they were a client. Now the word's got around.'

'Oh, for—' Phil stopped himself. 'Let me have a word with them, and let's put a statement together.'

'I think you should have a word with DCI Tayler before you do that,' the FLO intervened.

Things might have got heated, but at that moment Phil's mobile rang and he took the call. 'That *was* DCI Tayler,' he said as the call ended. 'They've got the car. It's been abandoned near Felixstowe.'

'If he's heading for that port, they've got him,' said the FLO. 'He may think the biggest container port in the country is a good place to stow away, but he has no idea how good the security is there.'

'It's huge, isn't it?' I said. 'Surely it can't be that hard for one man to hide himself in a place that size.'

'Don't you believe it,' she said. 'First, it's crawling with guards and sniffer-dog teams. Those dogs don't miss anything, in a container or out of it. Second, it's a massive, mechanised area where nothing moves except machines. If he tries to leg it to one of the ships, he'll stand out like a pea on a drum. Third, those ships are huge too. You don't just climb the sides of one of those to get on board. I tell you, if he's trying that route, he's made a big mistake.'

She was proved right. Before we went to bed that night, we had a further call from a tired but elated DCI Tayler.

'Got him!' she announced. 'I think you're dog lovers, aren't you?'

'Yes,' I said.

'Well, you can add a springer spaniel named Rocket to your Christmas card list. He sniffed him out halfway up a stack of containers in one of the sheds, and then cornered him when he tried to escape, which wasn't exactly in his job description but hey, who cares?'

'What next?' I asked, sitting down on the battered kitchen sofa with a sigh of relief.

'First, we question him, then we charge him, then he'll appear in the magistrates' court before being referred to the Crown Court for trial. I'll keep you posted, don't worry.'

As we were getting ready for bed that night, I started to grin.

'What on earth's funny?' demanded Phil, one leg in his PJs and hopping round the room.

'Pete hates dogs,' I said. 'It'll have really got to him, being apprehended by a spaniel!'

The next time we spoke to DCI Tayler was on that same kitchen sofa. Two days later she called round.

'I wanted to tell you this in person,' she said. 'Then I'll need you to make further statements down at the police station. But first things first.'

Her description of what had transpired after Pete was brought in was so graphic, I could see it all in my mind's eye.

***

The man Margaret Tayler first saw was dirty and tired. His clothes were smoke-soiled and his eyes red-rimmed. By the time he was sitting in front of her in the interview room, he was clad in a paper overall and had his solicitor sitting alongside. The solicitor had clearly instructed him to remain silent, but Margaret had a strong suspicion the advice hadn't been necessary. He spoke only to confirm his name, and then said absolutely nothing. Not even 'No comment'.

Long hours of questioning later, and he'd still said nothing. Apart from Margaret and Jim Henning, the only person to speak had been the solicitor, with complaints about how his client was dressed, fed, allowed to sleep, etc.

With time running out, Margaret and Jim had paused to regroup.

'He's not going to crack,' said Margaret, munching digestive biscuits with a gloomy air. 'I suppose we should have expected it. His smartest move is silence, and everything we've seen in the previous casework suggests he's both smart and forensically aware. I think the forensic evidence will let us charge him with arson, and obviously we've got him cold on possession of false identity documents. I think his ex-employers may be persuaded to charge him with misappropriation and or fraud, but I'm waiting to hear. What we're struggling with are the cold cases, of assault and possibly murder. There wasn't enough evidence then and, so far, we haven't anything new.'

'I've been thinking about that, and about DS Enys' comment on the file, about the science not being advanced enough. Things have changed a lot in the last few years, and I think it's worthwhile reinvestigating the materials we have in store from all those cases,' said Jim. 'Are you okay with me doing that?'

'Let me have a word upstairs,' she replied. 'I'll back you. We haven't anything else. In the meantime, I'll charge him with arson, possession of false ID and fraud. We can stick the other charges on the list when we think we can make them stick.'

***

That's how matters stood when DCI Tayler came to see me, to explain that, with luck, Pete would remain in custody until his trial.

'But I can't guarantee it,' she warned. 'Unless we can make more serious charges stick, he might get bail.'

We went along to the bail hearing at Norwich Crown Court. Phil hadn't wanted me to go, but I was determined. We sat in the public gallery with a very kind lady from the Witness Service, who'd done her best to manage our expectations.

Pete sat in the dock, looking down at the floor. He never, at any time, looked up or looked over to where we were sitting. His barrister stood to make what seemed likely to be, judging from the sheaf of paper in his hands, a long speech in favour of bail, but was stopped in his tracks. Someone had delivered a note to the clerk of the court. She stepped forward to give it to the judge, who raised his hand. The barrister reseated himself while the judge read the note. We watched with bated breath, then the Witness Service volunteer nudged me, and we turned to see Margaret Tayler enter the court and bow her head.

The judge looked up. 'Sir Anthony,' he said, addressing Pete's barrister, 'it appears that new charges have been laid. Specifically, fraud committed against his employers Messrs Hardy and Willis, and misappropriation of funds to the tune of several million. I understand bail is opposed by the police on the grounds that your client has property in the US of A and is a flight risk. You may wish to take instruction before we proceed further.'

'Thank you, my lord,' said Sir Anthony, and the court rose as the judge left the bench. I looked across at Pete, but he was still facing the floor.

Margaret indicated we should follow her into the public waiting room.

'There'll be a delay, then we'll be called back in, but I'm pretty confident now that he won't get bail.'

'What happened?' I asked.

'Hardy and Willis decided that keeping the scandal under wraps was a bigger risk than the publicity following a prosecution. Partly, I think, because feelings were running high in the company about a man who would take advantage of the death of a colleague. Especially in these circumstances. You can stay if you like, but I'll let you know the result.'

We opted to leave, and later that day she did indeed confirm that bail had been refused and Pete was safely behind bars until the trial, at least.

***

It was a long and tedious wait for the trial. I was amazed just how long it did take. In my innocence, I had imagined that a trial would follow a charge within a few weeks. In reality it was nearly four months before the trial date was scheduled. In that time nothing seemed to happen, and I was getting very frustrated. I should have had more faith in the team of Tayler and Henning because the latter, in particular, had not given up.

With DCI Tayler's support, he had gone through the evidence collections of three police forces and submitted samples to DNA testing. The results, slow as they were to come through, had him walking on air. The two of them called on Phil and me in the home we were renting on the edge of Norwich while we waited for the repairs to our fire-damaged townhouse.

'We have some good news,' she announced even before they were fairly in through the door, and ran her hands through her hair, making it even more chaotic than it was when she arrived. 'But I'll let DS Henning explain. It was his initiative.'

Jim Henning, perched on an uncomfortable kitchen chair, took the floor with a gleam in his eye. 'First, I should explain that I've been trawling the evidence collections in Truro, Stoke and Cambridge, and I sent certain samples away for DNA analysis. Quite a lot came back negative, but three were positive. The samples were found to be over ninety per cent probability belonging to Lynch.'

I hardly dared speak.

'Where were they from?' asked Phil, taking the words from my mouth.

'One, the oldest, was from the pillow found near your grandfather's body. You'll remember he was found face down on the bed. However, on one side of the pillow was saliva that was taken to be your grandfather's. Judging by comparison with the DNA sample we took from you, it was. On the other side were some small specks that turned out to be blood. They were from Lynch. The only likely explanation is that the pillow was used to suffocate your grandfather and that the backs of Lynch's hands were clawed during the attack. The body must have been turned over later.

'The second was from your work box. You remember they found a partial fingerprint on the box, but the CPS wasn't happy to rely on it to tie Lynch to the scene. With modern techniques, we've found skin cells and perspiration on the box that are definitely from him. This evidence that he knew of the link between you and Sir Harry gives him a motive. Taken together with his fingerprint found on Sir Harry's car, the evidence relating to the poison pen letters and his presence in the area at the time the brakes were cut on the Porsche, that might be enough this time. Jurys like a motive!

'Finally, I went back to samples taken from the scene when you were assaulted in St Ives, Cambridgeshire. This was harder, until I found that the cushion used in the assault and the spread from the bed were still in the evidence store. They'd been misfiled, but not mislabelled, so we're satisfied we've got the right ones.

'The cushion had nothing on it except your DNA. Not surprising given you said at the time you thought he'd been wearing gloves. The bedspread was more interesting. There were some traces of blood, probably from the dog attack you mentioned, and again they were Lynch's.'

'None of these on their own would be conclusive,' said DCI Tayler. 'But taken together with other evidence that was underrated or neglected at the time, it amounts to a consistent picture that justifies reopening these cases. In short, I've got the go-ahead to charge Peter Lynch with two murders and an attempted murder. Then we work like fury to assemble the case that will take him down.'

32

Trial and Retribution

In some ways, the trial in Norwich Crown Court felt like a rerun of the bail hearing. The courtroom looked very similar. The Witness Service support was on hand again – an elderly gentleman this time. And again, Pete entered the dock looking at the floor, and stayed looking at the floor for every moment that we were there to see him.

It took more than a week to hear all the evidence. I gave mine quite early on, so after that was able to sit in the public gallery and listen as the case proceeded. The expert witnesses were particularly impressive, especially the pathologist who had assisted the US authorities after 9/11 and gave evidence on how the bodies had been identified. The financial stuff went over my head mostly, although Phil said after that Pete hadn't been particularly smart, it was more that his company's procedures were lax.

I kept watching the jury, trying to read their views in their expressions. It was impossible. By the end I still had no idea which way they would jump.

After the closing speeches from the respective counsels, the jury were addressed by the judge and retired to consider their verdict. Trying to listen to the judge dispassionately, I thought that there was every chance Pete'd be convicted on the fraud charges and the arson attack, but less likely on the murder charges. Phil agreed with me. DCI Tayler was professionally impassive.

It was the following day before the jury returned. I could hardly breathe for anticipation. The middle-aged gentleman in the dark blue suit and pink shirt, who was the foreman, stood up and my heart stopped beating. The clerk to the court read out the charges one after the other.

The pink shirt inflated with a deep breath six times and six times a sonorous voice said, 'Guilty'.

I looked across at Pete as the judge thanked the jury for their work. He was still looking at the floor. I thought he must be getting a stiff neck. I missed a sentence or two, and the next thing I knew, the clerk of the court was inviting me to take the stand in order to deliver my victim impact statement. Suddenly this didn't seem such a good idea as when I'd been sitting safely in my rented sitting room, composing my thoughts. Why hadn't I opted for just a written version? Why had I been so keen to have my say? I heaved a deep breath, picked up my bit of paper and took the stand.

My voice was shaky when it began but strengthened after the first sentence. 'I was once Peter Lynch's wife,' I began. 'I have spent years being afraid, hiding from him. I have moved house twice, from one end of England to another and changed jobs, entirely through fear of him. I have lost a loved grandparent, a lover, a career, my dog and two homes. Worst of all, I began to doubt my sanity, to believe that I was imagining things. That no one would ever believe what I was saying. Only when I met an old friend and started a new life, did I begin to heal. Then the nightmare started all over again.' I stopped short. *Now* Pete was looking at me, and the dense blackness of his eyes was frightening.

'That's all,' I said. 'I can't say any more. I just want to be free of the fear.'

With a suddenness that made the whole court jump, Peter threw himself at the glass front of the dock, then started to climb. He was shouting and screaming his hate. Strings of saliva hung from his jaws as he scrambled and yelled, the words distorted and the sounds reverberating. I heard something like, *You'll pay, you vengeful bitch. You'll pay for ever*, when the dock officer reached up for Pete's wildly threshing feet, caught one, and pulled him violently back into the dock. Another security officer had reached me and ushered me back to Phil. The judge sat calm and still, his robes draped as though carved from marble.

I heard something about sentencing next week, and then Pete was pushed, still fighting and flapping, down the tunnel to the cells beneath.

Outside the court I stood, Phil's arm still around me, listening to DCI Tayler.

'Don't worry,' she said. 'He's going down for a very long time. You're safe now.'

I thanked her and DS, now DI, Henning, before Phil and I strode out to the car park and a life without fear.

As it turned out, Pete didn't go to prison for long. He was soon sent to Broadmoor to be detained in the secure mental hospital for the rest of his life. We were, now, truly safe.

33

MILESTONE 14: Plague

After all the upheaval of the fire, we didn't stay in our Norfolk townhouse for long. When the damage was made good, we sold it and bought a smaller property near the east coast. It had once been a small tithe barn and the conversion had been done with care. We added solar panels in the field behind the house and later, much later, a ground source heat pump. We worked on our garden, walked our dogs, became part of a village community and settled in to enjoy the culmination of our careers and, ultimately, our retirements.

We celebrated our silver wedding anniversary there with a massive party in a garden marquee. By this time Phil had grandchildren. Ffion had two boys and a girl, Andy had a successful restaurant in Suffolk and appeared regularly as a TV celebrity chef.

Five years later we were in the mood for something quieter. We planned to celebrate our thirtieth wedding anniversary with a holiday, but somehow the timing didn't quite work when we made the booking, so we went to Mexico a little early, in mid-March.

By then, it was already clear that China had a big problem with a new sort of flu. I, like probably a lot of people, thought it would be SARS all over again. A big problem in some parts of the world, but not a major problem in Britain.

We flew to Mexico from Gatwick, a little worried but not greatly, and determined to enjoy our holiday. If anything, we were amused by the few people we saw at the airport, wearing masks. And especially by the young men wearing them over their beards.

'Do they imagine their beards are particularly at risk?' I scoffed.

With my background in emergency response, I should have known better. I had, after all, often pointed out the folly of government planning for the last emergency rather than the next. Why did I imagine that public-health planning was any better, any more imaginative than animal-health planning?

You all know what happened. The Foreign Office advice changed to 'Do not travel' shortly after we had flown to Cancun. The challenge now would be to get safely home. Thus began the most bizarre holiday of our lives.

By the end of the first week, it was not so much a question of whether we would manage to bag a beach lounger, as which swimming pool would we have all to ourselves. Flights came out empty from England and returned full. The hotel did a magnificent job of trying to keep the holiday show on the road, but by the time it was our turn to return home, it was time for them to throw in the towel. We were on the last coach out and they closed the hotel behind us. I felt desperately sorry for the staff who bravely waved us off, now out of work for the foreseeable future.

The flight felt relatively normal, but the arrival back at Gatwick was anything but. Signs everywhere commanded us to keep our distance, and we were the only plane load of people making our way through the deserted terminal. The last bus of the day took us to the almost empty long-stay car park, and we collected our car for the long drive home.

The roads too were empty, even the tunnel under the Thames. Around Thetford we thought we'd better call at a supermarket to get some essentials. I knew our freezers and store cupboards were well stocked, but we needed things like bread and milk. After all the news I'd seen on the TV, the shelves empty of toilet rolls and hand sanitiser came as no surprise. Once we were home, we made a cup of tea, turned the TV on, and settled down for the siege.

Six days later we realised that sometime during our passage through the airport or in the supermarket, we had picked up some little passengers. First Phil, then I, lost our senses of taste and smell.

By the time I was reeling from the worst bout of flu-cough that I'd ever experienced, Phil was going downhill fast. I'd managed to get a pulse oximeter via Amazon, and was horrified to see that Phil's oxygen levels had dropped below eighty-eight per cent. I checked it on me, in the hope the device itself was faulty, but notwithstanding my cough, my levels were above ninety-five per cent.

'You have to go to hospital,' I said.

'No, I'm not leaving you,' he gasped, but I overruled him.

'It's not a debate,' I said. 'I'm ringing 999 now.'

The ambulance was prompt by the standards of the times. They checked my vital signs too but agreed that I was far less badly affected. They allowed me to say goodbye to Phil before they put the oxygen mask on his face and wheeled him into the ambulance. I rang Ffion and Andy, then retired to bed.

I had no idea that was the last time I would ever see him.

***

Two days later, after inadequate updates from hard-pressed nurses, I got a call on my phone and then another one on Zoom. The first was to tell me that Phil was about to be put into an induced coma. The second was for him to say goodbye. I begged and pleaded to be allowed to visit, but there was no way I was going to be allowed through the door. I asked if Ffion could go, but even she was excluded.

On a blurry iPad screen held in the shaking hands of deeply distressed nurses, I said goodbye to part of me. Twenty-four hours later I knew that he'd gone and needed no call from the hospital to confirm the news.

34

END POINT: Death of a Queen

On the evening of 8 September 2022, I was, like most of the rest of the country, watching the news. By then, the announcement didn't come as a surprise, but it still left a strange void. The monarch whose reign had encompassed my entire life was no more. I got in my car and drove the few miles to Scratby cliffs, where I could sit and watch the endless, patient sea rolling onto a Norfolk beach.

I remembered, among other things, the art teacher so many years before who'd told me that a life was the sum of your past experiences. *No,* I thought. *He was wrong. A life is a series of events, strung on a thread of decisions.*

At so many moments in my life, I'd taken decisions that had determined not just my path but those of people around me. If I'd just run away instead of swinging my satchel, perhaps that mad, sad pervert exposing himself to a child would have survived. Would that have been a good thing? Or would he have gone on to worse crimes?

If I'd stuck with Phil at the start instead of marrying Pete, or even married Bob the Bobby, would my grandfather have lived on in the care home? Would Ffion and Andy never have been born? What would have happened to Harry? I thought, with a wry smile, of the times I said, usually in the middle of an emergency, that failure to make a decision *is* a decision, and usually suboptimal.

Now, looking back with the benefit of twenty-twenty hindsight and reviewing *my* decisions, would I make the same choices again?

I didn't have an answer. The sea rolled in, the sky reflected the sunset behind me, and I looked at the flimsy clifftop barrier in front of my car. Then I started the engine, turned the car, and drove home.

There was a protective barrier in front of me much stronger than metal and stone: the knowledge that I'd been loved deeply and loved twice. Whatever time I had left, that knowledge would never leave me.

THE END

Afterword

Among other topics, this book explores the issue of abuse and control within a close relationship. It also touches on the loss and grief caused by a miscarriage.

If either of these issues strikes a chord with a reader, I strongly recommend a chat with one of the following:

Citizens Advice
03444 111 444   www.citizensadvice.org.uk

National Domestic Abuse Helpline
0808 2000 247   www.nationaldahelpline.org.uk

Leeway
0300 561 0077   www.leewaysupport.org

The Miscarriage Association
01924 200 799   www.miscarriageassociation.org.uk

Praise for the DCI Geldard Norfolk Mysteries

"An astounding tale that is guaranteed to keep you entertained to the very last page" - Featz reviews on Secret Places

"A page turner that would be enjoyable on screen as well as on the page" - Kate Weston, University of East Anglia, category judge, on Glass Arrows. *shortlisted for the East Anglia Book Awards prize for fiction 2021*

"A really brilliant series of books" - Rutherford Reads on Fires of Hate

www.heatherpeckauthor.com